Vellakari

By
Anna Siduri

HELLGATE PRESS   ASHLAND, OR

Published by
Hellgate Press
PO Box 3531
Ashland, OR 97520
hellgatepress.com
email: sales@hellgatepress.com

Interior design: Sasha Kincaid
Cover design: Patti Robrahn, L. Redding

.

ISBN: 978-1-954163-11-9
Printed and bound in the United States of America
First edition 10 9 8 7 6 5 4 3 2 1

Dedicated to all military personnel around the world who serve their country selflessly and honorably. To the heartwarming, welcoming people of South India who have become my family. To all those who travel far and wide in search of a better life, wild adventures, or a place to call home. And finally, to my sister Patti and husband Sumanth, my eternal supporters who never stopped believing in me.

IV   VELLAKARI

1

I t was captivating to stand in a place so genuine. No false admiration, nothing hidden or censored, just the quiet beauty of a city ravaged by conflict since the beginning of time. I stood arrayed in full battle gear, rapt in this dangerous, war-torn location... and felt strangely at peace, quite possibly for the first time in my life.

Deployment was just shy of a year and this mission brought me here... inside the Green Zone. The vast history of the area gave rise to my intrigue as savage as the unforgiving sun. Desert heat had crept to hazardous levels again and it was barely seven a.m.; its scorching, hazy air radiating tints of orange, a clear indication of a sandstorm fast approaching. Foul scents of burnt garbage and diesel infiltrated the neck gaiter covering half my face as I traversed the dismal city park. It resembled a city dump more than a place to take children.

Ahead, the Swords of Qadisiyah loomed in the near distance, a majestic landmark serving as the gateway to Saddam Hussein's former parade ground. Worn combat boots faintly crunched the sand with my cautious saunter beneath the arches. Massive sword-wielding steel arms crossed over like an entrance to the Garden of Eden. The mighty Hands of Victory they were called, and they glowed in the morning sunlight with intricate detail.

Stadium ruins emerged to my left as I wandered further; all windows blown out, bullet holes bestrewn remaining walls. The only noise present stemmed from blowing debris circulating the arena... and galling, relentless crows. The ambiance was surreal and eerie, yet so enticing. I could hardly believe I was within the Cradle of Civilization.

The indistinguishable click of a pistol advanced my succeeding step… and I froze in place. It didn't take long to figure out a gun barrel was pointed at the back of my head.

"Nahn hizb Allah! Alshiyeat al 'Islam!"

My heart raced aberrantly at the arrival of this unexpected visitor. I failed to remember the reason why I joined the Army in the first place, but in this moment, wondered what the hell was I thinking. There were limitless things in life I still wanted to do, and now feared I may never get to. The irritating pessimist in me prodded at a slim chance of survival… but the faint, near-fleeting optimist didn't want to give this asshole the satisfaction of taking my life away.

The city's loudspeaker suddenly blasted the Muslim call to prayer, contributing to the authenticity of the situation, though it wasn't hard to forget where I was. The man to my six kept spewing Arabic at a resounding volume, as if chanting in a rage. Though his words unknown to me, his hatred was easily interpreted from accusatory screams searing through the mere inches between us.

I firmly gripped my M16, finger inching slowly over the safety.

Okay, here we go, I readied myself. Time to do what you were trained to do. Let's fuck him up…

A deafening gunshot rang out at close range before I could turn, warm blood spattering onto my upper body in spurts. If there was ever a time when my life flashed before me, it was now.

"Oh, shit!"

It played out almost in slow mode as I hunched over and covered my right ear, now ringing from the blast. My eyes squinted under the bright glare while struggling to regain my bearings, my gaiter now drooped around my neck. Coming into focus, Master Sergeant Perez approached with all the speed of a tiger in pursuit of prey. Though his sizable, husky frame would otherwise intimidate people, his dimpled cheeks and thick black mustache gave onlookers the impression of a big teddy bear, and they would be correct. My ever-dependable section leader would do anything for someone in need, as has often been the case before, and it was a riveting relief to see him.

"Jesus Christ, Sergeant Don!" the familiar Mexican accent called out. "You almost gave me a heart attack!"

His M16 pointed at the man trembling on the sand as I straightened my back, breaths laden with shock.

"I'm so glad you saw me!" My hearing gradually started to return. "Thought I was done for."

"I am so sorry about that, Don," panic dominating his voice. "I was taking a couple pictures over there and then I look and see this guy had a gun on you."

"Wasn't your fault, Master Sergeant," I reassured him, breaths still erratic. "I should've been covering the area, but got distracted."

We both glanced down at the man, now bleeding out from his right shoulder. Our rifles remained in his direction as he struggled for his gun, which had dropped several feet away.

I sighed in relief. "Thank you for not killing him."

He nodded. "Iraqi officials will want to question him. Find out who he is."

A local guard raced toward us from the nearby Monument to the Unknown Soldier, his AK-47 battle-ready as he stopped to survey the scene. Perez spoke with him in fluent Arabic before turning back to me.

"Hang tight, Don. I'll call the Commander. He can notify the Iraqi government."

I gave a sharp nod, agreeing with his protocol, then he pulled out his cell as the guard returned to his post. I knew it had to be done, but I dreaded the idea of returning to base to face the consequences, being quite certain the Commander would not be happy about this incident.

I stepped back, analyzing the mysterious, craven attacker. He wore a long white robe with detailed leather sandals and a red and white-patterned ghutrah around his head. His ash-skinned face evinced a bristly beard and Middle Eastern features that had been slashed at one time, leaving behind a long, grotesque scar from eyebrow to chin. Judging from his fanciful clothes and excessive gold jewelry, I assumed he was a man of some importance.

Perez tucked his cell away and came up beside me. "Iraqi police will be here soon. Let's head to the flight line and get back to base before this sandstorm hits."

"Roger, Master Sergeant," I replied, now wanting to leave as soon as possible. "If I ever come back, I sure hope you're with me."

We were silent for most of the chopper ride back to Balad, the terrifying incident replaying in my mind despite efforts to block it out. My fingers trailed the base of my neck, and I cringed at the texture of dried blood splotches. At least the flight offered the opportunity to calm my nerves down some, even with the distracting loud rotary blades overhead. I glanced out from our Blackhawk helicopter over the boundless Persian Gulf. The water and desert seemed to extend forever.

"Hey Don, look." Perez broke my thoughts as if he knew I needed it. "There's a herd of camels down there. You see the white one?"

I smiled in awe at the white camel trotting amongst a herd of tan ones. "That's really cool. I've never seen a white one before."

"It's rare to see one in the wild. Some people say it's good luck."

We watched them lope along the desert until they faded off to a speck of dust in our view.

I leaned back, turning my head inward. "Thanks for the diversion. Aside from the obvious fact that we're in the middle of a war zone, it's still amazing to see normal life happening around the world."

"This is your first tour, right?"

"Yeah. Been in six years already. Contract's almost up."

"Oh, so you joined after 9/11."

"Sure did." My exhale sprouted modest frustration. "And here I thought the National Guard handled peacekeeping missions like assisting with earthquakes or Hurricane Katrina."

"Welcome to the suck, Don. We all end up in theater sooner or later, Active Duty and Guard alike. This war keeps sending soldiers back here three or four times. Some of these guys have kids they've never met."

"Is this your third tour?"

"Fourth."

"Damn." I raised both eyebrows. "How's your family handle that?"

"It's fine." His shrug wasn't entirely convincing. "Rosa's a devoted Army wife. She enjoys it, for the most part. And Jairo's still young enough to not really understand what's going on. Just three years left and I'll get my twenty. Besides, I really do love this shit. Far more exciting than a civilian desk job back home… and you get to experience things that most people don't. How many can say they've sacrificed all for something they believe in? Or fired a grenade launcher off a helicopter? I grew up a poor chico in Guadalajara and look at me now."

As a full-time, highly-decorated National Guard NCO back in San Jose, Perez's experience far exceeded my own, so I often asked him to share his stories. Our unit was well-aware of his accomplishments, but I always wanted to know about his grittier memories, such as how many people he's killed, what countries he's traveled to, or what the male soldiers acted like off-duty. I wasn't particularly close to my father, so on more than one occasion, I treated Perez as such, which he accepted graciously.

I sat contemplating his words of wisdom, trying to apply them to my own life when he pat me on the shoulder, most likely sensing my distress.

"No regrets, right?"

A slightly forced grin reflected my skeptical thoughts. "Right. No regrets."

He leaned over me, scanning the ground. "We're here, Don."

I took a deep breath, slinging my rifle over my shoulder. The Blackhawk descended closer to our home base, giving us an overview of metal container housing units and tents that extended for miles. Our mission had been brief, but seemed far longer due to the unfortunate event that transpired.

We landed on the tarmac and hopped down, racing across the flight line as an F16 fighter jet took off to our rear, long blue flames blazing out the back.

"Sergeant, you can head back to your CHU!" Perez yelled over the piercing sound of the jet. "Change your ACUs and get cleaned up, then hit the mess hall before going back to the office. I'll go speak to the Commander."

"Thanks again for this morning, Master Sergeant," my response bursting with incomparable appreciation.

He simply grinned and replied with "Hooah" before turning in the opposite direction.

Back at my room, I set my heavy kevlar on the bed and pulled a fresh uniform from the locker before following the sandy trail to the latrines. Eight shower stalls lined the far walls of the trailer, just large enough to turn around inside. With no one else using the facilities, I savored the quiet moment of hot streams cascading down, dissolving all traces of the murderous coward's blood. At the mirrors, I tucked a blonde hair strand under my patrol cap while adjusting the tight bun into place before heading out.

Hunger was just hitting me as I arrived at the mess hall. Outside the monstrous metal shed, I dropped the rifle's magazine and fired empty rounds into the clearing barrel before stepping inside. With the late morning hour, the usual long line was now gone. I grabbed a tray while observing the breakfast selection, which was the same nearly every day.

"Morning, ma'am." The flamboyant Iraqi cook smiled while pouring a spoonful of grits onto my tray. Food splotches and dirt clung to his apron and unkept beard stubble.

"Hey, Khalid. How's the kitchen this morning?"

He giggled. "Good, ma'am. Your smile very beautiful." An observation he conveyed every day, yet still brought a smile to my face. A fried egg and chopped mango was placed on my tray as well.

"Thanks, Khalid. I'll see you for surf and turf tonight."

He giggled again. "Ah yes, ma'am. Thank you, ma'am."

⚜ ⚜ ⚜

A ten-minute walk across base and I strolled into the one-room S4 office, a wave of cool air blasting out from the generously air-conditioned space. Three other soldiers from my section sat at their desks, and all heads spun toward me in anticipation.

"The Donegal Son returns!" Lieutenant Belinsky blurted out with his arms raised. "Way to waste a Haji, girl!"

While out on mission, behaving in a professional manner was something we all took seriously, but inside the office, our close-knit team spoke more informally. Our months of pre-mobilization training had brought us together like a family, though an occasionally obnoxious one.

Corporal Becker hurried across the room and embraced me in a tight hug as the door closed from behind. Gratitude didn't come close to how

I felt. Years ago, I never would've guessed my best friend since childhood would become my roommate during a war. She joined the Guard only a few months after I had and we've been inseparable since.

"I'm so glad you're okay, babe." Her deep, bosom voice brought much-needed alleviation.

"I'm fine. Just shaken up." I sighed, wanting to brush off all the attention. "Glad I had Perez with me." My glance over to his empty desk brought an immediate sinking feeling. "Where is he? He hasn't come back yet?"

"Nope," her answer ripe with trepidation. "Not sure if that's a good or bad thing."

I frowned. "With Ryder, that can't possibly be good."

"If anyone can handle him, it's you, babe. Did you get your passport?"

My mouth curved, remembering why I went to Baghdad in the first place. Even as a child, I dreamed of traveling the world, and was one of the reasons I joined the Army. I handed my new and very first U.S. passport over with all the elation of a compulsive shopper setting foot inside the Mall of America for the first time.

"Sweeeet." She flipped through the crisp, empty pages. "You ready to take the world by storm, babe? Go see how the other half lives?"

"Definitely." My excitement bloomed, but waned in remembrance of the earlier near-tragedy. "Getting this thing almost cost me my life. Better make use of it."

Perez walked through the door, his face displaying slight disappointment, but greeted me with a warm smile, nonetheless.

"Sergeant Don, the Commander wants to see you in his office."

"Oooohhhh snap, Sergeant Don!" Lieutenant Belinsky belted out, still tuned into our conversation. "Time to start burning shitters."

Lieutenant VonRutenburg sat motionless across the room, not offering any words of encouragement, which was expected. The enforcer of our group rarely showed emotional support and kept to himself, unless we made some minor error, at which, he was always quick to correct.

Corporal Becker offered her sympathy. "Good luck, babe. Maybe he'll be in a good mood and let this one slide."

I shot her an unconvinced look in response, my words dripping with sarcasm. "Yeah, right. We've all been here for ten months without any booze, sex, or good entertainment. Pretty sure I'm fucked." I held out my rifle. "Can I leave Xena with you?"

She nodded and took it. Perez gave another pat on my shoulder before I walked out with all the enthusiasm of a prisoner on death row bound for the electric chair.

⚓   ⚓   ⚓

Commander Ryder's office stood a few meters across the open-air office complex, a sandy area lined with metal office units, picnic benches, and tarps offering minimal shade from the hot desert sun.

Stepping up to his door, I paused to adjust my uniform. The last thing I needed was a patch out of place during an already tense situation, then knocked three times.

"Come in." His stern voice was as raw as it was intimidating, his tone more of a direct order than an invite.

I slipped off my patrol cap while entering, closing the door behind. The entire trailer served as his personal office. While still relatively small, most soldiers in our brigade packed at least eight in offices of the same size. Despite our instructions to bring minimal personal items overseas, the Commander managed to transport numerous awards and trophies from home, displayed proudly around his desk. He always did think highly of himself, whether justified or not.

My attention drew to him staring down, shuffling through paperwork. I stood at parade rest, waiting for him to speak. The rigidness in the room brought back memories of the gas chamber exercise during Basic Training, and the tumultuous retching that followed.

"How are you, Sergeant Donegal?" he finally asked without glancing up. "Have a nice time this morning?"

My prediction was correct: he was pissed. We were all well-acquainted with his usual calm before the storm. I was hoping he would ask me to sit down to break some of the tension, but he didn't.

"What do you mean, sir?" My casual response masked the calamity in my head.

His arms crossed his chest while leaning back in his chair, emerald eyes piercing mine. "You were almost killed by a Saudi terrorist this morning," his tone more sagacious. "You don't have any thoughts about that?"

I assumed I had ample time to think over my response during the flight back, but suddenly, I couldn't speak. My head dropped, scrambling to find the right words.

"Don't look at your boots, Sergeant!" he snapped. "Look at me. How in the fuck did a Haji get a gun to the back of your head in broad daylight?"

My gaze locked onto his face, words still unable to find themselves, but at least he moved the conversation along.

"Part of your mission was to obtain your passport from the Embassy. Tell me what happened."

My throat cleared. "I wanted to see some of the sights in Baghdad, sir. Perez was showing me around since he's been there before. We took a walk to Zawra Park before heading back to the chopper, but I went further out than I probably should have, and…"

He stared back, arms still crossed. "So, you both could've been killed because you were sightseeing?"

I swallowed in nervousness. "That's an accurate assessment, sir."

He sat up, removing a folder from his drawer. "I'm reducing Perez's pay for the next two weeks."

My eyes widened with guilt. "No sir, please. It wasn't his fault. It was mine."

"It was his fault, Sergeant. And yours. You both should've been maintaining your situational awareness. Just because Baghdad is now a Green Zone doesn't mean you can let your guard down. We're still in a foreign country and not everyone wants us here."

It was hard to argue with his logic, so I didn't bother with excuses as his drilling continued.

"I'm placing you on additional duty until your leave. You'll be on cleaning detail starting tonight."

Blatant dismay shrouded my face. Latrine detail was a shit duty for the most useless soldiers in the battalion and everyone knows those soldiers have fucked up badly. I actually would've preferred a reduction in pay to save myself the humiliation.

"Is there a problem, Sergeant?" his query smug as he considered my reaction. Ryder was not the type to have his directives questions, so I clenched my teeth and remained agreeable.

"No, sir. That's fair."

"Good." He exhaled while removing a paper from his folder. "On a more positive note, the man who attacked you turned out to be Payar Mohammad al-Nasser."

Immediate recognition registered in the photocopy he handed over.

"He's been on FBI's Most Wanted list since '98 when he and his brother, Abdel Karim, blew up the Khobar Towers, killing nineteen of our airmen stationed there."

I nodded and returned the sheet of my attacker's face. "I remember when that happened, sir."

"He's now being questioned by the Iraqi government in hopes of locating his brother. They're both Shia leaders in the Hezbollah terrorist organization and last we knew, they had fled to Iran."

I smiled coyly. "Glad to see there's a silver lining, sir."

He glared back. "And that's the only reason you're on extra duty instead of being demoted, Sergeant."

I nodded reluctantly. "Roger that, sir. This momentary negligence won't happen again."

"See that it doesn't. You're one of our best NCOs and the soldiers look up to you. Don't let me down again." He took in another breath while pausing, his expression softening. "So, your R&R is coming up soon. Are you planning to go home? Spend some time with your family?"

"I won't be going home, sir."

He raised an eyebrow. "Where then? Going to go see your roots in Scotland?"

"New Zealand, sir." Saying the name aloud brought a smile back to my face. "I'll bring over the paperwork for your travel approval by this afternoon."

The raised slant in his mouth told me he remembered my interest in seeing the country, which I expressed in detail some time back.

I elaborated. "I've never been outside the U.S. aside from this deployment and I don't know when else I'll be able to travel that far. Life gets hectic back home and travel plans often get delayed, but this is something I don't want to put off."

His pen tapped the desk, and expression thoughtful. "That makes sense. You'll get to see Cali again in a couple of months anyway." He paused for another moment and frowned. "I thought you always wanted to see Egypt."

"Oh, I still do. I mean, it's on my list of top places to see, but I'm getting sick of seeing sand. Hate brushing it out of my ass crack every day."

His laugh brought some much-needed repose and I smiled, glad that the hard part of the conversation was over. His hands linked atop his desk, gaze lingering long enough to be marginally uncomfortable.

"Was there anything else you needed me for, sir?" I asked, still standing at parade rest.

His eyes trailed over the length of my body in a manner that was clearly not intended to be discreet. "Are you still spending time with that young mechanic from 837th?" His tone was accusatory, and expression one of combined concern, disappointment, and jealousy. "What's his name? Private McDouchefuck?"

His insulting question caught me off guard, and my tone turned defensive in response. "It's McDee, sir…" pause to sneer. "…though you seem to already know that."

"I do," he confirmed with arrogance. "Nothing occurs in my brigade without my knowledge. Did you really think I wouldn't find out?"

I was taken aback by his divulgence, but quickly realized my relationship with a subordinate soldier was probably no secret amongst the battalion, even if it was just temporary. Now would've been the perfect time for excuses, if I had any.

"Sir, I…"

He shot up from his desk and charged toward me, his intentions suspect. I backed up against the door as his hand planted on the wall behind. He leaned in so closely that I felt his warm breath at my neck, a sensation I both adored and despised.

"Scaith," his whisper slayed my ear. "Why would you ever be with someone who doesn't deserve you?"

Upon hearing my first name addressed, I knew we were no longer on official duty, and my professionalism dropped in favor of spite.

"Why don't you ask your wife the same thing, Jason?" I whispered back in the same accusatory tone, a snarl emphasized at his name.

His fierce eyes bore down to mine. "I hate it when you sass me."

My lips curled to a cunning smirk, one he was acquainted with. "Yeah, I know."

Our eyes met and within a second, his hand grasped behind my neck, tilting my face as his lips pressed firmly over mine. I should've panicked, but the scent of his cologne and feel of his muscular chest were so inebriating, I welcomed it. When his hand soon found its way to my belt buckle, I shoved him back, shaking my head at my own feebleness.

"Stop, sir." My palm held firmly against his chest, keeping him at arm's length. "Let's hold off until we're done here. We already agreed."

A long sigh escaped him as his fingers ran over light chestnut, buzz cut hair. He seemed frustrated, but understanding.

"I get so hard when you say my name, Scaith. This feels like the longest deployment of my life and I could've lost you today." His hand reached up to stroke my cheek, then ran down my arm, fingers tracing the tactical American flag. "Don't ever do that to me again."

I now understood where his anger originated from. Our affair had lasted on and off since his reassignment as Commander of my unit three years ago. He also became subordinate to his estranged wife, the Brigadier General of Rear Detachment back home. At this point, I wasn't sure where our relationship stood, or his, though this incident may have reignited us... something I'd been trying hard to avoid.

He cleared his throat, returning to his desk as though it were a throne. "Here." He handed over a folder. "I need these memos typed up and back to me EOD."

I took it absent dialogue. His commandeering self had obviously bounced back, which was my cue to exit. I saluted and turned to leave.

"One more thing, Sergeant…"

I reluctantly spun around to see his demeanor turn more sentimental.

"I meant it when I said you're a good soldier, Scaith. I feel proud to have taken someone of your caliber and potential under my leadership. You've always worked hard and done the right thing."

"Until you, sir," my response emanating impudence.

His gaze dropped a notch. "I hope I'm not holding you back or clouding your judgment, because I don't want to do that to you."

I was tempted to agree, but decided against it. When it came to him, I never felt in control, but wasn't about to admit how utterly vulnerable his presence made me. His elevated ego didn't need more fuel to burn.

"You're not, sir. I'm in control of my own actions. I know what I'm doing."

"Good to hear. There's an E6 slot opening up soon and I'd like to see you apply. I know you only have four months of service left, but it would be nice to promote you before you get out."

I showed no countenance. "I'll consider it, sir."

He added, "If you bring your travel request documentation to me this afternoon, I'll approve it," his smile subtle. "I'd like to see you take that trip."

"Thank you, sir. I will." I saluted again and quickly left his office, feeling instant consolation once back outside.

⚜   ⚜   ⚜

Only Corporal Becker sat at her deck when I returned to the S4 office, her back facing me.

"Hey, where's everyone else?"

Her headphones dropped into her hands as her chair twirled around. "The LTs are at supply and Perez went to the gym. I'm already caught up on my stuff, so now just fucking around on this Facebook site and listening to some tunes."

"Good. I could use some peace and quiet." I settled into my desk next to her as she returned my rifle.

"How'd it go with Mr. Hot Head?" Her knowing, umber eyes revealed she knew what was going on, and smirked with bawdy approval.

I shook my head, flustered with discomposure. "Nothing gets past you, does it?"

"Not when you stroll in here with an obvious 'I just got ravaged' face."

Becker was the only person I trusted, having known about my affair with Commander Ryder since the beginning. She never judged me for it, even when I judged myself, and once again, I felt relieved to have her by my side.

"Nothing quite that taxing." I set the folder on my desk. "We haven't talked about anything other than work since before pre-MOB."

"I'm not surprised he came onto you again. You're hot, his wife's a power-hungry cunt, and he's gotta have some serious blue balls. I'm sure all these guys do. I know I do."

I chuckled softly. "How's it going with Specialist Vernon?"

"It's great. For now, anyway. She's clingy, but I always remind her that she's going back to Texas in two months."

"You're gonna break her heart, aren't you?"

She winked, her smile self-assured. "Won't be the last one, babe."

My attention turned back to my computer. After inserting my CAC card in the reader, I started typing up the Commander's memos until Becker reached under her desk, placing a bottle of detergent next to me.

Confusion swelled. "Uh, you want to go on a date to laundry later?"

"Open it," she stated enthusiastically.

I twisted the cap off and looked inside to see a clear liquid, inhaling a very strong alcoholic smell. "Whoa!" My head snapped back. "What the hell is that? Turpentine?"

She giggled deviously, a reaction well known to me.

Tsk. "What have you gone and done now?"

"It's homemade moonshine. I got it from Raj, that Indian contractor in transient housing."

I smiled in anticipation, grateful to have such a resourceful friend. "Pretty sure that stuff burned my nose hairs just now, but I could use something strong. Let's definitely break this out tonight."

She let out a humorous scoff. "Who says it has to be tonight?" She chugged the remaining water from her canteen and began replacing it with moonshine.

"Careful, hon. If VonRutenburg's anal ass comes in here and sees you, yours is grass."

As if on cue, Lieutenants Belinsky and VonRutenburg strolled through the door a moment later. I shot Becker my best 'See, I told you so' look before she swiftly concealed her contraband. It didn't take long before Belinsky's obnoxiously overpowering voice filled the office, ricocheting off the stark-white walls.

"You know why I hate these DoD civilians?" he boisterously entreated aloud to no one in particular.

"Do you want a list, sir?" I asked facetiously, but he kept grumbling as if he didn't hear me.

"Aside from them earning three times what we do and not having to carry a rifle and gas mask everywhere, they don't know how to do their fuckin' jobs. They just approved Specialist Bentz for forty percent VA disability. You know why?"

Becker and I shrugged while glued to our computers, hoping he'd sit down and shut up for once.

"Because he's got the shits!" he laughed maniacally. "I've had the shits since we got here. Where's my rating?"

"A little Saddam Soup never hurt anyone, sir," I teased him. "We've all been there. I lost like ten pounds the first month we got here."

Becker chimed in. "Maybe you're just not sucking the right dicks, KGB."

"Why don't you go suck some for me, Becker?" he quipped back. "Take one for the team."

She cringed in disgust. "No thanks, sir. I like my men with tits and no wieners."

Belinsky flopped down at his desk and kicked his feet up, nearly knocking over his laptop. There was a brief moment of silence until he pulled out a bag of Cheetos.

VonRutenburg turned toward me with his usual authoritative stance. "Sergeant, did you complete that HIPAA training yet?"

Brief panic arose as I had yet to check my email. "Uh, not yet, sir. I'm opening the attachment now."

"Make sure you get it done. Commander wants all the printed certificates by today. Don't turn it in late like you did with your Hazmat training."

His snide tone was infuriating, and annoyingly frequent, but I kept my opinion to myself. "Roger that, sir. Got it."

VonRutenburg always came off bossy, his sense of superiority to those he outranked evident. He joined our unit specifically for this deployment after completing ROTC. His family was said to own several upscale seafood restaurants in San Diego and were well-known in wealthy southern California social circles. Some people even claim they changed their last name from Rutenburg to VonRutenburg, just to sound more entitled. When I first saw him, I thought he resembled Jared Kushner, and I still do.

Belinsky was at least the entertaining one of the officers; a short, burly Russian-American with tawny hair and an eccentric personality. If he's bothered by the fact that we call him KGB, he doesn't seem to show it. He could spend an entire day expressing his obscene sexual fantasies over every woman he crosses paths with, though here in the sandbox, there weren't many.

I worked in silence, occasionally daydreaming of my upcoming trip to New Zealand. With an already-created list of things to do, I was ready to book my hostel stay pending flight approval. Perez entered the trailer just as I finished my online training.

"Hey, how was the gym, Master Sergeant?" Belinsky mumbled across the room through a mouthful of Cheetos.

Perez set his rifle in the corner next to his desk. "Packed. Everyone's bored with not much work left to do." He checked his watch. "It's almost noon. You guys wanna head to chow?"

Everyone got up except me. I opted to stay and finish a few things. Translation: Clear my head of distractions; namely a spineless terrorist who wasn't worth worrying about... and a certain other man who kept invading my thoughts.

After about two hours of cleaning detail that night, I took another shower and returned toward my room sporting my usual off-duty wear: a grey PT shirt and black shorts.

The sun was just setting as I swung the door open, revealing a petite African-American girl hovering over Becker… topless.

My lips twisted to a smirk as I cleared my throat, trying to face toward my side of the room. Being too late to retreat now, I embraced a more comical route than one of embarrassment.

"Hey, Specialist Vernon. Nice tits."

She sat up with a proud look on her face. "Thanks, Sergeant Donegal," her voice high-pitched and almost childlike. She pulled her hair into a bun with her entire upper body on clear display. Becker continued to lay on her bed, her hands interlaced behind her. The gaze she gave me begged approval of her latest fling.

I had to laugh. Neither of them had any shame, which I admired. One of Becker's finest qualities was her effortless dismissal of anyone's judgment, a trait I unfortunately lacked.

"Hey babe, Dee was here earlier looking for you," she informed me. "He probably heard about what happened in Baghdad. You know how emotional he gets."

"Okay, I'll head over there. You two can continue your… thing."

I pulled my PT jacket from the locker and headed out to the male housing area. Many soldiers were hanging out in front of their rooms while some were sneaking off to hook up.

In the few minutes it took to walk to Private McDee's door, it was already pitch black outside. His door cracked open before I could knock, his inviting smile showing off white teeth contrasted against beige Puerto Rican skin. His Army dog tags hung loosely over his bare chest and light grey sweatpants. Despite not working out much, I always thought he had a nice build. Though not the alluring Trojan that Ryder was, McDee's affections were comfortable and safe.

"Baby girl, get in here." He spoke with an adorable Texas drawl, as did many other soldiers from 837th, including Specialist Vernon.

After quietly stepping into his room, he slammed the door and hugged me. His distraught behavior over my near-death encounter was apparent. In comfort, I kissed the top of his shaved head, which stood a foot shorter.

"I heard what happened," his declaration hushed and apologetic. "Glad you're all right, baby girl."

I sighed, tossing my jacket on his bed. I had been there many times before, but he now lived alone since his roommate shipped home early for a family emergency. Lucky for me, what I wanted from McDee tonight didn't require an audience.

My hands slid around his back, my gaze falling to his silver puppy-dog eyes. "You know what, Dee? I'm done talking for today." My lips enclosed over his, and he happily obliged.

I couldn't have found a more perfect friend and playmate during deployment. He was young and energetic, easy to be around, and eager to please. At just twenty years old, he was seven years my younger, whereas Ryder was fifteen my senior. I cared for them both in different ways, but knew neither relationship was meant for long-term. Once deployment ended, McDee would return to Texas with his unit and I would be back in California with mine, an arrangement we were both content with. Though my thoughts occasionally drifted back to Ryder, I remained in the moment, releasing my cares and concerns away to this ever-willing recipient, returning to my own bed hours later.

2

I awoke early to a thunderous explosion.

Becker groaned while turning to her clock. "Why are the jets taking off right now? It's like four a.m."

Another blast rattled our room before the sirens went off shouting, "Incoming! Incoming! Incoming!"

"Oh, shit!" I jolted from bed. "Those are mortars! Get up!"

We snatched our rifles and darted out the door in our flip flops, trudging along the dusty path in earnest. Above us, streaks of red light blazed across the dark sky from the C-RAMS as missiles countered the incoming mortars. We dashed into one of the stone bunkers within our housing area along with hundreds of others. Several soldiers huddled in the same bunker as mortars continuously exploded nearby, the pitch black airspace made brighter only by the occasional flash of red.

"I'm hit!" a soldier shouted within the bunker.

"Keep your heads down!" I warned over the commotion.

The explosions subsided minutes later. We stood by for the "All Clear" announcement before crawling back out, and I turned to address the group.

"All right, safety check. Specialist Hoffman, how's your leg?"

Embedded shrapnel poked out just above his boot. "Fine, Sergeant. It's a flesh wound."

"Okay, I'll notify your section leader. You can head straight to Medical. The rest of you get to your sections for headcount."

The soldiers scampered off in different directions while Becker and I hurried toward Perez's CHU.

"Think I pissed myself," Becker joked, trying to make light of the situation.

"These guys are getting bolder," I noted. "Mosul has seen a big increase in attacks lately. They're not fucking around."

"So has Basra. Sergeant Jensen said a roadside IED went off right outside base when her convoy was there last week."

"Yeah, they're lucky no Humvees were hit. Apparently, there was another suicide, too. One of the British soldiers. Think it's high time to get us all back home."

Perez stood in front of his door talking with several soldiers.

"Morning, Master Sergeant," I spoke up. "Becker and I are checking in."

"You both all right?"

"We're good, but Specialist Hoffman went to Medical with some shrapnel to the leg."

"I'll let S1 know. You both stay in the area. The Commander will probably call a morning formation."

⚜   ⚜   ⚜

Becker and I utilized the gym for an hour before getting ready back at the latrines. We showered and met at the sinks, our same daily routine for the last several months.

"Hmm. I'm thinking a little makeup today." She finger-brushed her short brown hair while still wrapped in her towel.

"You wear makeup now? Since when?"

"Since Vernon gave me some mascara. It's nice to feel a little human again."

"True. I really miss having my hair down." I sighed pensively. "And wearing civilian clothes, and going out to eat, and taking road trips..."

"Just two more months, babe," she reminded me while sloppily applying mascara. "We'll head straight to Cinebar when we get home, get drunk, and never think about this place again."

While brushing my teeth, two young Privates occupied the sinks next to us, gossiping like they were on a reality show. Upon hearing the Commander mentioned, I couldn't help but overhear their conversation.

"…and then I saw him walk to the latrines this morning in a tight black t-shirt," Private Matthews bragged. "He looked so hot. Next time I see him, I'm gonna put on my white tank top without a bra and walk right past him."

Both girls giggled like high schoolers with a crush. Neither one could've been more than about nineteen, and were clearly from one of the subordinate units.

"I heard he's stabbing one of his soldiers," Private Reese responded, glazing on lip gloss. "One of those stuck up chicks from Brigade."

Becker's subtly curious look shot my way as she was also listening in on their conversation.

"Not surprised. His wife's like off fucking the Mayor of San Jose or something. And with a body like his, he can have any girl here he wants."

"Maybe we should transfer to California. Oklahoma sucks anyway. It's so boring there."

Slight jealousy arose the longer they spoke, but I brushed it off, mentally kicking myself for being so ridiculous and petty. The girls babbled on about some other guy for a while before leaving the latrines.

Becker turned to me immediately, her expression seeping with concern. "Sounds like we've got some Blue Falcons in our ranks. Do you think he's seeing someone else?"

I tried to shake off what I had just overheard. "I don't know, but it's none of my business. I don't own him, nor does he own me. Besides, he has a wife…"

"…who doesn't give two shits about him, babe," she cut in, trying to subside my obvious guilt. "You're the best thing to ever happen to that cocky prick. You know that?"

The latrine door opened with Sergeant Jensen poking her head inside. "Formation in fifteen minutes, you guys."

꧁ ꧂ ꧁

All eighty-nine soldiers were lined up in formation outside as Commander Ryder took headcount. The sun was just starting to rise, heating the morning breeze just beyond comfort. Birds chirped as they sat atop the blustering tarps.

"At ease," Ryder commanded, our arms relaxing down from parade rest. "Good morning, soldiers!" he addressed while pacing.

"Good morning, sir!" our response unified.

"How is everyone doing?"

"HOOAH!"

"Outstanding. Let's keep up those high-speed attitudes. I want to address a few things happening lately. First off, great job this morning for your quick response on the mortar attack. We haven't had one for a while and came out with a quick safety check and only two soldiers with minor injuries; however, we have had some other concerns recently. Last night, one of the 147th Chinooks went down while on mission near al-Asad during a supposed attack, but luckily no deaths reported. Also, yesterday morning a known Saudi terrorist held one of our soldiers at gunpoint within the Green Zone. I want to take this time to remind everyone that we are still on duty twenty-four seven and must maintain our military bearings. We are not out of the desert just yet, so let's not get complacent. That said, be sure you're always aware of your surroundings, never go out without a battle buddy, especially after dark, stay hydrated, continue showing proper respect to rank, and maintain your professionalism. Keep in mind we have five subordinate units from different states that report to us. Let's keep setting the example. Right now, transient housing is still operating in contraband, including illegal drugs, alcohol, and prostitution. You *will not* partake in these activities. Have I made myself clear?"

"HOOAH!" we shouted again.

My mind wandered as he continued covering various topics. His confidence and intense presence were what captured my interest from the beginning, and part of me hated him for it. He knew exactly how to use that charming personality to his advantage.

"That'll be all for now." He stood at attention. "Group, attention!" We followed suit. "Dismissed."

Formation broke as soldiers maundered off to their sections. Ryder brushed through the group, prudently passing me an envelope before continuing to his office absent a glance back. It quickly found its way to my pocket as I settled back at my desk.

The others flooded in slowly. Belinsky was rattling on about some hot Ugandan soldier while VonRutenburg didn't even pretend to be listening. Perez started chatted at his corner desk in Spanish while on the phone with his wife back home.

I faced the wall, ripping open the envelope, and inside found flight tickets to New Zealand for the following week. I gasped silently and pressed them against my chest, the realization kicking in that I was actually going. While opening my desk drawer to tuck it away, I also noticed a blue Post-It stuck inside.

Peeling it out, I mentally read the words, "My office, tonight - 9pm."

I jumped as Becker entered the office and sank to her desk, exhaling loudly.

"I tell you what, babe. I don't even remember what it's like to take a normal shit anymore. Here, it's like you've either got the shits or you can't shit at all."

"Uh-huh," I mumbled, quickly obscuring the envelope and its incriminating contents.

"What's up, babe? Want me to make you some coffee?"

I leaned in closely and whispered, "Do you still have some of that unauthorized ambrosia?"

Her smirk was all the answer I needed.

"Fantastic. What do you say to a little indulgence tonight?"

"I say 'fuck yeah.' I was thinking we could go to the bazaar later, too. Maybe bring Dee and Vernon along."

"Yeah, okay. Just make sure it's early enough. I need to pull a late cleaning detail tonight... around nine."

"Oh, that sucks." She turned to her computer, now back in the solace of her headphones.

⚜   ⚜   ⚜

I had rushed to pull an early cleaning shift, leaving enough room for evening "events." The bazaar was a far walk to the opposite side of base, a place where soldiers went to get away from the long, redundant workdays… and to get into trouble.

Becker handed over her canteen as soon as I arrived. "I believe you ordered this."

McDee and Vernon were with her, browsing through locally-made trinkets on display.

"You're my champion." I smiled after a long swig, waiting for the burning sensation to clear, then returned it to my mouth for another sip.

"So, will that be the only thing going down your throat tonight?"

I nearly choked, my glance over to her inquisitive.

"Oh, come on, babe. You're a terrible liar. I know you're not going to cleaning detail this late. You're seeing *him*, aren't you?"

McDee and Vernon joined us before I could speak.

"Hey, Sergeant Donegal. Look what I just bought." Vernon held up an exquisite, shiny gold ring, a colorful peacock gracing the center. "It's made with real gold from India."

"That's gorgeous. Think I'll go see what else they have."

McDee gaped at the canteen longingly as we relocated to the bazaar tables. "Baby girl, can I have some of that?"

For the next hour, we sifted through gold vases, leather wallets, miniature flags, and jewelry, then chatted and drank moonshine inside a bunker until we were all a little tipsy. McDee had his arm around me. I didn't remove it, but didn't let it go any further as I was about to ditch him for another man.

One more swig and I checked my watch. "Okay guys, I've gotta run. Got cleaning detail in fifteen minutes." I crouched up, stepping outside the bunker with an anxious McDee following behind.

"Hey, I'll walk back with you."

Before I could object, Becker stuck her head out. "She's fine, Dee. Get back in here."

"Yeah, I don't want to be late. I'll talk to you guys later."

With a quick wave I scampered off, leaving behind a slightly disheartened McDee.

.ᴼ.   .ᴼ.   .ᴼ.

I was a little drunker than I anticipated for, making the walk to Ryder's office feel excruciatingly long. A mint found its way to my mouth before reaching the complex, though I doubt it did much to mask my intoxication. Jason could always see right through me, which I found annoying, and strangely enough... attractive.

Without knocking, I burst through the door, quietly shutting it after. He glanced up from reading paperwork, his legs crossed while leaning against the desk. His ACUs were absent the jacket, showing off a perfectly toned chest and muscular arms bulging through his tan t-shirt. A tempting display.

Our eyes remained locked, his demeanor calm and composed. Without saying a word, he tossed his papers aside and removed the gun holster strapped to his thigh. With my rifle against the file cabinet, I locked the door, and the room stood dead silent. No conversation was needed as we both knew why I came. Invite or not, I consciously chose to be there.

I sprinted across the office, his hands gripping my head fiercely in overwhelming need. The warmth of his lips and dominating flicks of his tongue caused a moan from deep in my throat. He stripped my bun loose, allowing my long blonde hair to flow freely as strong arms circled my waist and spun me around, planting me atop the desk with his massive build towering over. His hands explored my often-concealed curves with possessive hunger, my body responding with almost painful insistence.

I paused to draw in a much-needed breath, and express my raw demand in a sultry whisper. "Fuck me senseless, Jason."

He wasted no time adhering to my request. My shorts dropped to the floor and panties ripped from my body in one searing swoop. As his fingers trailed up my shirt and over my breast, I reached down, unhooking his belt. Sliding my hand down his pants, I pulled out his immense, hardened cock; a paragon long missed. Seductive grunts fled him as my thumb traced his generous length.

"Goddammit, Scaith." He brushed a tuft of hair behind my ear. "Do you know what you do to me?"

I glanced up, my sassy smirk returning. "Yes."

His stiff flesh plunged forward, its thickness fulfilling with each strong, brutish thrust. I sprawled back, slipping out of my t-shirt and sports bra. He held my hips firmly, tugging me closer. As he traversed my body, papers toppled from his desk when his thrusts quickened, sending sensations of primal desire through me. His body was hard as oak, but skin smooth as porcelain, aside from some battle scars scattered across his chest and arms. My wrist slapped over my mouth to stay relatively quiet, though I wanted nothing more than to scream out his name.

He swept me up, moving us to his couch while still inside me. I was flipped over, gripping the frame as he rammed on in an almost animalistic nature. My head jerked back at his tug of my hair and I cried out in rapture, craving more of everything he was doing to me.

His cavernous breaths increased in speed and he moaned raucously as he came, squeezing my ass cheek so tightly that a handprint remained. I climaxed in the ensuing moment, his hands still gripping me in place.

We both collapsed to the couch, panting fiercely. A drop of sweat trickled down his cheek when he leaned back, his hands resting over his head. The office now sat in silence again with only the sounds of our fathomless breathing.

"Guess our PT for tomorrow is already taken care of," I teased.

He smiled, brushing hair away from my face. "I missed you, baby."

Sometimes his subtle tenderness, though a rare occurrence, felt relatively uneasy. I could only equate it to lack of emotion attachment, but at least he fucked like a Greek god. I returned to the desk, slinking back into my clothes as he sprang up in covetous confusion.

"Leaving already?"

"Yeah, I better get back."

"Why is that?" his visage turning moderately chilling.

Guilt was already overtaking my thoughts again. "Because, Jason... tomorrow you're still my Commander. Not much we can do to change that. We should keep these visits short given our circumstances." I held up my panties, now torn in half. "And you owe me a trip to the PX."

He laughed, clasping his belt. "Sorry about that."

I grinned. "We both know you're not."

"Nope. I'm not."

I tucked them into my shorts and pulled my hair back to a bun, fixing a few loose strands. Retrieving my rifle, I pecked Jason's cheek and glanced back at the floor, now enveloped in papers.

"Sorry for the mess," my apology flippant.

"It was worth it." Stroking the sides of my face, he claimed one more kiss before cracking the door open. "Goodnight, Scaith."

I silently stepped out.

"And no more drinking… or I'll give you more than just a slap on the ass," he stoically warned before shutting the door.

⚜   ⚜   ⚜

The evening air cooled my blushing cheeks, my footsteps breaking through the silence like a walk of shame. My impulse to get back soon was cut short when I abruptly halted, now guarded by someone emerging from the overshadowed tarp ahead.

"Perez?" My guess was confirmed as he stepped into the light. "What are you doing out here this late?"

"I'd like to ask you the same, Don," his face distinctly discouraged.

"I was submitting my travel request form for R&R next week." The ruse couldn't have been more unconvincing.

"You turned that in yesterday." He spoke temperately, yet with force. His eyes glimpsed behind me at Ryder's office, then recoiled back. "How long has this been going on? And don't bother trying to deny it. We all know what a bad liar you are."

"Were you following me?" I started to lose my cool.

Reaching into his jacket pocket, he tossed out a crumpled blue paper, and all my convictions sank. I knew exactly what it was.

"I went looking for a pen in your desk earlier." He sighed with frustration. "There's only one person here that uses blue Post-Its."

I retrieved it, but gaze remained at the ground. My options were slim, and there was nothing I could say to make the situation any better.

"The *Commander*, Don? Seriously?" he continued to scold me. "Ryder's actions are punishable by court-martial. Is that what you want for him?"

"Can you lower your voice?" I scanned the area for eavesdroppers and grabbed him by the arm. "Come on. Let's walk and talk."

"End this, Don," his voice saturated with worry. "Inform him tomorrow that it's over."

I took long strides. "I really don't want to have this talk with you."

"And you think I do? I'd rather this conversation not have to occur at all, or at least have it with anyone but you."

My pace increased. The sooner I was back at my room, the sooner I could escape his judgement.

"Don, I want you to listen to me. I know men like Ryder. They're used to getting what they want. I'm sure you're not the first beautiful young woman that's caught his attention."

Now I was seething. "What he does with his personal time is not my concern!"

Perez stopped and turned me toward him, slightly out of breath. "That's exactly the problem, Don. His personal time is *you*."

I looked away, desperately wanting to dodge his scrutiny.

His deep sigh indicated near-defeat. "At least consider what I've said. If you keep this going you could ruin your military career, as well as his. You don't want an Article 15 or dishonorable discharge to follow you for the rest of your life. You're so close to getting out. Don't waste your hard-earned years of service. Not for *him*."

I knew he was right. He usually was, and despite my denial, I always sensed it would come down to this. Ryder was like a drug I had trouble giving up, a temporary high with potentially devastating results.

"He's not worth it, Don. Trust me. You deserve much better than this."

I stopped myself from crying as the situation's emotional intensity got the better of me, and glanced up to him. "Thank you for giving me the chance to correct my own mistake. I couldn't ask for a better friend and leader."

I hugged him as he let out a relieving blow. "Chin up, Don. Just view this as a minor slip-up in the grand scheme of life's crazy adventures and experiences. We all need reality checks from time to time."

"Appreciate it, Perez." I let go of him. "That's a good way of looking at it."

"And no regrets, right?"

I half-smiled, still trying to avoid a tear from forming. "Right. No regrets."

After a vigorous gym routine to blow off steam, I showered and walked to the mess hall alone before the typical morning line started forming. In passing, a Sergeant I didn't recognize called out to me.

"Hey Sergeant, where's your battle buddy, huh?"

I ignored him, my stony face now plastered with a scowl. I fired aggressively into the clearing barrel, pretending it was the overweening Sergeant's face. Upon entering the mess hall, I sullenly grabbed a tray while awaiting the same boring breakfast.

"Good morning, ma'am," Khalid pronounced with his usual flirtatiousness. "You look beautiful, ma'am."

I managed a partial smile, just to avoid any disrespect. A full, unfeigned smile was too much to ask for right now.

Not long after sitting down, Becker dropped her tray across the table, her appearance suggesting she had just woken up.

"You're up early," she noted while yawning.

"Did you guys stay up late?"

She snickered. "Vernon and I did. Dee left right after you took off. He looked like a poor little lost kitten without his cougar."

I continued eating, giving no response.

"Oh no," she remarked, studying my off-putting behavior. "Did it not go according to plan last night?"

My head shook. "Not exactly."

"Did he try to stick it in the wrong hole again?" She chortled delicately, though her eyes remained fixed on mine, still waiting for an explanation.

"Perez knows," I sagely divulged.

Her eyes widened. "Oh, shit. What happened?"

I chugged my water canteen and let out a burp that could make any truck driver envious. "He told me to end it."

She paused in contemplation. "Is that what *you* want?"

I didn't answer, opting instead to poke at my food with a fork.

She sighed, as if privy to the battle I was having within myself. "Okay, you know what, babe? You're leaving in just a few days to this beautiful, tropical country for two weeks. It's the perfect time to let this situation settle. You'll probably come back with a clear and fresh perspective, so just forget about all this drama for now. When has worrying ever helped you?"

I did start to cheer up, kudos to her efforts. "You're right, hon."

"Too easy." She sat up, her smirk indecorous. "Now, tell me all the juicy stuff."

⚜   ⚜   ⚜

I worked in solitude for an hour before the rest of my section entered sporadically. Becker was working in the supply office for the day conducting inventory. In the middle of typing, Belinsky's awkward gaze caught my attention from across the room.

"Hey Donegal, you look like goat shit today. What happened? Have a bad date last night or something?"

My eyes returned to the computer screen. Everything about my appearance should've screamed "Do Not Engage," but he pressed on, despite my obvious disinterest in whatever he had to say.

His fingers snapped. "I've got it! He's not good at eatin' pussy." He cackled as though he were the most hilarious person alive. "Hey girl, I get it. I mean, some guys just suck at it… mind the pun. I'd be happy to help you out with that if you…"

My composure snapped, resulting in a calculator hurled in his direction. He ducked as it smashed into a hundred pieces against the wall. His widened eyes snapped back at me with his jaw dropped, his trembling palms darting up in shock.

Perez calmly spoke up from his desk. "Sir, maybe today isn't the best day for your jokes."

Belinsky's awoken vision now trailed downward, slowly turning back to his laptop. "Sorry, Don."

The embarrassment wafting off the overly egotistical officer was quite a revelation, one I found mildly appeasing.

VonRutenburg shook his head in revulsion. "It's like working with a bunch of children here."

For the next few hours, we all worked amidst uncomfortable silence.

⚓   ⚓   ⚓

The day prior to my scheduled flight to New Zealand had arrived and I was finishing up some last minute work in the S4 office.

"Sergeant Don, is the CONEX report completed for this month?"

I stood and turned to address Perez. "Already submitted. I emailed you my contacts for the transportation office. You might have to ship back some equipment, so just make sure these contractors attach RFID tags with enough battery power to last the whole trip. Some shipments are getting lost in transit or only make it as far as Dover."

An email alert popped up on my screen from Ryder, asking me to come to his office for my travel safety briefing. I grabbed my rifle and CAC card from the reader, locking the computer.

"Be right back," I informed Perez while exiting.

The weather was beautiful with the early afternoon heat tolerable for a change. I knocked on Ryder's door, which was already open.

"Sergeant Donegal, come on in and take a seat."

I left his door open and sat down. We hadn't really spoken since our late-night excursion. My plan to break things off was still etched in my mind, though I figured I could enjoy my vacation first before broaching the subject.

"This folder contains all your flight details, report times, copy of your passport, and a phone card. You already completed your online anti-terrorism and risk assessment training?"

"Yes sir, though it seems unusual to need it for New Zealand."

"It's standard procedure for every country, per the State Department. The C-130 will take you to Kuwait City at six a.m., so report in at least fifteen minutes early. From there, you have a layover in Dubai before reaching Auckland. All our unit's information in theater is included in that sheet, so don't lose it under any circumstances. You'll leave your military gear here and take only your two sets of civilian clothes, duffel bag, and any other personal items you need. You call me and report in as soon as you arrive at your hotel."

My smile beamed in anticipation for the arrival. "Can't wait, sir."

"I've also included the number for Carlson Wagonlit should you have any trouble with the booking arrangements."

I nodded. "I'll look over the details before tomorrow, sir."

He sipped his canteen. "So, what sort of things will you be doing there?"

I shrugged. "Oh, usual vacation things: Drink a lot, swim with dolphins… skinny dipping."

He chuckled. "Too bad I won't be there."

I silently scolded the naughty little slut inside me for continuing to flirt with him. "Am I all set to go, sir?"

"You are from *my* end, Sergeant. Just make sure you have everything ready and get enough sleep so you're on time. It'll be a long flight for you."

"Yes, sir." I stood up to leave but paused, my fingers twitching in anxiousness. "Um, actually, I wanted to tell you…"

His sudden unnerving manner was almost daring me as he tapped his pen, as though predicting what I was about to say.

"Yes?"

My words dissipated, and I shook my head in vanquish. "It's nothing, sir. Never mind."

"Then I'll see you in a couple weeks, Scaith." He shot me a cool-headed wink. "Have a good trip."

⚜   ⚜   ⚜

Perez released Becker and I from duty early, so I started packing my duffel bag back in our room while she sat cross-legged on her bed, browsing the net.

"Excited about your first solo international trip, babe?"

"Of course. Looking forward to a change of scenery from this ass-ugly dump. Just wish you could come with me."

"Me, too." Her solemn guise suddenly lit up. "Hey, I got you something." She pulled a small cloth bag from her pocket, handing it over. "I almost forgot about it."

"You didn't have to buy me something, hon. You're so sweet." Inside was a familiar gold ring with a colorful peacock.

"It's the same one Vernon bought the other day," she refreshed my memory. "I remember you saying you liked it. The Indian guy at the bazaar said the peacock is some Hindu god that represents safe travels."

I gleamed with appreciation, sliding the ring on. "I love it. Thank you so much."

A little while later, someone knocked at the door. McDee stood outside the doorway when I answered, still wearing his ACUs as though just coming from work.

"Hey baby girl, wanna go for a walk?"

I inherently wanted to dodge the question. "Uh, no. Not tonight."

My dismissive response seemed to crush his confidence. "But you're leaving tomorrow for two weeks."

I digressed. "I know, but I'm gonna get to bed early. I have an early flight."

Since reuniting with Ryder, I hadn't been spending much time with him anymore, so I couldn't help but feel a little guilty. He had been nothing but a wonderful friend these last few months and was always there when I needed him.

I stepped down from the trailer. "Come here, Dee." I hugged him, pinching his ass in playful apology. "I'll miss you."

"Miss you, too, baby girl," his disappointment starting to dwindle.

"Sorry I've been so distracted lately. I'll be back soon and we can pick up where we left off."

With that, he strolled back to his room as I returned to mine.

Becker's amusement surfaced. "Now who's breaking hearts? That was so adorable, I think I might vomit my chili mac."

"Here." I set my rifle next to her. "You're officially in charge of Xena while I'm gone."

"Sure. I'll take good care of her." She popped open a bag of cookies as I laid down, resting my head in my hand. "Speaking of big, stiff weapons, did you say anything to Ryder earlier?"

"No, I cowered out. Lost yet another battle with my conscience."

She crunched into a cookie and sighed. "You know what, babe? He's a major distraction for you. I know the sex and sneaking around is super-hot, but maybe it's time to end it altogether."

"You're right. I just wish I knew how."

"You seem to like the mysterious and forbidden, and always did things your way, even if they went against the rules." She paused. "I don't know. Maybe a real relationship is the answer."

"Whoa. This coming from the queen of non-commitment?"

She grinned. "Shameful, I know. But seriously, babe, since losing your mom and that... 'encounter' when you were sixteen, I don't think you've ever let yourself get too close to anyone again. I think it's your perception of Ryder that you like. He's temporarily filling some void, but what you really want is to travel the world and experience what's out there, see new countries and meet new people. You bide your time with these lists that you do until you can experience the real thing. You'll be getting out of the military soon with a passport in hand, so what's stopping you? Time to move on and start a new life, babe."

I closed my eyes, wishing life's decisions were simpler. "You're right. I have no excuses."

"And stop with the guilt, babe! I know what you're doing right now."

"Sorry," I mumbled.

"You *do* deserve to be happy. Your next adventure starts tomorrow, so get some sleep and quit worrying about any past mistakes."

I turned to her and smiled. "You're the best friend anyone could have."

She winked back. "I know."

A majestic orange glow cast across the parked aircraft when I arrived at sunrise. I took out my camera and snapped a photo, the first of my trip. About thirty other people were huddled in a group near the C-130, most wearing civilian clothes. Some were soldiers leaving for R&R, some DoD civilians, and some foreign contractors. I approached the Warrant Officer in uniform.

"Are you on the manifest?" he asked while glancing up from his clipboard.

"Yes, Chief. Scaith Donegal."

"Check. We'll start boarding in fifteen minutes. If you want chow there's MREs."

I shoved the tightly-packaged bag of overly-processed, questionable food into my duffel for later, and joined the group.

"Morning, Sergeant Donegal." A lively young man emerged with curly cinnamon hair and a black and white Adidas sports jersey.

"Hey, Private Williams. I barely recognized you in civilian clothes."

"Likewise, Sarge." He glanced over my baby-blue blouse and dark jeans. "You look great in civies. I mean, you always look great, but you know…"

I smiled back. "Where are you going for your R&R?"

"The Philippines."

"Wow, good choice. I'm heading to New Zealand for mine."

He seemed to already know that. "Have fun. I'm gonna be on beach the whole time," he described, slapping his hands in excitement. "I booked one of those huts right on the water."

"Make sure you don't enjoy it so much that you don't come back. I've heard of that happening."

He laughed. "Oh, I'll come back. Same to you, Sarge."

The Warrant Officer returned to announce boarding. We lined up on the runway, each grabbing a kevlar before following the ramp into the mouth of the C-130.

"These planes are badass, right?" Private Williams yelled over the noisy engine as we strapped ourselves in.

"Yeah, we flew in on one of these when we first arrived here."

The group settled in along with some cargo before the plane took off.

Our group departed in Kuwait City several hours later. I recognized the distinct white and blue Kuwait Towers a short distance from the airport, a landmark that had been the subject of a terrorist attack in '83 when the Hezbollah detonated a car bomb. I mentally connected that it was the same group responsible for the Khobar Towers attack of '98, as well as my own assassination attempt in Baghdad. Their terrorist activities seemed to be all over the Middle East. I snapped some pictures before entering the airport.

I waved goodbye to Private Williams as he proceeded toward a different terminal, then located my gate despite the flight to Dubai not leaving for a while. Being out of the war zone, I already felt better. I purchased a novel from one of the shops and read until boarding.

After a short layover in Dubai, I boarded the next leg and fell into a deep sleep, hoping to glimpse New Zealand when I awoke.

3

"I told you already! Are you even listening? I am a Diamond HiltonHonors member. I always stay in the presidential suite when I'm here."

"As I just explained, ma'am, the presidential suite is booked by another guest this evening."

"How did this slip past you guys? Do you know who I am?"

The woman opposite the front desk was a regular VIP guest, and a very unpleasant one. When in town for meetings, it was imperative that she have our best room. I guessed she was in her late thirties, but appeared older due to obvious stress and overexertion. Tonight, she wore a tight beige suit, pearl necklace, and her slightly greying auburn hair was pulled back in a clip.

I attempted to smooth the situation. "Ma'am, I can offer you one of our jacuzzi suites for the evening along with two complementary drinks in our restaurant lounge."

"No," she barked back. "I want to speak to the manager here."

"You are, ma'am," I told her with an attitude of irreverence.

She shrieked while snatching up her bags, bolting across the lobby. On her cell, I thought I overheard her request to speak to the Mayor before bursting out the revolving door.

Hazel swiveled from her computer. "You handled that well, boss."

My eyes closed briefly in disdain. "There always seems to be one like that every night."

"She acted like you were supposed to know who she was. Do you?"

"No. Well, I know she's some high-ranking military officer from Sacramento. She started holding meetings here a few weeks ago."

She recognized my affliction. "You want a soda or something?"

"I'm fine, but thanks for the offer." It was nothing a little alcohol couldn't cure later, I was tempted to add.

Hazel worked as the Night Auditor, and kept my sanity in check on more than one occasion. One would never guess she was almost seventy years old as her youthful, vibrant spirit always reflected her actions. With her husband recently passed, she chose to get out and work nights to keep herself busy instead of sitting home alone.

The lobby now sat quiet with just the peaceful waterfall cascading near the lounge.

"I'm going to make my rounds," I informed Hazel while grabbing my key card. "The floor is yours. I'm on Pager One if you need me."

"No problem, boss. I've got this."

I adjusted my navy-blue suit and white floral scarf, my high heels clicking against the lobby's white and gold marble floor. After inspecting all major departments of the hotel, I entered the restaurant, setting my elbow on the bar. The Restaurant Manager was the sole bartender, though serving only one guest at present. His ecru dreadlocks were pulled back in a loose ponytail, revealing epic gauge earrings and tribal neck tattoos.

"Hey Steven, how was Food and Beverage tonight?"

He glanced up from wiping down bar racks. "Yo, Scaith. It was busy earlier from that conference, but slowed down around ten."

I checked my watch. "Okay, it's almost midnight. I'm heading out for the night. See you tomorrow."

"Peace," he muttered.

I returned a missed call from Becker as I walked out to my car, juggling my purse and keys.

"Hey, babe. Done with work? I'm at Cinebar if you want to head over."

"Ten minutes."

.♠.   .♠.   .♠.

I located Becker inside the small dive bar, already nursing a dark beer. Passing by displays of pictures and movie memorabilia on the walls, I sifted through the groups of people, claiming the stool next to her.

"Grenache, please," I told the bartender, setting my purse down.

"Hey bestie, how was work?" She removed her white baseball cap.

I sighed with indignation. "Dealt with another self-righteous bitch tonight. Her ass was tighter than a Marine's haircut."

"You're a trooper to handle some of those crazy people, babe. They think money gets 'em whatever they want."

"Speaking of haircuts…" I noticed her fresh pixie cut, now shaved on one side. "I like it. Short hair looks good on you."

"Thanks. Got it done this afternoon."

I sipped from my wineglass just as the bartender set it down. "What did you end up doing tonight?"

Becker was a part-time Guard soldier, same as me. Her civilian jobs included a few different roles, such as caretaker to an elderly woman, dog walker, and plumber. She could do everything from fixing toilets to maintaining gardens. Since her family was wealthy, she chose to do random jobs just for fun.

"Had to go all the way to Lucille's house earlier 'cause she couldn't figure out how to turn her TV off."

"Sounds about right. She's a sweet old lady." I sipped more wine while surveying the room. "The place is packed tonight."

"Yeah, every Wednesday is ladies' night."

An eyebrow darted up. "Is *that* why we're here? So you can find some poon for the evening?"

"No, that was *last* night," her smirk contented and sly.

"You're unbelievable. Who was it this time?"

"Some nurse named Ivy with these gorgeous platinum blonde curls and huge tits. I met her at Splash Bar. She was obviously straight, but you know how suave I am."

"Glad you're enjoying yourself, hon. You've got skills, I'll give you that." I was bewildered. Her constant flings always caused me to evaluate my own situation, or lack thereof.

She stared in my direction. "Babe, when was the last time you got some dick?"

"Oh god. Not this shit again." I swayed my head, not wanting to discuss it.

"Don't tell me David was the last time. That was what... two years ago? You're probably re-virginized by now. Gotta clean out those cobwebs, babe."

"I really don't want to dedicate time to dating right now. I have a lot going on with a full-time management job, school, and the military. Also, I just to stay at home during my spare time where I can work on my projects."

"You live in a small apartment and barely own any furniture. What are these projects you're talking about?"

"Well, I create like, spreadsheets and lists of travel itineraries, world history and stuff." When said out loud, I realized just how nerdy it sounded.

"Okay, I'm seriously gonna start taking you out more often. What's the point of travel itineraries when you don't even travel? And here you're the perfect example of a golden California beauty with a rockin' hot body, blow job lips, crystal blue eyes, you're smart and successful..."

"Stop," I mocked her in a high-pitched, whiny voice. "I'm blushing."

"Come on, babe. We should be bagging you a couple cocks a week, at least. Just start sleeping around with hot guys and find out what you like."

"No way." My hand shot up in protest.

"Can I at least buy you a vibrator?"

"No!" I emptied my glass and ordered another.

"Fine," she suspired, giving up the skirmish. "Hey, Pam's graduating if you want to head up to Stanford next week. See what kind of trouble we can get into up there."

My interest piqued. "Sure. In Palo Alto there's a redwoods state park where we can go hiking, also a cactus garden and couple wineries we can hit up."

She frowned. "How do you always know these things? Every time we go somewhere, you know the places to go off the top of your head."

My grin broadened. "It's all those nerdy spreadsheets and lists that you seem keen on teasing me about."

I stumbled outside the bar an hour later, my ineptitude deriving more from fatigue than consumed alcohol.

I squeezed around Becker's waist. "Thanks for tonight, hon. I needed it."

"Anytime. And don't go home wallowing in self-pity. It's okay to enjoy yourself sometimes without feeling bad about it. I blame that one on your dad."

"I won't, or... I will," I groaned. "I'm a little tipsy."

Becker giggled. "You good to drive home, babe?"

"Oh, of course. Fine. I'm fine."

"Then I'll see you at drill this weekend."

⚜ ⚜ ⚜

The following late afternoon, I arrived for my hotel shift, heading straight to the General Manager's office. He was mid-bite into some chocolate cake with the crumbs sprinkling over his white dress shirt and maroon tie. Stacks of papers and boxes surrounded his desk, almost engulfing him.

I knocked on his door. "Afternoon, Bill."

His head rose up in embarrassment, and he briskly brushed the crumbs away. His shirt tightened at the mid-section as his large belly pressed against the desk. With glasses, he could easily resemble Drew Carey.

"Afternoon, Scaith," he uttered with his mouth full before taking a sip from his coffee mug. "There's leftover cake from that engagement party earlier if you want some."

"No thanks. Just wanted to remind you that I have military duty this weekend. I've already arranged for Patricia to cover the front office."

"Ah yes, shouldn't be a problem," his voice faint and scratchy, bloated face starting to perspire. "We don't have quite as many events this weekend, so Patricia should be able to handle it. I'll be around here for a bit this weekend, too."

"Perfect." I turned to leave as he alerted me to one more thing.

"By the way, a disgruntled woman called to speak with me this morning about you."

I rolled my eyes and pivoted back, a hand on my hip. "The presidential suite?"

"Yup. And you don't have to explain yourself because I told her the same thing you did. You handled it just fine. Everyone knows she's a ball-buster."

I was delighted by his indifference, but very displeased the woman had the nerve to call my boss in the first place. I smiled through clenched teeth. It was all I could do not to punch a hole in the wall.

"Thanks, Bill. I'll talk to you later."

My black pencil skirt swayed as I whisked through the back offices.

"Afternoon, ladies," I greeted my employees Lori and Jessica at the front desk. "I need the daily report and a pager, please. Make sure it's fully charged." I glanced over the events list for the evening. "We're at a hundred percent occupancy tonight. Let's make sure all gold and diamond members have key cards and welcome packets ready. Employees from Epic are here for a conference for the next few days, so place them in upgraded and renovated rooms if possible. And don't personally deliver anything to Ben Harrison's room. He's a groper. You can call Tony for that."

I turned to see the shuttle van arriving back from the airport, full of passengers.

"Lori, refill the water jug before all these guests come in."

Heading across the lobby next, I pressed a button on the pager as it beeped.

"Hey Tony, are you on this channel?"

It beeped back. "Yeah, I'm here."

"Okay, just letting you know I'm here if you need anything."

He paged again. "Actually, could you go up to room 515? There's a situation that you're better equipped to deal with than I am."

"On my way."

The elevator doors opened at the fifth floor, loud screams suddenly echoing from down the hallway. I turned the corner to see a man standing naked, pounding against his room door with one hand while holding his junk with the other. Several guests were poking their heads out to witness the commotion.

"Oh, fuck," I mumbled to myself. "Gotta be kidding me." I swiped a newspaper by the phone and approached the detestable, yet entertaining scene.

"Bridget, open the goddamn door right now! I'm not kidding!" He continued pounding. "She's just a friend from work, I swear."

"Sir, please take this." I slapped the newspaper to his pasty, hairy chest, and banged on the door next. "Ma'am, this is the Hotel Manager. Open the door, please." No sound came from the room. Swiping my master key card also proved futile as she had the bolt locked. I banged harder shouting, "Ma'am, if you don't open this door right now the police will be called!"

In a second, the door unlocked from inside and slowly jarred opened. The man shoved his way in as the newspapers scattered to the floor, slamming the door behind.

I shook my head and returned toward the elevators to a thunderous applause and whistle of validation. I laughed, throwing my hands in the air.

"I know. I know. They don't pay me enough for these things."

⚜   ⚜   ⚜

Hours later, I took advantage of a quiet period in my office to work on some reports when Jessica came in, her crimson curls bouncing delicately.

"Scaith, a guest is asking if he has to pay for his bottle of wine. He says he didn't like it."

"Did he drink the whole bottle?"

"Yes."

"Then of course he has to pay."

She returned to the front desk as I tapped my forehead in frustration. Tony entered through the backdoor, about fifty keys clamped to his utility belt jangling with each step.

My head tilted in preparation of inherently more bad news. "What now, Tony? Someone electrocute themselves in the bathtub?"

"Someone threw a diaper in the pool and clogged the pipes. I'm gonna have to drain it."

"How long will it take to have it up and running again?"

He scratched his balding head. "Overnight. At least."

I pinched the bridge of my nose while leaning back, evaluating the situation. "Okay, just try to get it back in use by early morning. Not much else we can do. I'll get a sign on the door and let my staff know. Thanks, Tony."

He left the office as Hazel walked in for her night shift.

"Ahh, my savior."

"Jesus is your savior, dear," her reply trance-like.

"Um, all right, Hazel. Thank you for that." I handed her a sheet. "Here's a list of things I need done before you run the midnight reports."

"Are you all right, boss? You seem frazzled tonight."

"Nope," I dissembled. "Just wishing I was ten people."

She sat down across from me. "You know, you're always trying to take on so much. It's okay to relax sometimes. We all know what a bright and talented young woman you are. You shouldn't feel as though you need to prove anything."

"Yes Hazel, I know that." I continued typing, trying to keep focus on my never-ending tasks.

"No dear, I don't think that you do."

My exasperation at the truth in Hazel's words gnawed at my temper, and my response to her was sharp. "I really need to keep working. Quit bothering me and get that list done soon."

She gave up and left, leaving me angst over my unintentional harsh treatment of her.

⚜   ⚜   ⚜

The National Guard Armory gymnasium was near-empty when I arrived early for drill. Dropping my backpack against the wall, I proceeded toward Perez, who was typing on his Blackberry. He peered up as I approached and put his Blackberry away.

"Sorry. You don't have to stop what you were doing."

"It's fine, Don. I was just futzing around. How was your week?"

I exhaled, weary of answering similar questions. "You know how sometimes you get sick of military life and look forward to civilian life? Then get sick of civilian life and look forward to military life?"

He nodded in acknowledgement.

"Yeah, it's the latter for me."

"It's the former for me. Duties have really been kicking my ass lately. I wanted to spend some time with my family this weekend, but looks like I'll be working through most of it."

"You're such a good family man, Perez. Rosa's a lucky woman."

"Thanks for saying that, Don. I don't always feel like I am. Here Rosa's pregnant and I can't give her my full attention."

"You have a very important job. I'm sure she understands that."

Lieutenant Belinsky could be heard across the gym making after-hours plans with some of the other officers. We took our places in line by section as opening formation drew close.

Perez leaned over. "Have you heard we're getting a new Commander this weekend?"

"Really?" I whispered back in surprise. "Where's Colonel Bennett going?"

"He's retiring. I'm sure he'll announce it first thing this morning."

"Bummer. Now we have to start the whole process over again. Once we kiss enough of one superior's ass, along comes another that we have to impress."

He laughed quietly. "Nice to know how you view me, Sergeant."

"You know I'm not referring to you, big guy."

Becker joined formation next to me. At one minute to the top of the hour, a six-foot, sixty-five-year-old Commander Bennett walked to the front of formation.

"Group, attention!" We stood upright until he put us at ease. "Good morning, 134th!"

"Good morning, sir!" we all shouted.

"I'd like to kick off this drill weekend by making a big announcement..."

I grumbled silently as I was hoping the news was just a rumor.

"Some of you may have already heard that I'm planning to retire next month. It has been an honor to serve as Commander of the 134th Combat Aviation Brigade."

My eyes moved to Becker. Judging from her expression, she hadn't heard the news either. He carried on with his speech as I partially zoned out.

"I'm humbled to be standing here with you all today. It has been an incredibly productive and heartwarming experience these last ten years with the wonderful soldiers of this unit. We have made memories together, good and bad, that have shaped our lives. I would like to thank my family for putting up with my absences for so many years throughout my career. After next month, I will be leaving you in good hands. Major Jason Ryder is a highly-respected officer who has just transferred from Sacramento and proven his dedication to our country. He served three tours and led countless counter-terrorism missions both here and overseas. He'll be arriving before noon and wishes to meet with every soldier one-on-one. A list has been set out with specific times to visit him in my old office..."

The downside of the archaic officers was unarguably their drawn out, overemphasized speeches.

We sat in the classroom after, awaiting some death by PowerPoint in the form of sexual harassment prevention, drug and alcohol abuse training, suicide training, and other topics we'd covered countless times over.

"What time do you meet the new Commander?" Becker inquired.

"Eleven. I think I'm the first one up. You?"

"Not until three."

"I'm assuming you didn't know Colonel Bennett was leaving."

"Nope," she replied with a heavy heart. "I'm gonna miss him. I've heard horror stories from other units that some Commanders are overly strict, like they give extra PT and have soldiers working long hours, especially in my brother's unit."

"Let's hope that isn't the case. We really don't need more on our plates right now." I read over the drill itinerary listed on the whiteboard. "Hey, we have the simulated shooting range operating this weekend. Good. I haven't held a rifle in a while."

The hours dragged on as the dry, redundant classes grew exceedingly tiresome. Close to eleven a.m., I left the classroom, swiping a break room coffee before resuming to the offices. I stalled as shouting reverberated from the designated room with something slamming harshly against the desk. A deeply heated argument ensued.

"... as if you actually care! I told you this event was important!" a woman's chilling voice screamed. "You know how that makes me look to the public when you're not there to support me?"

"This unit is my priority now, Melissa," a man responded, not giving rise to his tone. "Take your boyfriend instead. We both know you'd rather go with him anyway."

The woman stormed out... and I immediately recognized her as the disgruntled hotel guest from earlier in the week. Her military uniform displayed a one-star, indicating she was a Brigadier General. She huffed past me, knocking me into the wall while spilling my coffee. I briefly wondered if she had recognized me, but soon realized women like her never remembered the less important people. I glowered, tossing away the now-empty cup before tapping on the office door.

A man in military uniform glanced up sporting a chiseled jaw, muscular build, and tanned skin that seemed to glow from the sun. I stood surprised. I wasn't expecting a new leader that looked like this. If only every male soldier fit this description as well as he did.

"Is now an okay time to meet, sir?"

"Yes, come in." He motioned for me to enter while retrieving papers from the floor. "Sergeant..." he checked my name patch. "...Donegal. Have a seat."

Despite the quarrel he had just been involved with, he acted completely unfazed. As I sat down, I noticed a big coffee stain on my ACU jacket.

"Oh, could I take one of those, sir?" I indicated a tissue box behind him, and he handed it over. "Sorry, sir. That woman knocked my coffee everywhere."

"That was my wife." He stood up, emotionless while shuffling through a cabinet of folders behind the desk.

"Oh," I said softly, sinking into my chair. So much for successfully kissing the new Commander's ass.

He pulled my military file and sat back down. "So, Sergeant Donegal, how are you finding this unit?" He was prominently composed, as though he'd been doing this forever.

"Well, it seems good, sir, but I've never been with any other unit, so not much to compare it to."

"I see you recently received your E5."

I nodded. "I was promoted last month, sir."

"Congratulations. Being an NCO is a huge honor and responsibility. Are you currently in school?"

"Yes, sir. I'm taking some classes to get my MBA in Hospitality and Business Management."

His lips curved on one side, making him even more attractive, if that was even possible. "Glad to see you know what you want to do. You also have a civilian job?"

"Yes. A Night Manager at the downtown Hilton, sir."

"Oh, my wife held meetings there before we relocated."

I smirked scornfully. "Yeah, we've met."

He stilled, glancing me over. If he was analyzing my snarky retort, I couldn't say for certain. "Having all these accomplishments and ambitions by age twenty-four is impressive. Is there anything you feel should be improved at this unit?"

I pursed my lips. "The chow could use some improvement, sir."

He chuckled. "I believe that's a nationwide issue, Sergeant."

His eyes seemed to search mine, probably for thorough evaluation purposes. They held a sort of emptiness despite his intrepid, striking presence. I had no idea what was going on in his mind. The sense of mystery he held enticed me to no end and I found myself having trouble breathing properly. God, he was hot.

"Do you have any questions for me?" he asked.

Yeah, what do you look like naked? I wondered. Dammit. I had to inwardly nudge myself to stop with the perilous fantasizing. This man was off-limits in the truest sense of the word.

"Not at the moment, sir, but I'm sure I'll have questions later."

"Please do come to me with anything. My door is always open." He folded his hands on the desk. "Now, here's what I'll be expecting from you, Sergeant, as your new Commander: I want you to always be on time and ready to work, set an example to your subordinates and listen to yours, stay on top of your physical and mental wellness, keep up to date on your online training, and maintain your military professionalism, both in and out of uniform. The Army National Guard represents its community and people expect only the best from us. Let's always be our best selves. Tracking?"

I nodded once. "Tracking, sir. I'll do all that and more."

"Good. I'd also like you to pay close attention to what's happening in the news. Know what's going on around the world and take the time to learn history, especially military history."

I grinned, reminiscing on my conversation with Becker at the bar. "Done deal, sir. I already study history in my spare time."

He smiled. "Then you're already ahead of the game. That'll be all, Sergeant. Have a good drill weekend."

We both stood up. I saluted and quickly left the room, his beguiling green eyes still etched in my mind.

.⚜. .⚜. .⚜.

The rest of the unit had paused for break back at the classroom, so I flagged down Becker, motioning for her to join me in the restroom. Dragging her inside, I checked each stall, ensuring seclusion.

"What's up, babe? You look like you're flipping out."

I tilted against the sink. "The new Commander is…" I managed to get out.

"Yeah, you met him. How is he?"

I took in a breath, embarrassed by how unsettled I was feeling. "He got under my skin for some reason. In a… good way."

Her mouth dropped. "Babe, I *knew* your libido was in there, just waiting to come out for the right dick."

"It's *so* not right." Both hands slapped my own face. "I actually sat there visualizing all his clothes on the floor. What's wrong with me?"

"Haven't you ever lusted after unattainable guys before?"

"Never. And you know something else? That bitchy guest from my hotel the other night is his wife… and she's a one-star!"

Her smirk became insatiably devious. "Well, this just keeps getting tastier, doesn't it? Sleeping with her husband would be the ultimate payback, you know."

"No, I need to avoid him at all costs," I passionately asserted, pacing the room. "I'm not sure I trust myself around him. Things need to stay professional."

"You can't avoid him, babe. He's our new Commander."

I felt trapped between my duty and unanticipated desire for the man I met only five minutes ago. "I've never wanted to sleep with someone so much right after meeting them."

"Really?" she chuckled shrewdly. "It happens to me all the time."

"Yeah, but at least you…"

A couple soldiers entered the restroom, so we swiftly retreated. I kept shaking my head, trying not to think about him anymore, as if that would actually work. I detested the distraction. Self-control was always one of my best qualities… until now.

Becker now bounced with each step she took. "This is the best news I've heard in a while. My bestie wants herself some man-meat. It's about fucking time some guy makes you want to twitch your twat." She slowed down and grabbed my arm. "Hey, is that him?" She pointed out a couple male soldiers conversing further down the hallway.

All I could do was stare, and twist my mouth in agony. "You were right. Guess I can't avoid him."

Her eyebrows raised. "You really weren't kidding. I don't even like wiener, but he's kinda making me wet right now. I bet he's got a fat dick."

"Shh!" my whisper sharpened. "Not here. And this stays between us. We can grab drinks tonight and finish this conversation."

She giggled. "Oh, yes we will."

⚜   ⚜   ⚜

The rest of drill weekend elapsed without me seeing Ryder more than a few times in passing, which I was highly relieved about.

On Sunday night, I popped in a movie while preparing a dinner of pasta and vegetables, looking forward to a solitary night in my apartment. It had been another balmy summer day, so I relaxed in white jean shorts and a rose-colored tank top with my hair hanging loose.

Ten minutes into Raiders of the Lost Ark, my cell rang. "Scaith, here," I answered.

"Hey, Sergeant Donegal. It's Sergeant Jensen."

"Oh, hi. What's going on?" I asked, mid-bite.

"Just letting you know you left your bag here after drill. Looks like there's some important homework you may need."

"Oh, shit." My palm slapped the side of my head. "I *do* need it."

"Yeah, I figured. I would drop it off but I have to be somewhere, like right now. I'll set it in the commons area by the offices and leave the back door unlocked for you."

I thanked her and snapped my phone shut, slipping into white flip flops before shoving the rest of my dinner aside. It seemed to be the story of my life. The moment I had time to just kick back and relax, something urgent always required my attention.

⚜   ⚜   ⚜

I parked behind the armory and crept through the back door. Being too dark to sufficiently see where I was going, I opened my phone, giving just enough light to locate my bag in one of the cubicles. When I slung it over my shoulder, powerful arms circled and grabbed me, shoving me into the wall with a loud bang.

A piercing scream escaped my lungs as my bag dropped to the floor. The overhead lights switched on to reveal Commander Ryder, now changed into gym clothes. He appeared as shocked as I was. My palm rose to my chest as my heart beat wildly.

"Sergeant Donegal, what are you doing here after-hours?"

I answered through rough breaths. "I left my backpack here, sir."

He frowned. "Why didn't you just call me? I could've brought it to you."

I found his question somewhat unorthodox. "Uh, I didn't know you were still here, sir, nor would I ever expect a superior of mine to correct my own mistake."

My answer seemed to amuse him. "You should be more careful sneaking into a dark building with a trained soldier."

I sneered at his not-so-subtle misogyny. "I *am* a trained soldier, sir. Just... maybe not as physically strong as some." I retrieved my bag from the floor, tossing it over both shoulders this time.

My gaze snapped up to his as he made no attempt to hide his obvious stare. I discreetly glanced down, reminding myself that I was wearing next to nothing, not even a bra as I didn't anticipate running into anyone. Being alone with this man was exactly what I was trying to avoid, and the last thing I expected to happen tonight.

My face rolled away nervously as I rubbed the side of my head, minor pain stemming from my temple.

"Are you hurt?"

"I'm okay, sir. It's just my ear smacked the wall pretty good. You caught me off guard."

He stepped up in front of me, slowly tucking a swath of hair over my ear. His eyes practically perforated mine as his fingers pressed under my chin while inspecting me for injuries. My heart pounded as his deep breathing disrupted my senses, his irresistibly virile physique just inches from mine. If his lips got any closer to mine, I couldn't guarantee propriety in my ensuing decision…

His step back was quick and sudden. "You're fine, Sergeant," his presiding voice low and direct. "You can get going. I'll see you next month."

I nodded and retracted my steps out of the armory with a sense of urgency, wondering if we just had a moment or if it was willfully concocted in my head.

⚜   ⚜   ⚜

Upon rising from a restless night, I went to the gym and attended my economics class at the university. A turkey sandwich from the student cafe sufficed for lunch before sitting through one more class.

Driving to work later on, I rang Becker while en route.

"Babe," her usual monotone answered.

"Hey, what do you think of Drunken Truth or Dare tomorrow night?" my random idea spilled out. "I'm off work all day and can rent out the presidential suite. Maybe get Dan, Cody, and Ellie to join."

"Sounds awesome. I'll call and arrange details. I do have to visit Lucille when she goes to bed at seven, but can come after."

"Eight sound good?"

"Sure. We'll meet you in the lobby. Can we bring our swimsuits and maybe go for a night swim?"

"Yeah. Go ahead and bring 'em."

"Oh and babe, I have one more *really* important question to ask you. Like, *really* important." She sucked in a breath. "So, our new Commander…"

I rolled my eyes sportively. "Yes, Becker?"

"Did you masturbate to him yet?"

My phone snapped shut.

⚜   ⚜   ⚜

Our group met up at the scheduled time wearing comfortable sweatpants and t-shirts over swim gear. I opted to dress a little nicer since the Hilton was still my workplace, so I rocked some black slacks, a flowy white blouse with red heels, and a long, dangling gold necklace.

Cody flipped sandy-blonde hair from his face. "Hey Scaith, where've you been lately? You've been missing all our parties."

"I've been working, Cody. Remember what that's like?"

We all crossed the lobby in a non-orderly fashion and piled into the elevator, Dan and Cody discussing a new PlayStation game while carrying bags of games, snacks, and alcohol.

"This is going to be a long night, isn't it?" I observed aloud.

"Here's hoping!" Becker vocalized her expectations.

"Let's just make sure we don't trash the room tonight, guys. My credit card's holding for incidentals."

"No guarantees, Scaith," Ellie stated mischievously.

I unlocked room 700 on the top floor, the presidential suite. They all gasped as I stepped aside, revealing the elegant grandeur of the space.

"Whoa, Scaith!" Dan exclaimed. "This is the biggest, fanciest hotel room I've ever seen. Can't believe you never brought us here before."

I shrugged. "I was planning to at some point."

They continued exploring the room, so I offered details, as though giving a tour. "So, we have a full bar on the far wall, crystal chandeliers, the double king-sized bed folds down, a stocked kitchen with…"

"I think we've got the idea, Scaith," Ellie playfully interrupted. "We know you're a hotshot Hotel Manager. And you're looking gorgeous tonight. Maybe we should play Spin the Bottle, too."

"Just a reminder, Ellie, there's also guys here."

She squirmed uneasily while twirling her black, shoulder-length hair. "You're right. Never mind. Worth a shot, though."

Both Dan and Cody were former employees of the hotel. Ellie was a friend of Becker's and fellow stud lesbian that she'd met at Splash Bar.

"Okay Dan, truth or dare?" Becker asked, now well into our game.

"Truth," he replied.

"Whose voice would you like to make love to? Patrick Stewart, Yul Brynner, or a young James Garner?"

"Why not Sean Connery?" a miffed Ellie interjected.

"Yul Brynner, but wearing those Ten Commandments costumes."

"Oh, I second that." I added, fanning my face.

"Scaith, truth or dare?" Dan asked.

"Truth."

"Naked poster for your bedroom of Tom Selleck, Morgan Freeman, or David Hasselhoff?"

I raised my wineglass. "Morgan Freeman!" They cheered in agreement as I turned to Cody. "Truth or dare, Cody?"

"Dare!"

"Run down the hallway naked, all the way to the other side and back."

"Oh, hell yeah!"

He showed a little more enthusiasm than I was expecting. He stripped down to his bare-assed self as the lesbians roared in laughter at the sight of his small, wiggling wiener.

"Just keep that thing away from our mouths, Cody!" Becker firmly insisted before he raced out the door.

"Okay Leah, you're in the hot seat now," Ellie told her. "Truth or dare?"

"Truth." Becker crunched a Dorito.

"If you could know every person that's ever rubbed one out to you, would you want to know?"

She laughed aloud. "Good one, Ellie. I would say 'yes,' though I already know a lot of them. Plowed them already, too."

Cody burst back in and danced on the table, still absent clothes... then Dan joined in. When the phone to the room rang, I unsteadily rolled to my feet.

"Scaith here," I answered, still laughing from diminutive intoxication.

Hazel's voice faintly came through the other end over the shenanigans and music playing in the background. "Scaith, I apologize. I know you're not working tonight, but there's a man here asking to see you."

"That's fine, Hazel. I can come down." I cleared my throat, composing myself. "Did he give his name?"

"No, he just said he'd wait for you in the bar."

"I'll be down in five." I hung up and glanced over at my friends. "Sorry to sneak out early, but I have to meet a guest downstairs. You guys can keep playing. I'll be back up later."

They were having so much fun, they barely noticed I was leaving. After a quick hair and makeup fix in the bathroom, I returned downstairs.

Exiting the elevator, I waved over to Hazel at the front desk, who smiled back while answering a call. I flipped open my phone and checked text messages, my high heels tapping the polished floor with each step as I strolled into the dimly-lit lounge.

When I paused and looked up, recognition surfaced. Commander Ryder was sitting casually at the bar with his Blackberry, dressed in affluent business attire. I gasped under my breath, quietly snapping my phone closed. I slowly ambled over as he sipped his scotch, soon turning in my direction. A presumptuous smile flashed as he put his phone away.

"Good evening, Scaith," his voice low and suggestive.

My head shook in confusion. "What in the hell are you doing here, sir?"

Though I was shooting for high-spirited and buoyant, I must've come off more discourteous, as he seemed taken aback.

"Oh, shit." I rubbed my forehead, hardly believing I had just affronted a respectable, high-ranking officer, who also happened to be my new boss. "Sorry, I didn't mean to..."

"You've been drinking tonight," he observed.

I found his tone bordering on judgmental. "I'm allowed to drink, sir."

"It's Jason tonight, Scaith."

"Jason," I repeated softly. The name matched the man perfectly. His sex appeal was easy to get lost into. Part of me wanted to escape and hold onto my dignity while the other part wanted to tear his clothes off and savor every inch of that sculpted body.

He set down his drink, his attention wholly on me. "I was here earlier for a business meeting. Figured I would say hello to you."

His snifter was almost empty, so my attention shifted behind the bar. "Hey Steven, another scotch for this gentleman... and house charge it."

"That's all right, Steven. I've got it," Jason cut in, tossing his credit card on the bar. "And a bottled water for Scaith." He faced me and leaned on the bar, fingers loosely interlaced. "I assume you're not working this evening."

"No, I was upstairs playing some games with my friends and..." He waited for me to finish, but I instead cleared my throat and said, "Never mind."

I sank onto the stool beside him as Steven handed me a bottled water, which I twisted open immediately. Soft jazz played throughout the lounge, torturing all sense of morality further. Jason's gaze was still on me as I scrambled for something to say. It wasn't every day that I sat down and had a friendly conversation with an officer of his stature.

"So... uh, how are you liking command of your new unit?" Yep, I sounded stupid, as expected.

Steven set down another scotch, which Jason raised to his lips. "Is work really what you'd like to discuss tonight?"

And that was my confirmation. This wasn't just in my head. He saw right through me, so I decided to play along, my red heel brushing his thigh as I crossed my legs.

"Did you really have a meeting tonight?"

His swindling smirk said it all. He finished his scotch in one gulp and signed his receipt before leaning over.

"The feeling is mutual." His lips grazed my cheek. "You look stunning, Scaith." With that, his footsteps faded off as he walked out.

I let out a long breath, not realizing I had been holding it in. Steven was grinning behind the bar. Guess no one at the hotel had seen me with a man before. He stopped me as I stood to leave.

"Yo, Scaith…"

He gestured to a business card on the bar in front of me, which I picked up. Jason's cell number was sprawled on the back with a message that read, "Call when you're ready."

I trotted to the lobby to find that Jason was already gone. Ridiculously loud banter resonated as my friends came scrambling out of the elevator, skipping to the pool.

"Scaith, come on! Let's swim." Becker slid off her loose t-shirt, her boobs bouncing amuck in her purple bikini top.

"Actually guys, I have something I need to do. Is the room clean upstairs?"

"Yeah, we took care of it," Dan said. "Come join us in the pool if you change your mind."

I raced back to the room and immediately slunk to the sofa, tapping the business card still in my hand. I pulled out my cell and took in a slightly-panicked breath. Against my better judgment, my yearning for him consumed my compunction as my fingers leisurely dialed the number, his stimulating voice answering on the first ring.

"Ryder."

I paused, wondering if I should back out or not, but the allegorical devil on my shoulder won.

"It's Scaith," I finally said gently into the phone.

I waited for response, listening to his slow breathing.

"What room number?"

My eyes closed, lower lip quivering. "700."

"I'll be right up."

4

AUCKLAND, NEW ZEALAND
MAY, 2009

I exchanged my cash for New Zealand currency after a grueling, but exciting flight. A cab brought me to the Yaping House, a hillside mansion from the late 1800s and my lodging for the next two weeks. I took a picture with the view of Mount Eden in the background, a volcano lying dormant for millennium.

I stepped up to the porch and entered with my duffel bag. The main foyer had a hardwood staircase, rustic chandelier, old Persian rugs, and a resource table with an antique phone and bowl of fruit. The sunporch to my left accommodated travelers on their laptops and a small kitchen resided to my right. An elderly man with a cane and striped scarf descended the stairs as I called up to him.

"Hi, are you the caretaker?"

A minute later, he reached the main floor. "Yes," he finally replied, his voice weary and haggard. "Would you like a bed for the evening, miss?"

"I already booked a reservation. It's under Scaith Donegal."

"Ah, yes. Please follow me."

Mattresses covered most of the room he led me to, every possible inch of carpet space accounted for. A man snored away on one while a woman sat on hers, eating a granola bar.

"Oh, it's co-ed," I hesitantly observed. "New experience, I guess."

He explained the details of the stay and said, "I'm Darrel. I live upstairs if you need anything." He turned to leave, as though he had gone through the same process a thousand times before.

I dropped my duffel to the corner bed, glancing out the window at birds playing in a small pond. Back in the foyer, I searched through pamphlets, coming across a private touring and adventure company that specialized in hiking and canyoning. Using the desk phone, I dialed the number for Ryder's international work cell, leaving a message of my safe arrival. I called the tour company next, booking a one-day hiking excursion for the following morning.

A desktop computer sat available in the sunroom, so I checked my email next. There was a message from McDee on MySpace saying, "Miss you, baby girl. Hope you arrived safe."

I was about to respond when weariness hit me all at once, a side effect of the long flights and time zone change, so I promptly returned to the communal bedroom for the night.

.⚘.   .⚘.   .⚘.

A lengthy, hot shower felt exhilarating and refreshing the next morning, especially since I didn't have to share the bathroom with twenty other girls. I put on a white tank top, jeans, and teal scarf with gold-printed leaves, then threw on some makeup with a high ponytail before heading outside.

My tour guide soon pulled up in an old Jeep and hopped out. He was a polite, adventurous-looking man in his mid-fifties wearing a grey button-down shirt with khakis. Something told me this guy had been places in his life.

He held out his hand to shake mine. "G'day, dear. I'm Ross," his New Zealand accent thick with just a hint of Australian.

"Nice to meet you, Ross. Thanks for coming on short notice."

He brushed it off. "Eh, don't even worry 'bout that, dear. That's how I like to live my life. Always on edge. Never know what the day will bring ya."

Approbation glinted in my smile. I knew I had found the perfect person to show me around. I pulled out cash to pay him right away, but his hand raised in opposition.

"Oh, put that away for now, dear. It's adventure time. Get in the Jeep."

He drove us down the hill through the nearby town of Mount Eden.

"So what sort of things are we doing today? I didn't see any specifics listed in the pamphlet."

"Well that, my dear, you'll come to find out when we get there. We've got several places to be."

"Have you lived in Auckland your whole life?"

"Nah, when I was younger I lived in Australia's outback for a time. Came back here for a girl, a pretty young thing like you, then she grew ugly and unpleasant."

I laughed out loud. "Tough break, huh?"

"Well, we make our beds and lie in it. I have the beauty of the world at my fingertips and I like to share it."

"And I appreciate you sharing it with me."

"So, where ya from, dear? You sound American, but your name suggests a Scot."

"You're spot on, Ross. Born and raised in California. Mother was from Los Angeles and my father's from the Isle of Skye."

"Ahh, I went up there through the highlands many years ago and base jumped off Ben Nevis."

"Wow. You're into extreme sports. Bet you've got some cool stories to share."

"Too right, that." He slowed the Jeep down. "I'm gonna show you the biggest spider in New Zealand here in a sec, dear. It's called the Avondale spider."

"Ugh, as long as we don't have to get too close. Not a fan of spiders."

"Not at all. It's so big you can see it from the road."

"What? Really?" I looked out the window, up to an enormous black spider statue impaled on a pole, scaling at least ten feet high.

I smirked. "And you're a jokester."

"Well I try, dear."

I continued gazing out the window at the peaceful green countryside cruising by. "I see you guys have a lot of wild chickens running around."

"Those aren't chickens, dear. They're pukekos."

"Really? They're so cute. Will I get to see a kiwi at all?"

"Of course, dear. In fact, we'll see some today."

He drove on for a while and parked at an overlook area adjacent a tribal visitor's center. The sound of waves crashing greeted us as we stepped out of the Jeep. I straddled the edge, peering out over one of the most mesmerizing places I had ever seen, my mouth dropping in awe.

Ross nestled next to me. "That there's Piha Beach, dear."

Metallic black sand glistened below as though crystals were contained within, the water a perfect indigo and lavish beach surrounded by lush green hills that rolled with the wind. A towering black rock stood mid-point, resembling a mighty sitting lion. The location was just too beautiful for words, and I captured a multitude of pictures, wanting to always remember this moment.

"We're in the heart of the Waitakere Ranges. We'll head up the foothills next and do some trekking."

"I'm loving this already, Ross. Lead the way."

We passed through the visitor's center and back through the trails, hiking through the thick foliage.

He picked a leaf along the way. "Try this, dear. What do you get?"

I chewed into it. "Black pepper."

"Correct. That's called horopito."

"That would make a fun salad."

We carried on up the mountain as he introduced various wildlife, minerals, and flora before reaching a remote waterfall, its strong surges of water shimmering down into natural pools. We were well into the jungle by now and the view was enthralling, and exceptionally tranquil.

"Welcome to my office, dear. We're at the Kite Kite Falls. I come here every week for canyoning."

"You repel down that?" I asked over the roar of falling water.

"Oh absolutely, and some waterfalls higher than that."

I took out my camera.

"I can take your picture, dear," he offered.

He captured shots for me as I smiled modestly before the falls.

"You can take your top off if you like," he casually suggested.

"Wait, what?" His question stunned me, and I self-consciously wrapped my arms around, covering up what I could. "Are you serious?"

"Of course. Europeans ask me to take theirs all the time. There's no one around for miles and this is a lovely backdrop."

I glanced around, eventually acknowledging that he was right. "Hmmm." With a moment of contemplation, I timidly removed the clothes upwards my waist, tossing them to the dry rocks below.

"That's the spirit, dear. Have a go."

I felt cold and exposed at first, then loosened up the more pictures he took. Before long, I was swimming under the falls, posing like a water goddess… and I felt free. Free from judgement and the need for acceptance. This body was mine. This life was mine. In that instant, I existed alone, safe from the cruelties and control that occasionally disrupted my life by those needing to feel superior. Here, no one could get to me with unrealistic expectations and say I was doing it all wrong.

"There you are, dear," he called out over the cascading rampage. "You look lovely."

I swam back to shore, a proud smile elevating my face. He tossed a towel from his knapsack as I rung out my long, soaked hair. "You really are prepared for anything."

"You always have be prepared, especially when traveling. Never know what you'll end up doing."

He watched me dry off, though not as a creeper would. He seemed to enjoy the step forward I took after the shame of my exposed self nearly caused me to miss out. It was nice to feel appreciated for the small victory.

"I've never done anything like that in public before," I revealed to him, fully clothed again. "That was a lot of fun."

"Well, if you can call this public, dear," he respectfully rebuffed, glimpsing around. "You're out in nature, your natural environment. Of course you had a nice time." He fetched his knapsack. "Now onto more fun."

．♦．　　．♦．　　．♦．

We stepped out into Mission Bay for lunch, a bustling seaside neighborhood of swimmers, bikers, and tourists, the streets lined with resorts, restaurants, and beach activities. We navigated the busy sidewalk to reach the Hook Line & Sinker cafe.

"They have great burgers here, but you being American, you ought to try something different." We settled in, perusing the menu. "The key to expanding your palate and becoming more worldly is to try new things when you travel, things you can't necessarily find anywhere else. Have you tasted green-lipped mussels before?"

"Never heard of them."

"Right. We'll get some Drunken Mussels... and make room for Hokey Pokey ice cream."

After lunch, Viaduct Harbour was our next stop. His docked speedboat rocked from the choppy waters as I bobbed down inside.

He stood over me, unraveling the looped rope. "Right then. Time to get up close and personal with the sea. Have you got your togs on, dear?

"My what?"

"Togs. Your swim wear."

"Oh, uh... no. Didn't bring one."

"Eh, no matter. Just be prepared to get wet."

He started up the engine, driving us out to the bay. I captured pics of the Auckland skyline from various angles while Ross pointed out local sites along the way.

"This here island is Rangitoto, the largest volcano out of some fifty in the Auckland area. It was inhabited by the native Maori tribes that worshipped fire gods. Over there is the Auckland Harbour Bridge over the North Shore."

Thrill-seekers were actively bungee jumping from the ledge. "I see people are quite the extreme sports fanatics here."

"Actually Queenstown on the South Island is the place to be for all that," he called back over the noisy motor and splashing sea. "They have skydiving and bungee jumping like nowhere else in the world."

I went to take more pictures when I noticed a large fish gliding beside us. "Hey, is this a baby dolphin?"

He glanced back. "That there's a hector dolphin, smallest marine dolphin in the world."

"Whoa, that's cool we managed to see one," I exclaimed, catching some pics before it veered off.

Ross drove us out further amongst sailboats, cruise ships, and freighters. After cruising around in seemingly endless circles, he stared down at the water for a while in silence.

"What's up?"

His head turned back to me. "Ready to get wet, dear?"

I glanced out over the now-still water, confused. "For what?"

A massive whale suddenly leapt above the water next to our boat. My eyes followed him in the air, blocking the afternoon sun with my palm. It was a glorious display, glistening droplets spinning off his monumental form in all directions. He seemed to pause midair before plummeting back down.

"Oh, shit."

A booming splash battered against our boat, nearly tipping us over and drenching to the bone. I raised my arms as water dripped off every inch. Ross laughed, and I joined in.

"That was amazing!" I enthused.

He nodded in delight. "They're impressive creatures, that."

⚜   ⚜   ⚜

"Well, this has been an incredible, fun-filled day, Ross," my gratitude expressed as he drove his Jeep. "One of the best of my life. I don't know how to thank you."

"No need, dear. I'm having as much fun as you are. We do have one more stop before day's end."

He pulled up to a country farmhouse with a younger man emerging to greet us, his hair darker and muscle less pronounced than Ross.

"Hamilton, this is Scaith," he introduced us.

He shook my hand. "Welcome to New Zealand, Scaith. Come on back."

We were led into his barn-turned-brewery with a small, homey bar in the corner. I inspected the simple, but adequate ambience of the interior.

"The place looks nice, Hamilton. Is this open to the public?"

"I rent it out for events, otherwise just my closest mates and special guests come here."

He strolled around the bar, setting out two pint glasses as Ross and I sat. "I've got homemade beer and cider in the chilly bin. What'll it be?"

We all raised our poured glasses. "Chur bro," they said as we all clinked in celebration of a great day passed.

After a long conversation on the country's history, funny stories, and things to see and do, Ross and I left, stopping first at the property's fenced area.

"Last thing, dear. Have a look in there."

He opened the gate to a wooden enclosure and I glanced inside… and saw hundreds of kiwis.

⚜   ⚜   ⚜

I was back at the hostel just before dark. I hugged Ross, profusely thanking him once again.

"*Kia kaha*, Scaith. That's Maori for 'stay strong.' Call again when you're back in New Zealand, dear."

"I absolutely will."

I noticed more travelers occupying the house when I entered, many employing their laptops in the sunroom, one guy playing guitar. A delectable aroma deriving from the kitchen drew me in, and I was instantly famished. A slender woman was removing some sort of casserole from the oven. Minuscule, dense braids coiled her burgundy hair that hung beyond her black tank top to her vibrant tie dye pants. She discerned my gaze as she set the dish on the stove.

"Hello, there!" Her voice consumed exuberance as she waltzed over, shaking my hand. "We haven't met yet. I'm Gin."

I smiled back. "Scaith. How are you?"

"American?"

"Yeah, got here last night."

"Lovely. We arrived this afternoon from London. My boyfriend Clark is playing guitar out there."

"You guys on vacation?"

She nodded. "We're backpacking for the next few months."

"Wow, a few months. That's incredible that you can do that."

"How about you, love? Why are you here?"

"I'm actually deployed to Iraq right now. Just taking my two-week leave… a little breather."

"You're U.S. military? My little brother was in Afghanistan last year with the British Army." She stepped into the main hall. "Clark, come and have your supper, darling." She turned back to me. "Would you like to join us? I made cottage pie."

"Oh, thank you, but I can order something for delivery."

"It's no trouble at all, love," her insistence genuine. "You *aren't* imposing and we have plenty."

"In that case, yes." I grinned, looking forward to that amazing-smelling dish.

Clark entered the kitchen wearing a red flannel shirt with stygian jeans, slightly ripped at the knees, and his rich, espresso hair was pulled into a man-bun with several necklaces dangling below, one a guitar pick. We situated at the table, getting to know each other while making plans to hang out at some point during our stays.

⚜   ⚜   ⚜

A casual stroll into town the subsequent morning was more for running errands than sightseeing. After a haircut, I bought more clothes and some groceries from the farmer's market. Gin was just waking up when I returned to the hostel.

"Hello there," she mumbled while yawning. I found her very amiable and engaging. Even when weary, her conversations were pleasant and cheerful.

"Want some coffee, Gin?"

"Well that sounds lovely. Thanks." She sat at the table in the kitchen, yawning again.

I prepared a French press coffee. "Where are you both heading today?"

"I'd like to see Waiheke Island. There's lots of wineries there."

My attentiveness escalated. "Hey, that place is on my list of things to do."
Her inviting smile beamed. "Then join us, love. Please."

I couldn't sway from feeling like I'd be a third wheel, but she didn't seem to mind, so my affirming smile gave her her answer.

⚜   ⚜   ⚜

The pristine gulf waters surrounding Waiheke Island rivaled the scenic beaches as the locality's leading attributes. It was a beautiful day to be out wandering with a cooling currant fusing the warm sun rays, forging the perfect climate. Departing the ferry, we passed by the main village boutiques, stopping at the first winery we saw. A server greeted us on the patio, distributing menus and a glazed bowl of olives. I ordered a shiraz as they shared a bottle of sauvignon blanc.

"It's absolutely perfect." Gin sipped her wine, mesmerized by the ocean view.

"*You're* perfect, darling." Clark kissed her cheek sweetly.

"Scaith, love, do you have a boyfriend back home?"

At that, I was already anticipating a second wine order. "No, but I do have 'situations.'"

"What's that, then?" Clark quipped.

"Not sure," I laughed.

"Are you looking?" Gin asked. "Might there be a perfect bloke out there waiting for you?"

"Um…" My wineglass rapidly returned to my lips. "I'll have a couple more of these and get back to you."

"Fair enough, love."

"Hey, how about some conversation starters to kick us off?" I suggested. "There's this Chat Pack game where we each ask a thought-provoking question that we all have to answer. It helps us get to know each other better, such as 'What bad habit do you want to get rid of?'"

"Oh, I always skip breakfast," Gin started.

"How do you do that?" I questioned. "I would die without my morning sustenance."

"Does coffee count?" she half-joked.

"Well, I don't drink enough water," Clark chimed in.

"And I probably drink too much alcohol."

"That's not a bad habit, love," Gin enlightened me. "You're talking to two Brits."

"True. Then over-thinking things would be my bad habit. Now it's your turn to ask, Gin."

"Hmm. What dish do you like to cook?"

"You already know I make a smashing-good steak on the grill," Clark responded to her.

"I like making veggie scrambles," I answered.

"And I enjoy making meat pies." Gin turned to Clark. "Now you, love."

"All right, what is a relationship dealbreaker for you?"

"Kids," I responded without a second thought. "Don't wanna birth 'em. Don't wanna raise 'em."

Gin went next. "A hairy arse. Dated a guy with a *really* hairy bum. I could swear I was snogging a gorilla." We all laughed.

"A social media addict," Clark derided. "My ex couldn't slip away from her cell phone to save her bloody life."

I asked the next question. "Okay, what's something kids teased you for when you were younger?"

"They called me Virgin all the time, because of my name Virginia. Kids are absolutely rancid, aren't they?"

"I was a chubby little fucker, so often teased about that."

"That's hard to picture," I told him. "For me, it was my ears. They stuck straight out, so kids called me an elephant."

We sought out another winery an hour later. Along the way, we foraged one of the boutiques, chock full of homemade soap bars, perfumes, and other local trinkets. Clark anxiously returned to us from the restroom.

"The woman at the counter just told me about a nude beach up the path. You ladies in?"

"Absolutely!" Gin's excitement blossomed. "Scaith?"

Under normal circumstances, my bashful reluctance of exposing myself at a public beach would've stopped me, but I was self-reminded that this was a new me now.

"Yes, of course! Let's go."

⚜   ⚜   ⚜

There were only a few others when we arrived at the secluded nude beach, some people lying in the sand just soaking up the sun. The three of us stripped down and raced into the waves with no cares in the world. Gin and Clark splashed each other before making out like college kids on Spring Break. I admired Gin. She was a woman who seemed to have it all, a free spirit with a life of adventure and endearing boyfriend who loved her.

She swam over to me. "How are you finding your vacation so far, love?"

I glanced out to the ocean. "I never want this to end. This feels like real life."

"That's because it is, love. There's so much to experience in this life and if you want it, you must take it. Freedom is never free... or easy. Sometimes, it's just your mindset that has to change before you can change your whole environment."

"You know, this isn't really something people do in the U.S. It gets frowned upon and shamed. Things get censored or forced to stay hidden."

She smiled adoringly. "No wonder you're out here in the world, then. You were like a tiger in a cage, wanting to roam free in the wild."

My lips twitched at her analogy. "Exactly."

⚜   ⚜   ⚜

Gin and Clark slept most of the three-hour bus ride down to Rotorua while I read more of my book. We had made plans to see the geothermal town together and were now arriving at our destination.

We dropped our overnight bags at another hostel and headed to Te Puia, a plethora of geysers, boiling mud pools, a cultural center, and Maori village. The potent air reeked of sulphur from the hundreds of geysers littering the area. I threw on a black wool sweater as the cool breeze blew stronger than in Auckland. Gin and Clark both got traditional New Zealand tribal tattoos while I skipped one in favor of a cultural dance show.

We checked out Rainbow Springs Nature Park next and hiked the trails, passing by beautiful springs and wetlands, flowing with exotic fish and birds.

"Scaith, have you seen a kiwi yet?" Gin asked.

"I did. They have like fur instead of feathers. They're super cute."

"The people here are called Kiwis, too."

"Yeah, I heard that." I pointed to a bird in the koi pond. "What's that one?"

"It's a swan," Clark answered.

"Really? I've never seen a black swan before."

Gin picked a leaf. "Here, love. This is one of those silver ferns that you see printed everywhere. It's the symbol of the All Blacks rugby team here."

"It's not silver, though," I told her.

"Turn it over."

I complied and saw that the whole backside looked like someone had taken a silver marker to it.

"Now you know where the symbol comes from."

After seeing some alpacas, emus, wallabies, and a kunekune pig, we stopped for a late lunch and hopped back in a cab.

"Scaith, we have a fun surprise for you," Clark told me.

"Oh, okay. I thought we were just gonna hang out at the hostel tonight."

"That's what we told you, love," Gin said. "Believe me, this will be fun."

We soon drove into a parking lot past a sign that read, 'ZORB Rotorua.' Outside were large translucent balls rolling around the lawn and people within.

"No way! We're going zorbing!?"

"Sure are, love," Gin confirmed. "We haven't tried it yet either, but always wanted to."

"This is incredible. It's like a bucket list item."

We entered the site and arranged for our zorbs. Soon after getting the hang of the movement, we were running races, knocking into each other, and floating atop a pond… and I slept that night with a smile on my face that never left.

⚜   ⚜   ⚜

My bed neighbor's farts roused me from slumber in the morning, his head popping up for a tick before proceeding to snore.

In the kitchenette later, I made some beans on toast with peppermint tea before our two-hour bus ride to the Waitomo Caves. Once again, Gin and Clark slept the whole way while I regarded my novel.

Our tour guide led us on a boat ride through the subterranean Ruakuri Cave, filled with limestone formations and thousands of glowworms. The bioluminescent insect larvae illuminated the dark cave like stars in a crystal-clear night sky. It was a spectacular sight, like nothing I had ever seen. My gold peacock ring glowed under the blue luster, and I wished Becker could be there with me.

Back in Auckland, we ended our night at the Garden Shed bistro in Mount Eden, splitting some fish cakes over steamed fiddleheads and mushed peas with Manuka honey cocktails. They had also ordered a plate of grilled huhu grubs, a New Zealand delicacy which I passed on trying, though had to admire their tenacity.

⚜   ⚜   ⚜

My scheduled departure from the land of kiwis arrived much sooner than I wanted. The trip had been packed with many more adventures, most of them joined by Gin and Clark. I reminisced on the panoramic coastal view from Sky Tower the night prior, a lasting memory I took for the flight home.

Outside the Yaping House, I bid my farewells while waiting for a cab. "I'll miss you both so much."

"Likewise, love," Gin solemnly stated. "You're an absolute treat to get to know."

"Where's the next port of call for you guys?"

"Southeast Asia," Clark declared. "That's the plan anyway, but who knows."

I sighed when the cab pulled up, not wishing to depart yet. "Well, I have you guys on Facebook now. Will definitely keep in touch."

I hugged them again and hopped in the cab, bound for the airport.

⚜   ⚜   ⚜

Another long flight awaited me as my itinerary had a return layover back in Dubai. I occupied my time on the plane with a couple movies and finished my book, dozing off some time later.

I awoke with a sudden jolt after what may have been hours later, something I promptly equated to minor turbulence. Scanning the cabin, most of the other passengers were either sleeping or unfazed, so I rested my head again, hoping to sleep longer when a second bump hit, this time far worse. The passengers now reacted with panic as the Fasten Seatbelt light switched on. Numerous cargo bins had swung open, heavy luggage striking people below.

The aircraft descended speedily as the flight attendants raced to their seats. A woman screamed from the rear while a man scuffled back from the lavatory. I gripped the seat in front of me, trying to stay upright as the plane shook rashly, then emergency oxygen masks released. I remained gripping the seat while slipping one on, murky smoke quickly filling the cabin.

I gasped at the scene from the window, trembling with fright as the trees below gradually materialized. We were going down fast, my stomach flipping from the quick descent.

In unison, all flight attendants called out, "Heads down, stay down! Brace! Brace! Brace!"

I bent over, covering my head as others did the same. The flight attendants repeated their emergency warning.

A torrent of fear flooded over as I realized we were inevitably going to crash. There was no way the pilots would be able to get us out of this. It was occurring too fast me to even process. I shut my eyes and drew in a breath, immensely ill by the thought it be could be my last, and braced for impact as everything went black.

5

San Jose, CA, USA
June, 1998

"Hey Dad, I'm gonna head to class. Leah's picking me up."
I stood observing my father, his eyes affixed to the TV. Though already dressed for work, he didn't appear in any hurry to get there.

"Dad?" I repeated, my nerves nettled.

His head shook in disgust at the news channel. "American airmen were just killed in Saudi Arabia. These foreign bastards."

Although a foreigner himself, he held a sense of pride for the U.S., having been his home for so long, though I wasn't sure 'pride' was the correct word. Pomposity maybe.

I turned to the TV. The newscaster was disclosing information about several terrorist bombings taking place, one being a truck bombing near the Khobar Towers that was serving as quarters for coalition forces. A picture of two Middle Eastern men appeared on the screen displaying Abdel Karim, leader of the Hezbollah extremist group responsible and his brother Payar Mohammad al-Nasser, both now on FBI's Most Wanted list.

"That's interesting, Dad. I'm just letting you know I'm leaving."

Though I did find the news intriguing to learn, I had places to be. When he finally faced me, it was to sneer at my outfit.

"Is *that* what you're wearing to school, lassie?" his Scottish accent laden with disapproval.

It wasn't the first time my father's opinion of my clothing choice was less than glowing. I glanced down at the ensemble I had put together:

a red tube top, mini jean shorts, and jeweled sandals. I thought I looked adorable.

"Yeah, Dad. It's hot outside today. You would know that if you were on your way to work right now." I shut the TV off, tossing the remote aside. "You can watch the news later."

Most of his time consisted of watching the news, engendering him more and more senile. Maybe it was a generational thing. He grumbled in dissent, but ceased his badgering, so I dipped before he could change mind.

⚓   ⚓   ⚓

Leah's silver Dodge Viper pulled up. Her family made extensively more money than my father did, so the car was a sixteenth birthday gift. Though only holding a learner's permit, it never stopped her from going out. With her parents habitually away, they've never even noticed. My dad was a computer programmer for a paper company in Cupertino whereas Leah's parents were both doctors at the university hospital. Leah didn't fit the typical Silicon Valley girl persona. One would never guess she was spoiled her whole life as she had far too many Down to Earth attributes to be considered high-maintenance.

"Hey babe, did your dad actually let you wear that?" she asked, driving us away.

"He didn't want to, but I think he's starting to realize I'm gonna do what I want now anyway. He's probably sick of trying to stop me."

We were both attending summer school, though for contrasting reasons. Leah's sparse attendance and poor grades brought her the extra classroom time while despite my good grades and perfect attendance, my father still deemed it unsatisfactory. At least we had someone else to roll our eyes at during the teacher's lame jokes.

"Our parents will be in Cabo this weekend, so Pam agreed to buy us some wine coolers. She's hosting a pool party and said we can bring some friends as long as we promise not to embarrass her."

"Are you sure she wants us there? You're notorious for your embarrassment. Remember last summer when you grew out your pubes for like six months, then jumped in the pool naked when Greg was about to go in for their first kiss?"

Leah laughed, reminiscing on her bold stunt. "That was so great. She got me back though. She told our parents about my Playboy stash."

I smirked. "My life would be seriously boring without you."

⚜   ⚜   ⚜

We pulled up to Alameda High School and stepped out.

"Hey, that's Tracy." Leah pointed out a dainty brunette on the steps. "I'm gonna say hi."

"Okay, but hurry up. Class is in like five minutes."

I entered the classroom without her and took my seat, a sudden chill making me shutter from the air conditioner cranked too high. Only seven other students were attending the same class, our friend Derek one of them. He whirled around, caressing his sepia, slicked-back hair.

"Whatcha girls doing this weekend, Scaith?"

"Leah's sister's havin' a party. I'm sure she'll invite you."

"Wicked. You'll be there?"

I recognized his insinuation. "Yeah, I'm going."

His grin bashful and weighted with hope. "Maybe I can get your help on our oral presentation for next week."

Though I've never viewed Derek as more than a friend, I've cherished his multiple bona fide gestures.

Our teacher stood engaged in the chalkboard, ferociously writing notes. His grey receding hairline contradicted his early-forties age range and his sweater could've come straight from Bill Cosby's closet. Leah still hadn't shown up yet when the bell rang.

"Good morning, class. Today for current events we'll be covering the terrorist attack that has just taken place in the Middle East and whether or not our government should now use excessive force while acting in accordance of the law to apprehend these suspects." His eyes bounced about the room. "Who are we missing?"

Leah stumbled in and scurried to her desk next to me in the far back.

"Miss Becker," his voice raised an octave, unsurprisingly. "This is your third tardy so far this summer. Consider this your final warning."

"Sorry, Ernest," her response mocking and defiant.

He looked marginally offended. "That's Mister Wiener to you, Miss Becker. You ought to ensure you're using proper respect to those in charge. Try working on that."

Her smirk was malign. "Mister Wiener, right. Got it."

When he returned to the chalkboard, Leah rolled her eyes and leaned toward my desk whispering, "Wiener Teacher severely needs to get laid."

I could hear Derek giggling softly in front of me. I whispered back, "You think a guy named Ernest Wiener has a chance of getting laid? Shame on his parents, like for real. Who would do that to their own kid?"

As Mister Wiener lectured, I caught him leering at my shirt a couple times as he spoke. Hmm, I thought, feeling a little embarrassed. Maybe it is too revealing. Guess I should've changed.

"Babe…" Leah whispered again, her pencil poking me. "Your headlights are on."

Derek's head spun around at overhearing Leah's comment, his eyes darting to my top where hardened nipples poked through the thin fabric like shard glass.

"Shit," I murmured, tugging my backpack to block the teacher's line of sight… and Dereks'.

"Miss Donegal, what are your thoughts on this latest act of terrorism? How do you feel our government should handle it?"

I grabbed my pencil, focusing on an answer. "Well, uh, we have to start at the root of the problem and see what's causing it. All throughout history, violence has been answered with violence and it hasn't stopped. These radicalized extremists feel empowered to take action in the name of their beliefs, but we should focus on coming together, understanding and accepting our differences across cultures, religions, and ideas, as long as they don't hurt other people. I don't know the exact answer, but… I don't know, maybe I'll join the Army someday and find out." I laughed, but I was partially being serious.

He smiled proudly. "Impressive answer, Miss Donegal. I can see you've thought this over." He continued his lecture.

Leah leaned over again and smirked. "Butt licker."

.·ê.·   .·ê.·   .·ê.·

That evening, Dad picked me up from the Rosicrucian Egyptian Museum where I worked part-time. I relished my first job, processing customer tickets and giving tours of exhibits that felt like being transported back into a colorful and mysterious ancient Egypt.

"Hey Dad, you want to go out to that Mexican place? It's Friday night and I don't really have much at home for dinner."

He gave a passable shrug. "That would be fine, I guess."

Upon arrival, we snacked on chips and salsa inside the El Amigo restaurant a block from our house, a spot our whole family used to frequent. The ambiance always brought back memories of a happy childhood. When asked about work, Dad's answer surprised me.

"Measurex isn't doing very well, lassie. It looks like there could be a big layoff."

The news was concerning, but I did find ease in his seldom-seen openness and vulnerability.

"Sorry to hear that, Dad. Have you started looking for other jobs, just in case?"

He shrugged again.

"You know what? I can help you build your resume. I took a class on it and I'm actually really good."

He simply nodded and continued eating. Another idea came to mind that I shared, just to make our night out a little less stale.

"How about we give you a whole new look, too? Let's go to the salon and get you a new haircut, maybe buy some more stylish clothes."

His fingers brushed through his rippled, reddish-brown hair.

"You haven't been out on a date since mom, so I'm also thinking…"

"It's not the right time for that now, Scaith!" he scolded me.

I froze in place, stunned by his icy response. I peeked around, feeling somewhat humiliated, and my discourse turned nearly inaudible. "Fine Dad, but I think it's time to move on by now. It doesn't mean you're betraying the memory of her. She wouldn't want you squelching in your grief. She'd want you to live your life." I switched topics when met with yet another long stifle, and poked at my tamales with a fork. "Well, anyway, can I go to Leah's house tomorrow and go swimming?"

He sipped his horchata. "Is this going to be a party?"

I paused to ensure my response wouldn't subject him into a frenzy. "Pam is just hosting a girls night with pizza, swimming, and a movie."

"All right, that's fine. Just don't wear what you wore to class today… and your curfew is nine."

I nodded in agreement, but if he'd said no, I'm sure I would've found a way to be there regardless.

⚜   ⚜   ⚜

Leah drove me to her parents' house, an elegant mansion in the ritzy Santa Teresa neighborhood. Cream-colored furnishings filled the copious space with a stark-white kitchen, blue-tiled backyard patio, pool and hot tub, big-screen TV, and fireplace with a cozy seating area.

Pam was preparing appetizer platters when we entered the kitchen. Her auburn hair fluttered to her shoulders, bridging to a white see-through tunic over a pink floral bikini. She recently turned twenty-two and was attending college at Stanford University while still living at home.

"Hey, girls. I got those wine coolers you wanted in the fridge. There's strawberry and pina colada. Also picked up some Zima."

We popped open drinks and helped chop fruit and veggies.

"Is your brother still in military training?" I asked them.

Leah responded. "Yeah, he's up at Fort Leavenworth. Got another month or so to go." She swigged her Zima.

"I was thinking about joining the National Guard someday," I told them. "It sounds cool. You can shoot guns and travel while still working a regular job."

"Oh, I would do it with you, babe. I was thinking about joining, too."

I crunched into a carrot while chopping. "Who all is coming tonight?"

"I know Tracy, Nichelle, Derek, and Nate are coming for sure, and a bunch of Pam's college friends."

Leah was the socialite between the two of us, which I preferred. Guests started showing up within the hour and the party eventually turned forty deep.

We all sat in the hot tub that night with our wine coolers.

"Thanks for inviting us, Leah," Nichelle avidly expressed. "I love coming to your parents' house."

Leah wasn't paying much attention to her surroundings as she was too busy wooing Tracy.

"Dude, there's so many hot older chicks here," Nate told Derek, his eyes searching the pool area while sipping his beer.

I countered his comment. "Sorry Nate, but I'm pretty sure college chicks don't want to go out with teenage boys."

Nichelle joined in. "Well, there's some cute older guys here. Maybe I'll get a kiss tonight."

Nate closed in on her plump, porcelain face, latching onto her platinum hair. "Just say the word, angel."

She briskly shoved him away. "Ugh, so gross."

Nichelle was the hopeless romantic of the group, never having been kissed. She was holding out for the perfect moment and perfect boy to come along. Derek and Nate were typical teenage boys, hopelessly immature and actively on the prowl for girls to lose their virginity to.

Leah pried away from Tracy for a moment to talk to me. "Babe, how's your dad holding up? Is he finally dating now?"

I languished. "No, he doesn't wanna talk about it. Seems to make him sad."

"Scaith, your dad is cute with his accent. *I'd* go out with him."

"Ew! I don't want that image, Nichelle. That's nasty."

Her eyes rolled. "Whatever, party pooper. Let's go to the pool, guys. Someone has a bug up their ass."

Nichelle and Nate headed to the pool while Derek stalled. "You coming with, Scaith?"

"No, I'll stay here a while."

He twitched. "All right. Guess I'll see you later."

Leah was making out with Tracy now, so I headed toward the kitchen instead of joining at the pool. Pam was busy mixing drinks inside.

"Hey, Scaith. I'm making some Aloha Punch with vodka. Want one?"

I welcomed the inviting orangish-pink cocktail, admiring it's pretty color. I ate a few pinwheels and headed back out with my drink as Pam brought out a tray for her guests. Leah and Tracy had fled the hot tub, bound for her bedroom upstairs, so I climbed back into the now-vacant whirlpool. I sipped my strong, fruity drink, treasuring the quiet moment alone until Greg and his friend splashed inside, acting deranged and hysterical.

"Man, it was sweet," his friend bragged. "I boned her right in the locker room after the game. She was begging me for it the whole time."

Greg laughed and gave him a high five, chugging his beer. "Way to go, man. Glad somebody got to enjoy that piece of ass."

He spotted me next to him, his aesthetic blue eyes taking in my lime-green bikini, and emerging glimpse up to my face somewhat distrustful. It wasn't completely out of character for him, just more enhanced than usual.

"What's up, Scaith? How you doin'?"

I inched away in expanding suspicion. "I'm fine. Where's Pam?"

"I dunno." He shrugged and guzzled more beer. His sun-kissed blonde hair and bronzed body made him a cliché surfer boy, and he was a popular football player in college. Though girls often feigned for his attention, I took pride in being one of the few that didn't find his sleazy antics charming.

He turned back to his uncivilized friend. "What about Rachel, dude? You hit that yet?"

"Man, she bailed the other night. I took her out, paid for expensive dinners, and then she said she was tired and wanted to go home. What the fuck, man?"

I checked around the backyard nervously, most guests drunk by this point. I stood up to leave, but Greg forcibly pushed me back down with a splash.

"Stay a while, Scaith. Have another drink with me and Terrence." A sinister look was exchanged with his friend, the situation growing increasingly tense.

I slammed my drink down and rose again. "I have to use the bathroom."

They scrupulously watched me get up from the tub, their ravenous gazes making me want to go take a shower. I hurried off to the house and attempted the bathroom door, which was locked, then ascended the stairs to use the one attached to the master bedroom. I slabbered water on my face in an attempt to simmer down before heading back out.

When I opened the door to leave, Greg stumbled through, slamming it behind. I gasped in alarm and stepped back.

"Get out of the way, Greg," I demanded, trying to sound menacing. "I'm leaving."

He leaned on the sink, barely holding himself up. "Nah, Scaith. Let's hang out. Come on now."

His breathing was hefty, reeking with alcohol. He leisurely approached and attempted to slide down my bikini strap.

I panicked, swatting his hand away. "Stop it, Greg! Move!"

He became more agitated. "No! I know you want me. I can see you staring at me all the time."

"I'm not! You're Pam's boyfriend!"

The thought of him touching me was repellent, yet his harrowing hands moved to grip my waist, digging hard enough to leave bruises.

"I'm not her boyfriend. We're just having fun. She knows that." His body pressed to mine, grabbing me hard in the crotch.

"Get away from me!" I screamed, smacking his bare chest with my shuddering fists.

"Stop being a tease, Scaith. Gimme that tight little virgin pussy."

He leaned in to kiss me and I slapped his cheek, leaving a rouge mark.

"You like it rough, huh?" his tone becoming ominously frightening. "That's how I like it, too, baby."

A handful of my hair was tugged rapaciously, then I was shoved to my knees. I winced in pain as his swimming trunks dropped down.

Leah suddenly stormed in with purpose. "Get the fuck away from her, Greg!"

She knocked a vase over his head, shattering it as I protected my head, blocking the sharp flying debris. He toppled to the floor face-forward with his bare ass exposed, which in another mood, I would have found funny.

"You okay, babe?" Leah wheezed frantically.

I was catching my breath as well, my hands slicing the air from shock. "What the hell was that? I never thought Greg was…"

"A shithead? A gross, cheating dirtbag? I knew all those things. Been trying to get Pam to realize it, too."

I slapped the sides of my head, cringing in horror at what could've happened had she not shown up when she did. Greg started to move and was met with my fierce kick, knocking him back to an unconscious state.

Leah laughed. "Fucker deserves it. Let's get you home. I'll explain this to Pam later."

⚜   ⚜   ⚜

I checked my watch as Leah drove me back. "Shit! It's almost nine."

Leah frowned. "Well, you won't be *that* late, babe."

I squeezed my fists, trying not to freak out. "This is my *dad* we're talking about."

"Good point. Can we sneak you in through your bedroom window?"

"Maybe. Let's go around back."

Leah passed by my house, both of us making note of the lights on inside. Parked in the alley, we walked a short distance to the back fence. She helped me to the top from a trash can, the task trickier from slight intoxication. Climbing over, my foot swayed to a branch of the plum tree.

"Think I got it," I whispered.

"Okay, go," she whispered back. "Stay quiet."

It snapped, hurtling me several feet down with a loud thump. I could see my father stand up from his recliner through the window. Darting around the deck, I yanked off my window screen, bouncing inside while mindful of the rhododendrons and rose bushes below. I crawled into bed as my father checked in on me before closing the door, and I took a reposed breath, avoiding punishment for the time being.

⚜   ⚜   ⚜

Mass was an unfavorable Sunday morning requirement in my dad's household. I entered the kitchen wearing my best prude dress and prepared some chai and scrambled eggs.

"How'd everything go last night, lassie?" Dad asked from behind his newspaper. "No problems?"

"Nope. We had fun." As terrible of a liar as I was, I somehow always managed to get things past my father. "Now I'm ready to get my Jesus on."

Entering the cathedral later, I considered whether people actually wanted to be there or came simply out of guilt. I couldn't imagine sitting through anything more boring. Most of my prolonged hour was spent absently pondering the statues and paintings glaring back at me during redundant sermons in Latin.

My father chatted with Blair after the service, an Irishman and the only friend he had that I knew of. I never spoke to anyone there my age. Aside from most attendees being upwards of sixty, we had nothing in common. I didn't believe in this facade, nor did I understand the hype surrounding it.

Dad's conversation ended and he turned to leave, but I stopped him abruptly when I discerned someone's dallying gaze.

"Dad, Linda's staring at you again," I said quietly.

He sighed, his reaction blase.

"Seriously, go talk to her. She's in full-blown bedroom eye…"

His head spun. "Watch your mouth, lassie. We don't speak like that."

I grew frustrated at his stubbornness. "Fine. *I'll* step in and do something about it then."

I approached the freckled, fair-skinned brunette, ignoring Dad's hushed outcry of opposition behind me.

"Good morning, Scaith," her tone winsome and well-mannered. "You look pretty as always, sweetheart."

"Thanks, Linda. Hope you're having a blessed day." I silently laughed at myself for how ridiculous I sounded. "I like your dress. Light blue is a great color on you."

She glanced down and smiled, enjoying the flattery. "Why, thank you. I got it on sale at the thrift store."

"You like to go shopping?" My face brightened, though I was possibly conjecturing a little too much exaggerated enthusiasm.

"Oh yes, though, I don't get out much. I've been spending a lot of time in my garden."

"You like gardening? I've been getting all my produce from the farmer's market…"

I subtly glanced back at Dad while parleying. Though maintaining his distance, he gauged us like a hawk, but I kept on.

"In fact, uh… I'm planning to make a pot roast tonight for dinner, using all fresh, organic vegetables. Why don't you join us?"

Her smile perked as she glanced over to Dad. "Hello, Graham." She waved and turned back to me. "I would absolutely love to. Are you sure?"

"Of course. We love having special guests over. I'll give you our address. Let's see…" I peered around, snatching a Bible from the pew and flipping it open.

"Oh dear, please don't use…"

Her plead fell on deaf ears as I ripped the first page out, placing it atop the book.

"Gotta pen?"

I jotted our address down beneath the words Holy Bible. We arranged a suitable time for her arrival and said our goodbyes, then strolled back to a cross-armed father, my strides airy with jounce.

"You'll thank me later, Dad."

⚜ ⚜ ⚜

Silence surrounded us most of the ride home, though surprisingly, Dad spoke up first.

"I can't believe you did that, Scaith."

Snark shielded my reply. "I can. You obviously needed the push. When were you planning to make a move?"

"That's not the point. It wasn't the right time."

"I know. It's never the right time, is it? Were you planning to wait until you're in a nursing home to start dating again?"

No response.

"She's a nice lady and it's clear she likes you. You don't have to marry her, just practice getting back out there."

Still no response. He was really starting to piss me off, but I veered to a more comforting nature, hoping for better results.

"Dad, four years of self-loathing isn't healthy for anyone. Just go out with Linda. Mom would want this for you."

"You don't know what she would want!" he cracked. "You were too young to understand."

My veiled vehemence surfaced. "No, I wasn't, Dad! I remember everything! And *felt* everything! You think you suffered alone?" I turned away to cry candidly. "You lost a wife and son, but I also lost a mother and brother. We have to deal with it the best way we can. Denial isn't helping, Dad. I can't…" sob "…I can't keep being strong for both of us."

He promptly pulled his rusted '82 Cadillac over, exhausting the engine. His unexpected ensuing hug advocated more contrition than a Catholic priest.

"I'm so sorry, lassie," remorse dousing his eyes. "I don't want to shut you out. You're all I have left."

I sniffled amid raging tears. "I'm right here, Dad. I'm not going anywhere. Okay? I need you to be strong. I can't deal with this on my own."

His head buried in my shoulder, voice crackling in despair. "I miss them so much."

I held him tighter, vowing to not let go until he was ready. "I know, but I'm still here. All right? We can do this together."

Seeing my father this emotional was a first, and left me wondering if this could've been the breakthrough I was ardently anticipating.

Back home, I raced to call Leah right away.

"Oh, you're so clever, babe."

"Learned from the best. So just be here by 7:15 to get me. And one more thing… does Pam know how to make pot roast?"

6

My eyes peeled open to a dreary, cloudy day. Through blurred vision, smoke filled the air in a long trail from somewhere close by, and my cough was rough, sharp pain stemming throughout my body with each labored breath. I tried to stand amidst my weakened, throbbing head, but quickly toppled back down. Something sharp protruded from my upper right thigh, and when I reached down, I felt warmth. My fears were confirmed as I brought my hand up to my face. Blood... so much blood.

What the hell happened? I boggled. My ears were ringing like cicadas before a rainstorm, but I could faintly make out screams and a blaring, sputtering engine. My head turned slowly toward the devastating noise, aircraft rubble coming into my line of sight. A totaled fuselage lay amongst the tall grass and trees not far away.

I remembered the crash... and was evidently thrown from impact site, rendered unconscious. Most of the plane's body was still intact except for the tail end, several scattered fires blazing amongst its blackened ruins. I tried to stand again, but to no avail, the sharp pain almost too much to bear.

A dark-skinned, impressively slender man in a bandana came into view with a machete in hand, racing in my direction. He dropped to the ground and leaned over, inspecting my injury. I looked up to his ripped white tank top and wrapped plaid rag at the waist. He tore at my pants around the wound with his machete, revealing a substantial slab of embedded glass. He glanced over to the plane wreckage, the fires still burning with people calling out for help. He clasped my hand while trying to move me, but I cried out in pain.

"No! It hurts!" I objected and flopped back to the grass.

He frantically gestured to the plane. "Ma'am! Ma'am!"

"Do you speak English?" I mumbled, my voice scratchy and barely decipherable.

He didn't respond; instead, lifted me up. I cried out again, but gripped around his neck as he raced downhill.

"Wait!" I hollered. "There's more people back there!"

We didn't get very far when the plane exploded behind us into a massive bright light and blast that could be heard for miles. I screamed in shock as the man kept running, cradling me in his arms while parts of the plane flew past. He jolted, as though pelted by a piece of the wreckage.

The man continued for a good half hour, running through thick shrubs, tall grass, and across a raging river. I wailed again when a thorny bush scraped down my arm along the way.

When he slowed down, I turned to see people gathering into a crowd around us. Behind them, a small tribal village stood within the jungle, laden with stone huts and wooden shacks covered by torn cloths.

I was sprawled down onto a cot inside. Three or four women stood over me, observing my wound while conversing in a foreign language. They hastily gathered water pots and rags as the man attempted to extract the glass from my thigh.

I screeched like a banshee. "Stop! It fucking hurts!" I sat up, my mind scrambling, but the women shoved me back down. "Hospital!" I pleaded. "Take me to the hospital!"

Two women constrained me as the glass was quickly pulled out in one fell swoop, my vision immediately fading off as I barely remembered my agonizing scream.

⚜   ⚜   ⚜

My eyelids later fluttered up to a semi-dark room and immediately trailed down to my thigh, now wrapped in a cloth. The pain had lessened, though my headache still loitered, mind groggy and delirious. I was clearly in a mountainous tribal village, but still unsure of where exactly it was.

A woman entered the hut in maroon clothing resembling an Indian sari, but far less elegant as it was worn with numerous rips throughout. She carried a stainless steel jar filled with water.

"*Thani*, ma'am."

I quenched my extremely parched throat. Behind her, kids poked their heads inside, giggling in curiosity. The woman clapped her hands in reaction, shooing them away. Another woman came in with a dented tray of snacks. I saw pomegranate seeds, a mini banana, and some boiled peanuts. I wanted to try and communicate with these women more, but realized how hungry I was and scarfed down the entire plate contents.

They removed the empty plate as I asked, "Where am I at?"

I was met with blank stares, but heard something conveyed in their language, their arms gesturing.

I pointed outside. "The plane… uh, where did it land?" I asked slowly. "Which country?"

They talked amongst themselves while I glanced around the sordidly quaint lodging, wondering if this was actually a bad dream. Moments later, I was handed a small cup containing a hot beverage.

"Thank you." I took one sip… and figured out where I was. "This is chai," I blazoned aloud, more as a realization to myself than statement to them.

They bobbed their heads side to side, pointing to my cup. "Chai, ma'am. *Ahmahm*. Chai."

I set the cup down so I could take it all in, now seeing the hut in a new light.

"Holy shit," I cursed under my breath, my mouth partially covered. "I crashed in the jungles of India."

The women grinned in recognition. "India," one of them confirmed.

I sat up a little higher, taking in a breath. "Uh, okay, I need to call someone," I informed them sluggishly. "A phone." I gestured with my hand at my face.

They swayed their arms, as if objecting. *"Elay. Elay."*

I rubbed my forehead in exasperation, soon realizing a phone would be useless. My cell was back in California and all contact numbers for Iraq were in that folder, which was now burned up. The only number I knew by heart was Becker's, and she wouldn't get home for another couple of months.

I laid back down, feeling too overwhelmed to deal with the revelation. A couple men in tight beige uniforms entered the hut carrying black fighting sticks, sporting pornstaches to rival Ron Jeremy himself. They appeared to be policemen or some kind of government officials.

They walked over, glancing down to my bandaged thigh. I hoped they would shed some light as to what would take place next.

"Which country, ma'am?" one asked with an eminent Indian accent.

"United States, sir."

They spoke only amongst themselves with one writing in his notepad, then both turned to leave.

"Hey, wait!" I implored them, but they were gone.

⚜   ⚜   ⚜

All I could do was wait, listening to the constant outdoor sounds of chopping wood, birds chirping, foreign languages being spoken, and kids playing. Women occasionally came in to check on me, bringing food and water.

A woman I hadn't met yet set foot inside wearing an elegant, shiny sari that was several shades of blue with gold trim. The material appeared expensive. Gold jewelry adorned her with fresh jasmine flowers tied into her long, jet-black hair. Her skin was a rich caramel, her eyes smoky dark and lips lined with violet-red lipstick. She was a very beautiful, exotic-looking woman.

"How are you feeling, ma'am?" her accent thick, but clear enough to follow.

I smiled and sat up. "Glad to see someone knows English here. I just survived a plane crash in the middle of the jungle of a country I've never been to, so I guess you can assume how I'm feeling."

"You are from U.S.?"

"Yes. I'm a soldier stationed in Iraq. I was traveling back there when my plane landed, well… here."

"What's your name?"

"Scaith. You?"

"I am Sharvani," her answer formal.

"Sharvani," I repeated. "How come you know English so well and they don't?" I gestured to the villagers.

"I am from the city. My parents live in the town of Gudalur nearby and I'm visiting."

"What happened with the plane? Did anyone else survive?"

"No," she informed me casually. "Everything destroyed."

I exhaled while glancing down, feeling remorse for the other passengers and their families, but ever thankful to have survived somehow.

"God saved you," she told me, as if answering my thoughts.

I scoffed, unconvinced by her dubious claim. "Okay, well, I don't believe that. I just happened to be thrown from the plane."

"No, you wear Murugan." She pointed to my gold peacock ring. "God of safe travels protected you. You will come and stay with my family now."

I couldn't decipher whether she was asking or telling me. "What's the next step here? Can you take me to the U.S. Embassy?"

"That is in Chennai. That is very far. We are in the Nilgiris."

I rubbed my eyes from exhaustion. "I'm sorry. I don't know what that is."

"It is a district of the state of Tamil Nadu. We are in the mountains here."

"Yeah, I can see that." I sighed in distress. "And probably no good cell service, right?"

She motioned for me to stand. "First, we go to Gudalur. We have place you will stay."

I saw no point in objecting. She seemed to know what was going on and I didn't necessarily want to stay in a remote village so far removed from the grid. More than anything, I wanted my wound to heal so I could walk on my own. The limitation frustrated me to no end.

Hobbling outside, I held onto Sharvani's arm and squinted, blocking the bright sun while passing a group of kids. They giggled and kept relaying something to me while pointing.

"Hey, what are the kids calling me?"

"*Vellakari*. It means 'white girl' in Tamil. You are the first foreigner they have ever seen."

"Oh." I smiled and waved at them cordially as Sharvani climbed onto a neon-yellow moped.

"We're riding on this?"

"Yes, get on and we will go."

"Um, okay." I slowly swung my injured leg over the seat behind her and settled in, groaning slightly at the added pain it caused. The villagers had crowded around us to say goodbye, so I waved and thanked them.

"*Nandhri*," Sharvani said to me.

"What's that?"

"*Nandhri*," she repeated. "It means 'thank you'."

⚜   ⚜   ⚜

Astonishing sights flooded my senses as she drove through the town of Gudalur, passing small wooden shops and colorful Hindu temples. She swerved constantly to avoid hitting cows, goats, stray dogs, pedestrians, and other vehicles. So much life scurried about and people drove however they wanted, all of them staring in my direction as we sped past.

Across town, Sharvani pulled into a driveway extending uphill to a factory or warehouse of some kind. Just beyond it, a white mansion stood amongst coconut trees and a waterfall. An elderly Indian couple came out to open a finely-detailed black and gold gate. We stepped off the moped inside the property grounds, Sharvani now speaking to them in what I assumed was still the Tamil language.

"Scaith, these are my parents."

I extended my hand. "Nice to meet you."

They both smirked, bobbing their heads shyly from side to side.

"Watch me." Sharvani demonstrated the proper greeting by placing her hands together, as though praying.

"Oh, I get it." I mimicked her movement. "Like *namaste.*"

"Not like that, actually. That is greeting in Hindi. They use that in North India. In Tamil Nadu, we say *vanakkam.*"

"*Vanakkam,*" I repeated, smirking immaturely. "Sounds like 'Wanna cum,' so should be easy enough to remember." Sharvani's reaction was blank, and I realized it was a quip perhaps only Americans could appreciate. "Forget it." I cleared my throat, moving on.

A man around my age came through the gate carrying a long bamboo stick, and I recognized him right away.

"Hey! This is the guy that saved me yesterday."

He handed the stick to me, pointing to my injured leg.

"He wants you to use it to help you walk."

I set it on the ground, wobbling for a few steps. "That's a nice sturdy cane. Thank you so much."

I went to hug him and he cowered, his hands curling to fists. He smirked and turned away, hiding his amusement.

"He is being shy."

"Oh, I'm sorry." I backed up and smiled. "Aww. He's so sweet."

"He works up at the tea factory."

"What's his name?"

"Mani."

He returned to the factory as I went with the family toward the house, following suit of footwear removal at the doorway. I tiptoed inside, taking in what an Indian country home was like with the walls dusty pink and dark stone flooring scattered with multi-colored rugs.

"Sit. Would you like tea or coffee?"

"Oh, anything is fine." She stared as I sat on the couch, waiting for an answer. "Um, okay. Tea, then."

With the women now in the kitchen, her father sat watching TV from the other couch with his back facing me, news playing at a deafening volume. Random objects sat atop the shelves: books, lightbulbs, and a statue of an elephant Hindu god, which I assumed was Ganesh. A slingshot hung on the wall next to several framed pictures, Sharvani's image in one of them. She stood next to a man, her red and gold sari even fancier than the one she had on now. Matching garlands of white and red flowers draped from their necks. In the photo to the right, an adorable boy smiled for the camera, his ears somewhat jutting out.

Sharvani and her mother returned with a tray of chai cups and settled in beside me.

"So, what are your parents' names?" I asked Sharvani as she handed me a cup.

"Ravi and Manjula, but here, you would just call them Uncle and Auntie. It is giving respect."

"Sort of like Sir and Ma'am in the U.S.?"

"Yes, like that."

I pointed up to her picture. "Is this your wedding day?"

"Yes. That was in Coimbatore where we live. It is four-hours' drive from here."

"Is that your son?" I referred to the picture of the boy.

"No, that is my brother. He was ten years old in this picture."

My eyes drooped down, suddenly saddened by the past memories the picture triggered. My face must've given it away as Sharvani acknowledged my sharp decline.

"What is wrong?"

I rapidly forced myself back in the present and cleared my throat. "It's nothing." Sipping the chai, my attention swung toward the TV with identification of my plane's wreckage on the screen. "Oh my god! That's the plane I was on!"

Images of a blackened jungle displayed with hordes of debris scattered, some flames still burning. The video footage was taken from overhead with roughly twenty locals hard at work, sweeping up the area.

"What are they saying?" I asked her to translate.

She watched the screen. "They are saying the plane crashed due to bad maintenance... and there were no survivors."

"But..." I edged my seat, looking dumbfounded. "That's not true. I survived it. I'm right here."

"The police should talk to them, but service is not good here. I must return to Coimbatore soon. My brother Aryan will be here in two days to help you."

"Two days?!" I set down my chai to avoid dropping it. "Sharvani, I really appreciate you guys helping me, but I can't hold off much longer. I need to contact my unit in Iraq. I was supposed to report in by now. They're going to think I'm either AWOL or dead."

"Everything will be fine." Her level response stunned me, but perhaps I was just scared and overreacting. Wouldn't be the first time. "You will stay in the workers' quarters at the factory."

"Wait. I'm not staying here?"

"No, my brother is coming and he is not married. We do not have unmarried women stay in family homes. It is considered scandal."

"Wow. Guess I'm not staying here then. Don't want you guys to be the town gossip."

She laughed. "We are already. By now, everyone would come to know that we have a foreigner here."

I shook my head, still convinced I was dreaming. "This is all so unreal."

She went to go change as her mother returned to the kitchen, her father still watching TV, off in his own world. He leaned back and let out the loudest, longest, and wettest-sounding fart I had ever heard. It startled me, and I covered my mouth, trying not to laugh. I expected him to show some sign of embarrassment, but it never came, just continued sitting as if no one else was around.

Auntie returned with a plate of food. "Idly sambar."

I thanked her as Sharvani came back out, now wearing a t-shirt and jeans. "I have some clothes you can wear. They should fit you."

"Thank you. Is there someplace I could take a shower? These clothes are about to stand on their own."

I followed Sharvani back outside a short while later, limping against the bamboo stick. It was now raining lightly in a soft, cool mist.

"It's a little chilly here," I observed aloud. "I thought India was supposed to be really hot."

"It will depend on where in India you are and what time of year. Right now is monsoon season and we are in the mountains. Too much rain for many days. Causes flooding and landslides."

Across the field and up toward the factory housing area, she led me to a shadowy stone room with a toilet, built as a hole in the ground. Beside it sat a bucket of water and pitcher. It replicated some kind of ancient Roman bath house. Something black and slimy caught my eye next, wiggling by the water bucket.

"Is that a leech?!"

"Yes, there are leeches here. You must be careful."

"And, uh... toilet paper?"

"You have water there." She pointed again to the bucket.

I had been in unsavory living conditions before at various military bases, but nothing quite like this. I scratched my head and gave a drawn-out sigh. "So, I use that pitcher to pour water over myself?"

"Yes. Now follow me."

I followed reluctantly, wondering what other surprises she had in store. She opened the door of a small room with her set of keys and I followed inside, expecting the worst.

"Hey, this isn't too bad," I retracted as I took in the simple space. The bed seemed suitable, wooden shelf sufficient, and a single lightbulb buzzed on the wall.

She handed me the key. "You can shower and change. In some time, my mother will come dress your injury. I must go back home now, but my mother knows some English words. She will check on you."

I was a little nervous to see her go. "Thank you, Sharvani. And please thank your family as well. It's really something that you guys would take in and care for a stranger."

⚜ ⚜ ⚜

I returned to the 'shower room' after she left, anxious to rinse off my several-day stank. When closing the door behind, I noticed there was no functional lock.

"Oh, great," I mumbled.

Tossing my filthy clothes aside, I scraped the leech away using the handle end of my toothbrush. Crouching down, I dunked the pitcher into the water bucket, picking out a few bugs before pouring it over my head. I gasped and jumped back as the water was freezing cold.

After a brisk, teeth-clenching bath, I slipped into a long orange tunic. Sharvani's mother was arriving as I stepped out, pointing toward the housing unit, so I waved and followed inside. She applied a yellow paste to my wound that smelled like turmeric mixed with ass and stuck leaves on top, re-wrapping it with a fresh rag.

"Sleep," she said, pointing to the bed.

"I will. Thank you, ma'am… or Auntie." And she left.

The bed was one of the most uncomfortable I had experienced, though I was grateful to have it. Something caught my eye after a while as I laid back, the critter dangling from the ceiling. I bounced up and shrieked when I discovered it was a snake and leapt out of bed despite how much it hurt my thigh. Grasping my bamboo stick, I whacked and managed to toss it outside, then slammed the door while exhaling, scared by the notion that it could've been poisonous. Regardless of whether my sleep schedule was off or not, there was no way I was sleeping tonight… period.

．．．

Sharvani's mother served a plate of dosa and spicy coconut chutney in the morning before proudly showing me around her backyard. It bustled with papaya and mango trees, sub-tropical flowers, and exotic vegetables. She pulled a monstrous fruit from her storage shed to show me and I was shocked to see it was several times the size of my head.

"Is that a durian?"

"Jackfruit," her voice dainty and adorably accented. She started chopping it up on a stone slab with a machete.

"Geez. Watch your fingers there, hon."

The pods inside were smooth and tasted like fresh cotton candy. I knew she didn't understand me, but she seemed to be enjoying the minimal back and forth conversation we were having, and I was grateful we could communicate on some level despite not speaking the same language.

I hung around for a while before wandering about the area, still using the bamboo stick as a crutch. Back up the hill, I peeked inside the factory to see a huge operation going on, loud machines running with a strong scent of tea drifting outside. Around back were several water buffalos and goats grazing... and I wished I had my camera.

Oh shit, I thought. My camera. It had all my New Zealand pictures. Dammit!

I tried my best to brush the fervid disappointment away as I should've been grateful for just being alive and not worrying about my travel photos, but the loss plain sucked. Guess I would have to enjoy my trip in memory only.

I shuffled down a path leading deeper into the jungle, spotting plants, insects, birds, and other animals I had never seen before. I also noted a couple white grave headstones tucked away, lying just beyond a sizeable fruit tree.

A little further into uncharted territory and a man pranced out from the jungle to stop me. He motioned to be quiet and pointed back, so I stood tall, trying to see what he was pointing at. Only a short distance away, I saw what appeared to be a large rock, until it suddenly moved.

I gasped quietly while still as a statue, and smiled. "An elephant."

7

Another day passed that had been relatively uneventful. There wasn't much to do besides roam the area and eat meals. I chose not to return to the jungle. Encountering a wild elephant was already a close call, and while incredibly tempting, I thought it best not to revisit. Surviving a near-death experience for a third time would definitely be pushing my luck.

I stood up and stretched, my fingers sliding over bumps on my back, which I equated to bed bugs. I carefully knocked out a few light exercises and headed to the shower room, getting a little more used to the routine.

I was busy shampooing my hair when I turned toward the sudden glare of morning sunlight, and the silhouette of a tall man stood in the doorway, his eyes wide as baseballs.

A scream of holy terror shot out from my lungs at the sight of him viewing my naked body on full display. My palms rapidly grasped my tits as I bent over and stepped back, knocking over the water bucket while almost tumbling to the ground.

The man's hands rose up, covering his sight. "Sorry! I'm sorry!" He stepped out, slamming the door behind him.

I fell back against the cold wall, breaths going haywire from shock. How embarrassing, I thought. One of the tea workers just saw my… everything.

I rushed to finish bathing, adrenaline now running wild. After slipping into black stretch pants and an unflattering grey shirt entirely too big on me, I poked my head out, ensuring my peeper was gone. To my discontentment, he wasn't. He stood casually near the factory while in conversation with Mani and another tea worker.

"Oh, fuck my life," I mumbled before tiptoeing out the door. The pressure of bumping into him again face to face was more than I wanted to handle. I moved quickly, hoping he wouldn't see me, but too late. Mani pointed in my direction and the man spun around. I nonchalantly kept my head forward, but could see him jogging toward me out of the corner of my eye.

"Hey!" He came up alongside me. "I apologize for that. Have to admit it was pretty funny, though." His English was solid with a smooth, modest accent.

I continued walking, stupefied by how coy he was being. He spoke as if we were old friends. "Maybe for you it was. Why didn't you knock?"

"Did not expect to see someone in there. No one uses that washroom."

"Except for you and I, apparently."

"Where are you heading to, *Vellakari?*"

I wanted to tell him it was none of his business, but he was being nice enough, and seemed harmless. I didn't want to come off as disrespectful simply because I was mollified by his unintentional mishap.

"There." I pointed down to Auntie's house.

"The Visu cottage?"

I realized I didn't know their last names. "Yeah, sure." Luckily, I was closing in on the house and didn't have to speak to him anymore. "Well, I'm here now and I'm sure you have to get back to work, so bye!"

I darted through the open gate and entered the house, taking in a deep breath while sitting down. Encountering the mystery man left me feeling strangely ruffled up. Uncle was sitting over on his couch again, watching TV. Auntie walked in the room, so I smiled and waved as the Indian man casually strolled through the door behind me.

"*Vanakkam, Amma.*"

He hugged her as I sat in silence, confused. He turned back to me with his grin beaming.

"Good morning, Scaith." His hand reached out to shake mine. "I'm Aryan Visu. Welcome to my family's home here in India."

I gaped at him for a moment, putting the pieces together. "You're Sharvani's brother?"

His hand dropped to his side. "Yes and these are my parents."

"So, you don't work up at the tea factory?"

"No. I own it."

Oh great, I ruminated to myself. The man helping me get back to Iraq is the same man that just saw me naked. Feeling rather inarticulate and red-faced now, I repositioned myself on the couch, analyzing him. Since I was trying hard to avoid his gaze before, I hadn't taken the time to glance him over.

He exhumed a seemingly confident stance, one which I couldn't help but find agreeable. He stood taller than most Indians with a slim, but densely rugged build. His thick raven hair was slightly waved, skin a soft caramel like his sister. His nicely trimmed beard and hazel eyes popped out as appealing signature features and his ebony button-down shirt fit aptly over dark jeans. There was no denying his elevated level of attractiveness and I thought that if I was stuck with this guy for a couple more days, maybe it wouldn't be so bad after all.

He sat beside me sporting a presumptuous smirk, as though he found our interaction together amusing. His amiable smile exhibited full lips and perfect stark-white teeth. Of all the Indian men I had met so far, none came close to looking as sharp, classy, and distinguished as Aryan did.

"What's wrong, *Vellakari?*" he acknowledged my distraction.

"Nothing." I turned away, feeling unhinged.

He frowned when his eyes hovered over the ridiculously oversized shirt I was forced to wear. "You need some new clothes."

I sulked in defense. "All my stuff is gone. I didn't have anything else to…"

"I know," he interrupted. "I'm aware of what happened."

Auntie pointed to my head and said something to Aryan in Tamil.

"She says you need to dry your hair or you'll catch cold."

She left briefly and returned with a towel, which I used to dry off with both mother and son observing intently.

"You know, I'm not real comfortable doing these everyday things out in the open like this. If I were back home, I would've gotten ready in a nice bathroom all to myself and put on clothes that fit… audience free."

"But you're not back home, Scaith. Indian families do all these things. It's not like U.S."

"And how do you know what the U.S. is like?"

"I live there."

I paused, my attentiveness sparked. "You do?"

He nodded. "Arrived here yesterday actually, at the airport in Coimbatore."

"Where do you live?"

"Kentucky. I co-own a bourbon distillery in Lexington and have a home there. I'm here for the next few months visiting family and managing the estates. After we eat, I'll take you into town for supplies." Auntie brought plates of food. "This is called dosa."

I returned the towel in exchange for the plate. "Yes, I've had it for the past couple days."

He grinned and bobbed his head. "South Indian breakfast is usually the same: Dosa, idly, upma." He ripped off a piece and scooped it into chutney, molding a perfect ball before popping it into his mouth.

"You're good at that," I noted.

He shrugged. "I am Indian. Been doing it a long time. Where are you from in the U.S.?"

"California."

"Mmm." He took another bite. "I've been to San Diego. Went skydiving there."

"Another extreme sports fanatic, huh? I was just in New Zealand. The tour guide said Queenstown on the South Island is the place to be for that."

"I've heard. I'm going to go there someday."

As awkward as our first encounter was, I was finding Aryan fascinating and comfortable to talk to.

"So, you were in military?"

"Correction. I *am* in the military… and need to get back to my unit in Iraq as soon as possible."

"I can bring you to the Consulate General in Chennai, but it won't be open again until Monday."

"What day is it today?"

"Friday."

"Oh fuck!" I blurted out before processing. I glanced at both of them while clearing my throat, feeling a little unsettled by my sudden outburst. "Sorry about that. Guess I've got a vulgar military mouth."

He continued eating, giving off a diminutive snicker. "It's okay. She doesn't know that word."

"Sorry to keep pushing the issue here Aryan, but is this my best option?"

He nodded. "It's a twelve-hour drive. I have some things to do this weekend, but can take you after."

"Any quicker ways to get there?"

"The bus ride would be around sixteen hours with over a hundred people crushing you."

I emitted a long sigh. "Okay, guess I'd rather you take me."

I had no choice but to trust his judgment. This family was already assisting me above and beyond what most people would, and presented to be genuinely honest.

"Once you finish, go pack your bag and bring everything you need with you," he instructed. "I have a better place you can stay for the next couple days."

"All right. Where's that?"

"My house."

⚜ ⚜ ⚜

Aryan drove us to Gudalur on his Royal Enfield, parking alongside a sitting cow on the road. The scene before me shifted my senses into overdrive as I removed my helmet. Murky water flowed down the sidewalk as several stray cats and goats picked at trash jumbled amongst the area. The streets were noisy with constant honking, stray dogs barking, and cows mooing. There were so many people traversing the area, all of them staring in my direction once again.

Aryan laughed. "They are jealous of me." He situated our helmets into place. "How is your leg now?"

"It's better. Just a slight limp."

"You can get those stitches taken out in another week."

"Yeah, I'll get it done at Medical back in Iraq."

"Come with me."

He guided me along the sidewalk, both of us dodging people at every step. He stalled a couple times to chat with people who knew him, all his conversations in Tamil. They seemed intrigued to learn who I was.

We entered a clothing shop that sparkled with chandeliers, displays of detailed gold necklaces, and traditional jeweled Indian dresses. I never would've guessed a place like it to be in the middle of this town... and found it somewhat comical even. The women wore elegant fabrics of bright colors and glittering materials when outside, the streets were grimy and befouled, like lotus flowers blooming in mud and sand.

"You're probably most interested in the clothes towards the back, not the Indian clothes. You'll find t-shirts, jeans, and maybe a few western-style dresses."

I browsed the clothes in back, instinctively checking the price tags. "These are really expensive, Aryan. I can't ask you to..."

"That's in rupees," he educated me. "Compared to U.S. dollars, it's not that much."

Before shopping any further, I turned to discuss payment with him. "Listen, I *have* money. I don't have access to it right now, but I promise I can pay you back for all the things you're doing for me."

He swiftly brushed off my concerns. "It's fine, Scaith. You're serving the country I also reside in. I'm happy to assist."

At that, I smiled with staggering respect, and thanked him once more.

We stopped by the produce market next, picking out fresh fruit, vegetables, and raw nuts.

"Do you want meat?" he offered.

"Sure. Now that I think about it, I haven't eaten any meat in the last few days."

"Most people here are either vegetarian or only have meat once a week."

The butcher shop was situated down a shadowy alley. A couple whole skinned chickens hung from hooks in the walkway above a blood and intestine-covered dirt floor.

"You want goat or chicken?"

A live goat stood chained to the back of the shop, bleating wildly. "Uh, chicken, please."

We returned to the sidewalk, heading back to his motorcycle carrying raw, unprocessed meat wrapped in newspaper.

"That was quite an experience just now," I told him.

He grinned, seeming to enjoy my reaction to things. "Everything here is fresh. Never frozen."

"I bet it tastes a lot better. Do you cook?"

"Yes, I can make curries and…"

A young Indian woman was instantly up in Aryan's face, screaming obscenely in Tamil. She whipped out a paring knife, pressing it to her wrist while shouting over to me as well. Aryan attempted to pacify her, but I took action, knocking the "weapon" from grasp while shoving her facedown. I locked her flailing arms behind her as she squirmed to bite me. Several women in saris approached frantically, dragging her away as she continued snarling toward us.

Shock and reverence dominated Aryan's stare, his brows raised. "Impressive, *Vellakari*. You had no trouble detaining her."

"Not much there to praise, Aryan." I brushed myself off. "I can't imagine an easier target than that petite little thing." We kept walking, my adrenalin still pumping. "What was that all about? Why was she upset with you?"

He shrugged, callously glancing away. "She's no one important."

"Well, it seemed to have something to do with *me*."

He continued on void of response, so I didn't poke further.

Back at the motorcycle, his leg swung over as he revved up the engine, handing a helmet back to me.

"We're heading further up the mountain," he called back. "It's almost an hour drive and gets steep, so hold onto me."

Once reaching the border of town, we scaled upwards, the overall view turning simply serene. The foliage condensed at higher elevations, road now almost entirely encircled with trees. People walked along the side of the street carrying jars or piles of timber atop their heads.

My arms tightened around Aryan's waist as he sped along the sharp corners. "Aryan, can you hear me?" I called though my helmet.

"Yeah," he called out, turning back slightly.

"What are these trees?" I pointed up to the forest of tall, mystical-looking trees, the bark a smooth, milky white.

"Eucalyptus."

"Amazing. The scent is incredible!"

"Look over here." He pointed out several tan monkeys with red, wrinkled faces playing along the road's shoulder and up in the trees.

"Macaques!" I stated in recognition. "Aww, they're very cute."

We eventually entered a picturesque city filled with pastel-colored houses, lined in terraces along the hills. The locals dressed nicer and the streets cleaner than in Gudalur. A vastly steep hill led us to a navy-colored house, bordered with an elaborate silver gate. It was huge when compared to the surrounding houses along the way.

He parked under the overhang and removed his helmet, brushing back rich, wavy hair. "Welcome to Ooty, *Vellakari*."

Barking dogs raced up, jumping with excitement. One was a golden lab, the other resembling a German shepherd.

"This is Spydo and Chestnut."

"Hello babies." I pet them profusely, having missed seeing animals I could touch. Spydo knocked me off my feet, his tongue slaying over my face repeatedly.

"Spydo!" Aryan pat his thigh and whistled. Both dogs went running to him as I stood up, wiping my face with my shirt. "Sorry. They're normally with my neighbor."

I chuckled. "That's okay. I like their company." I glanced up to his house. "This looks like a nice place. You live here alone?"

"Yeah, it was my grandfather's house." He grabbed the bags, leading me through the front door and into the main hall while the dogs remained outside.

"Hey, aren't you worried about the scandal of people knowing you have a woman here?"

"Nope." He tossed his keys on the table. "I don't care what people think."

I glanced around to see the interior was saturated with hues of cadet blue, pewter, and charcoal… a fitting space for a bachelor.

"It's almost time for lunch. Are you hungry?" He placed the bags in the kitchen.

"I'm actually a little tired."

He nodded. "Traveling up here will do that, and it's obviously been a rough couple of days for you. Grab your bags. I'll take you to your room."

I followed him upstairs to a spacious bedroom, painted rich merlot with a floral wardrobe and attached bathroom.

"My sister and her husband stay here when they're in town. It should have everything you need."

I set my bags on the bed and smiled, eyes combing the cozy space. He stared over at me for a moment, probably ensuring I had everything I needed.

"Oh, I have something that belongs to you." He pulled something from his pocket. "Here. This is yours." An SD card was placed in my hand.

I frowned with ignorance. "What's this for?"

"It's the memory card from your camera."

"My camera?"

"Your camera was completely damaged, but the card wasn't. My employee Mani found it during cleanup duty of the crash site."

"What? How did you even know it was mine?"

"I checked the pictures on my laptop this morning."

I gasped, unduly excited by my New Zealand photos having been recovered. I raced over, embracing him with an unyielding hug. He seemed surprised, but hugged me back. I did however, step away promptly, somewhat embarrassed by my forwardness.

"Sorry. I'm just so happy to have these back. You have no idea."

"Of course. Would be terrible to lose travel photos. Looks like you had a nice time."

Pictures suddenly propelled through my mind of being topless by the waterfall, and I became mentally fraught with reticence as there was no way he would've missed them.

"Well, I'll let you rest now. I have a few things to take care of this afternoon, so I'll be out. If you need anything, my uncle's house is just down the hill, third one on your right." He headed to the doorway.

"Wait a sec," I called after him. "Do you have internet? Maybe I can reach out to someone through email. Let them know I'm alive and well."

"It won't be hooked up again until next week. I just returned after months of being away, but we can call the Consulate on Monday when we leave."

"Okay." I sat on the bed, a wave of exhaustion hitting me all at once.

"You look tired. Get some sleep and I'll see you soon, *Vellakari*." He shot a dashing smirk in my direction before disappearing around the corner.

I laid back on a bed so comfortable I could've tarried for days. Visions of the plane crash kept flashing through my mind. Something about it didn't feel right, but soon passed as I drifted off to sleep.

·❦· ·❦· ·❦·

For the first time in months, I slept without interruption. Rolling out of bed, I searched the quiet house, curious about the inner workings of the surprisingly compelling man that was hosting my unplanned stay. He hadn't come home yet that I could see so I took a proper shower, the hot streams generating a relaxed, idyllic sensation long missed. The cabinets stored a blow dryer, toiletries, and some makeup.

"Perfect," I heartened to myself. "Thank you, Sharvani. I owe you one."

Wanting to feel pretty for the night, I dolled up my face and hair before slipping into my new white floral summer dress, just long enough to cover my hideous wound.

I left the room after deciding to be nosy and snoop a bit. Across the hall, I found what appeared to be Aryan's bedroom. The walls and decor were dark, though void of any depressing undertones. It was moreover bachelor elegance. His immaculately clean closet housed some very nice dress shirts and pants, and peeking into the bedside drawer, I sifted through stacks of old photos, recognizing his family members in many. Some showed him playing with friends as a child, a few elephants, monkeys… and a wild Bengal tiger.

I silently laughed at myself. Here I was in the bedroom of a man I didn't really know, riffling through his underwear drawers. It should've felt uncanny, but turned out to feel surprisingly congenial.

The front door opened. I tucked the pictures away and fleetingly bounced back to the hallway to see Aryan standing in the foyer, checking his cell. He glanced up as I fringed the top of the staircase. His expression showed a flicker of surprise as he took in my appearance, a smile rousing his lips.

"You look beautiful, *Vellakari*."

I reveled in the response I was hoping to hear. "I have *you* to thank for that, Aryan. Your home has everything I could need."

"Am happy to hear that." He stared for another beat. "You must be hungry by now. I'll start dinner."

I descended the stairs. "Can I help you at all? I'd love to learn how to make an authentic Indian curry."

"Sure. Come on."

I followed him to the kitchen, sitting down to chop onions and tomatoes as he pulled a bottle of molasses brandy from the cupboard.

"Would you like one?"

"I'd love one. Wasn't sure if drinking was a common thing here, but I guess you do own a distillery after all."

We cooked and conversed until we had an aromatic chicken curry, coupled with fluffy basmati rice. His glass raised and I followed suit, us cheering simultaneously.

"To surviving plane crashes," he enlivened.

"And to landing in a beautiful place." My sip was unsparing, and I dug into dinner like a starved vagabond, practicing with my hand as a fork. "So where did you go this afternoon?"

"I was just checking on my properties. Making sure everything's running smoothly. I have a coffee plantation across the valley and rental property in the city."

"Whoa, you've got businesses all over the place. How do you manage all that by yourself?"

"By having good staffs." He knocked back some more brandy.

"It's actually staff," I politely rectified.

"What's that?"

"Staff isn't plural. You would just say staff with no 's' at the end."

"Oh, is that how it's said?"

"Yeah, but not a big deal. Your English is already really good."

"Tomorrow is Saturday. My estates will be closed, but I do have some work to do. You're welcome to join me if you'd like. I'll be out for a walk early morning."

"Sure. May as well see more of India while I'm stuck here." At my thoughtlessly candid wording, I was worried I deemed unappreciative.

The strong booze was already befuddling my better judgement, so my comments grew increasingly bolder.

"Hey Aryan, that girl from today..?"

"Yeah?"

"Sorry if I'm being intrusive, but what was the deal? I've never seen anyone threaten to slit their wrists before. I'm really curious to know what that was about."

He continued eating. "She wants to marry me, but I don't want."

My brows heightened. "That's pretty extreme. Why did she do that? Did you sleep with her?"

I construed his silence as confirmation.

"You did, didn't you?" I derided with inconsiderable irreverence. "You probably took her virginity and then left her. Now she's gone crazy because she's ruined for any other man, right? Is that what happened?"

"No, Scaith. I did not sleep with her." The serious credence in his tone prodded at my regret for bringing it up.

My head lowered. "I'm sorry, Aryan. It's none of my business. Didn't mean to jab at you."

His regaled grin came as a relief. "It's all right. I know how blunt Americans are."

"If I do overstep, just let me know."

"I won't. You should act as you are. Who am I to stop you?"

Though appreciating his reassuring words, a change of subject was in order. "How did you come to own all these businesses?"

"I inherited land from my grandfather. It included the tea and coffee plantations, as well as this house, but they weren't well-maintained. I revived and kept them going."

I smiled. "That's very honorable. Keeping your family's legacy."

"How is the military for you? You mentioned Iraq."

"Yeah, my unit's deployed. They've probably heard the news of the crash by now, which is why I need to reach them. My best friend is there and I don't want her to worry."

"We'll get that straightened out. The local police met with you, right?"

The creases under my eyes became more pronounced. "They saw me briefly, but didn't even ask who I was. They just..." My eyes drifted above him to a sizable black spider creeping along the wall, and I leapt from my chair.

"Oh god! There's a huge spider!"

He stood up and grabbed a towel, swatting it down. Fists shielded my mouth as I quaked with dread, squirming at seeing the blood-curdling creature fall dead to the floor.

"Thank you for that. I *hate* spiders… and that one was bigger than any I've ever seen. Thought being further away from the jungle I might not see any."

"No, you will always see a lot of bugs here. This is India."

I sighed, settling back in my seat. "Guess I'll work on getting used to that for the next couple days."

He smirked almost derisively. "But I thought you are in Army."

"Yeah, but that doesn't mean I don't have fears. Sometimes people misconstrue our characters and view us as invincible, but we're not." I couldn't help but envision how sexy Aryan would look in a military uniform. "You'd probably make a great soldier. You're into all these extreme sports, like skydiving. You could be a paratrooper."

"I considered joining the Indian army, but I don't like being told what to do."

"You're a free spirit, huh? I'm the same way… or at least trying to be."

That night, we watched a Tamil movie together with English subtitles while he occasionally worked on some paperwork. I don't remember ever watching a movie with a man so smolderingly attractive before. To say I struggled to keep my eyes on the screen instead of him was an understatement indeed.

꙰   ꙰   ꙰

I pulled my hair into a ponytail as I entered the kitchen in the morning. Aryan was already savoring a chai and British biscuit at the table.

"Morning, *Vellakari*. You want chai?"

"I'll just take some water, please."

He poured me a glass of steaming water, and I sat motionless while observing it, distinctly perplexed.

"It's hot," I stated the obvious. "And pink."

"We boil our water here and add some kind of root, but I don't know the English name for it."

"Interesting." I sniffed the floral, earthy fragrance, relating it to likely some Ayurvedic medicine, and took a sip.

"Did you sleep okay?"

"Better than I have in months. Of course, that's easy to do when there aren't bombs and fighter jets going off all the time."

His interest seemed to pique at the topic. "How often does that happen?"

"Every day. Most don't get close enough to the camp perimeter to be a danger, but any that do are destroyed by our missiles." I shrugged. "Guess you just get used to it after a while."

He smiled in a way I deemed a bit flirtatious. "You're a badass, *Vellakari.*"

"Me? *You* jump out of airplanes for fun. That would scare me a lot more than mortar attacks."

"You've never been skydiving?"

"No, but I would try it sometime. It's a popular bucket list item."

"I highly recommend, obviously. I live for it. It was life changing for me."

I smiled back. "It's always nice to discover what you love in life."

He handed me a copper water bottle later as we left to take a walk, Spydo and Chestnut tagging along down the driveway. From the road, I saw countless tea fields with crops and farm animals grazing in the valley below. For the most part it was quiet, aside from distant traffic originating from the city.

"This is some place, Aryan. Must've been incredible to grow up here."

"It was fun. I remember my friends and I were chased by an elephant right down there." He pointed out a spot in the lower valley.

"Wow. You were like Mowgli from Jungle Book, huh?"

He laughed as though it wasn't the first time he's heard it. "Yes."

"Wild elephants can be dangerous, right?"

"They can be very aggressive and unpredictable. It's usually the males, especially if they're protecting babies." He stopped to pick a branch, bending it in half. "Watch this." He blew through the tiny hole, producing natural bubbles into the air. I was fascinated and had to try it out for myself before we continued walking.

"Do many foreigners come here?"

"Not usually. Africans come for school. Sometimes we have Australians and Europeans touring. If Americans come, they're usually in Delhi, Rajasthan or Agra to see the Taj Mahal. That is in North India."

"It seems like South India is very different from the northern part."

He grinned with contentment. "It is."

We stopped at a monastery and were greeted by an elderly nun in a habit. She and Aryan exchanged communications before we crossed the courtyard. She proceeded to milk a cow that was tied up to a tree, filling the tin can I didn't even realize Aryan was carrying.

"So this is what a trip to the grocery store for milk looks like."

As we headed back, I made an observation of something else I thought unconventional. "I see there's quite a few churches here."

"There's more of a Christian presence in this area than Hindu."

"Do you follow any of the religions out there?"

"No. I believe in what connects to my senses. Anything beyond that is up for debate."

"Me too. My father is a devoted Catholic, but I view all of them as forms of mental slavery and control. I'll pass. We need more logic in the world than we need religions."

"I agree. How did you get your name? I've never heard it before."

"My mother was from California. My dad moved there in the seventies from Scotland and they married. When I was born, she wanted to name me something that represented my dad's heritage, so she chose some warrior woman from Scottish mythology. She trained a legendary figure in martial arts and eventually settled down and got married. There's a ruined fortress within the Isle of Skye where she supposedly lived. That's the area where my dad is from."

"It suits you. Do you have any siblings?"

I paused, not wanting to open up about my life's worst evocation just yet.

"Sorry." He stood contrite, detecting my heartache. "That a tough topic?"

I looked away, days of pent-up stress hardening me. "Yeah, sort of."

"That's okay. You don't have to tell me."

Back up the hill, a middle-aged, heavyset woman in a turquoise sari approached us on the road while waving, and she and Aryan spoke.

"My neighbor Leela is inviting us in for breakfast," he conveyed.

"Really? She doesn't even know me."

"Doesn't matter. You're a visiting foreigner. She wants you to come meet her family."

"That's so nice of her."

He turned back to her, bobbing his head. "Mmhmm. *Sarri. Sarri.*"

We entered her home as the dogs raced off to chase a huge red squirrel. She introduced her husband and kids while serving breakfast. My gaze met Aryan's from across the table.

"Dosa and sambar. This is fast becoming my favorite meal."

He smiled in accord. "It's always been mine."

We ate over loud Indian music videos playing in the other room and Leela's chatter. Something she said caused Aryan to burst into laughter. I also sensed some embarrassment.

"She wants me to tell you that she used to change my diapers."

I laughed. "That's so cute. She's like the adopted mom down the street. I take it you used to visit your grandfather here often when you were young."

"A lot. I really like it here."

"Are your grandparents still alive?"

"No. They both died some time back. I buried them close to the tea factory in Gudalur."

"Hey, I went for a walk in that area and saw a couple graves. They were hidden back in the jungle a bit behind this huge tree. Was that them?"

He nodded as a group of guys charged through the front door. He chuckled, slapping his face before greeting them in Tamil. He clearly knew them. Though not expecting them, he didn't indicate any surprise at their arrival.

"Scaith, these are my friends. They all came to meet you."

"People just show up at other people's houses unannounced?"

"Yes. It is like that here." He introduced them. "This is Steny, Sham, Mangesh, but we all call him Mango, Nishant, Sanjeev, and Kelvin."

"I'll never remember all that, but it's nice to meet you guys." I gave a brisk wave as they roughhoused together from excessive excitement.

"Most of them know English. We meet up at Leela Auntie's place a lot when I'm in the country. This is where they can freely eat beef, drink, or escape their wives for a while."

Most appeared to be around Aryan's age, maybe thirty or so, except for Kelvin, who looked about nineteen.

"Nishant and Sanjeev are the married ones. Both love marriages."

"Love marriage? Is there any other kind?"

"Arranged marriage is still common here."

Nishant chimed in. "Usually the parents arrange to meet their parents first. If Hindu, they should come from same caste and background."

"The parents arrange it?" I asked, astounded. "That sounds horrible... and like a mountain of pressure."

Sham joined in. "No, it is fine like that. All our parents were arranged. Now people are starting more love marriages."

"What's this caste about? Is that like a social standing? People being classified into groups?"

Sham explained further. "Starting from long back, everyone had to marry in same caste. It depended on your job."

"Essentially how much money the person made, right?" My head shook in opposition. "That's awful. Dividing people into organized groups is never a good idea. Rwandans were separated into groups and look how well that turned out. It ultimately led to genocide."

Aryan spoke up. "My sister wanted to marry from different caste. Our parents had a hard time dealing, but allowed because she was already twenty-seven."

"I'm twenty-seven now, so I guess that makes me an old maid, huh?"

"Yes," Nishant concurred.

"You weren't supposed to agree with me, you know," I teased.

Leela served chai as we relocated to the balcony, the delicate breeze wafting through my long hair over the view of the rich green valley.

"How do you like India, ma'am?" Mango asked.

"I love what I've seen so far. Still can't believe I'm here."

"Don't go back," Mango beseeched. "You can stay here."

His comment regaled me. "Are you kidding? I have to go back. I have family, friends, responsibilities..."

"You are married?" Nishant verified.

"No, I'm not."

Aryan's gaze sideswiped briefly at my response.

"In military, you can shoot with guns?" Kelvin asked, his voice shrill.

I smiled with cognizance. It was clear Aryan had already told them a few things about me.

"Yes. I'm trained to use several kinds of guns. In Iraq, we carry a long assault rifle called an M16. Do you guys have an Army here?"

"Yes. There is Army base near Ooty."

The conversation of cultural comparisons carried on. By the time Aryan and I were leaving, I had received numerous invites to come over and meet everyone's families. Their hospitality and curiosity was incredible, and I was made to feel right at home.

"Your friends are great fun," I apprised Aryan back at his house. "They like to talk about their country."

"I'm glad you're getting to see the real India." His black t-shirt was suddenly removed and tossed aside in the foyer. "I need a shower." He removed his watch as well. "Want to meet down here in an hour?"

I couldn't even begin to unravel his words. His frame bore resemblance to an Adonis statue as he stood at the base of the staircase. My mind was transfixed by his durable arms, hardened chest, muscular back, his skin a dark sable...

"Scaith?"

"Huh?" My eyes popped back to reality, blinking several times.

"Is an hour enough time for you to get ready?"

"Uh, yeah. That's plenty. I'll... meet you down here."

I breathed deep as he headed upstairs, my esurient self trailing closely behind. I took in his firm, shapely ass as it was just begging to be stared at, and I undeniably enjoyed what I saw. If there were a perfect model for the ideal Tall, Dark, and Handsome man, Aryan was it. Combine that with brains, brawn, and… damn, I'm so screwed.

I returned downstairs later, after an alleviating cold shower, wearing a black and white-striped top over skinny jeans. Aryan arose from the couch, shutting his laptop as I approached.

"You ready?" He bumped into me as he reached for the front door, his hand grazing my boob by mistake. "Oh, I'm sorry."

I followed him outside, smiling sheepishly at his unintentional cop-a-feel, which he pretended to be unfazed by.

We hopped into his red TATA car, my standard of living readjusting to the passenger seat opposite what I was accustomed to. He drove the short distance to pick up his uncle, who was quite a handsome geezer for his age. I could see Aryan resembling him when he got older, far more than his own father.

"Scaith, this is my uncle, Gangatharan. He's my mother's brother."

I joined my palms. "*Vanakkam*, Uncle."

They both looked equally impressed.

"Your sister taught me," I enlightened Aryan.

Gangatharan's hefty accent was almost unintelligible. "How are you finding India, ma'am?"

"Love it. Didn't even need a visa to get here. Just literally dropped in." I sniggered at my own dumb joke.

⚜   ⚜   ⚜

Aryan's elegant estate encompassed well-manicured hedges, fountains, and a British colonial plantation overlooking acres of coffee fields.

"Scaith, you can have a look around the gardens," Aryan suggested as we stepped out of the car. "We'll be inside for just a moment."

I strolled the grounds alone for a while, following along a stone trail of rose bushes with a scenic overlook. A short distance away, I recognized Aryan's home balcony from this viewpoint. In the valley below sat small huts of wood and straw. A vintage blue train chugged along the mountainside behind, a trail of slate grey smoke extending behind. There was so much to see just from this one spot.

"That's the Ooty train." Aryan came up beside me. "It runs for a few hours through the mountains. The British built it for transport when they occupied this area. Now it's used by tourists."

"It's simply majestic seeing it run along the mountain like that. Just beautiful."

"That's the Toda village down below, the tribal people of the area."

"Does every town or city have its own tribal village?"

"Usually. The one Mani lives in is called Kurumbar, where you were found. These people have their own languages, but can also speak Tamil."

I watched the Toda villagers collecting sticks and vegetables from their land. "I think we can learn a lot from people so closely connected to nature. Living in the city, we tend to lose that essential link, buying groceries at a store and taking pills when we're sick while forgetting where things actually come from."

Aryan stared over in contemplation, perhaps scrutinizing my ramble. "What's up?"

Another brief pause. "You're not like other American women I've met. You're more… practical. Not superficial at all."

I felt put on the spot, assuredly sentimental from being in this amazing place. "Guess I've just wanted to travel for a long time. There's so much we can learn from each other, all over the world. We have wars and conflicts over simple differences when in the end, I think we all want the same things: love, happiness, acceptance… The difference is in how we all try to obtain those things."

Aryan was still observing me with novelty. "We should get inside. It's going to start raining soon."

🛕   🛕   🛕

We arrived in the city hours later for some sightseeing, Aryan dropping off his uncle prior. Our first stop was the chocolate museum for a tour and sampling, purchasing a container of assorted pieces before leaving. He certainly knew his way to a woman's heart.

He drove up the street after and parked to the fore of a signless shop, dragging me through a creepy, dark alley of hanging clothes, scurrying rats, and dispersed rubbish.

"You're not planning to murder me, are you?"

"What would be the point of that, *Vellakari*? I could instead sell you for very much money."

My eyes rolled sprightly. "That's nice, Aryan."

Something smelled like doughnuts as we came upon a small shop, several men inside mid-baking process. One rolled dough as another formed balls. Trays were then handed to the next guy as he took a long paddle, shoving them into a deep clay oven and crisping to golden brown within minutes.

"Ooty is known for its chocolate… and varkey."

A man handed me one. "Varkey, ma'am. You try."

It was warm, coming fresh from the oven, and flakey with hints of butter and sweetness. "Mmm. That's really good."

"People here eat varkey with afternoon chai," Aryan described on.

"It's fun to experience things that are off the beaten path, like not typical tourist attractions. Get to see how the locals live."

I didn't have to twist Aryan's arm when I asked to see a Hindu temple next. It sat further in the jungle just outside of the city, painted bright colors with a monstrous golden deity centered like a guardian.

"Which god is this?" I asked, climbing the steps.

"Murugan."

"I've heard of him. The peacock, right?" I looked at my ring. "Your sister said he protected me during the plane crash."

Aryan smirked absurdly. "Yeah, she believes in all that."

We entered a vibrant room inside the outdoor complex where people were bowing to multiple statues. Several monkeys raced across the tiled floor playfully.

"I'll show you pooja. Just follow my lead."

A shirtless priest sat wearing a long white cloth with powdery markings across his forehead and chest. Aryan bowed as the priest hoisted a golden plate, a glimmering flame within. Aryan covered the flame, touching his palms to his face three times as I followed suit, our foreheads then tapped with red-powdered dots. The priest gave Aryan an apple and for me, jasmine flowers before we both bowed once more.

I roistered in the unique experience as we walked back to the car. I found the traditions fascinating, wondering where they all came from.

"Glad you enjoyed that." Aryan knew my blissfully contented face by now. "Oh, here." He stopped and picked a leaf from the bushes nearby, gifting it to me.

I glanced down and smiled. It was in the perfect shape of a heart, causing me to optimistically wonder if Aryan was suggesting something, but when I looked up, he was already gone.

⚜ ⚜ ⚜

Our daytrip concluded at a historical restaurant once frequented by British colonials. The walls were embellished with black and white photographs of game hunters and men riding intricately painted, jewel-adorned elephants.

A waiter greeted us in a traditional turban and garnet suit, his brimming mustache curved up at the ends.

"Welcome to India, ma'am." He set down glasses of hot water.

"This place has good biryani," Aryan advised, scouring the menu. "It's a South Indian rice dish."

I was agreeable, trusting his recommendations. He turned to me after placing the order.

"Our waiter speaks Hindi. He's down here for work from Assam."

"You speak Hindi, too?"

"Every state speaks different languages. I also speak Kannada and Malayalam and can understand some Telegu and Urdu."

"You speak like seven languages? That's crazy."

He nodded, as if it was common for everyone to know that many dialects. "We're close to the borders of Karnataka and Kerala."

"So you wanted to learn their languages. That's smart." I sat elucidating his distinctive character. I was enjoying his company and hoped he was enjoying mine. "You're a fascinating person, Aryan."

He smirked and sipped his water. "So are you, *Vellakari.*"

We both smiled, having a brief moment of mutual appreciation... or possible attraction.

"How did you end up in Kentucky?"

"I went there on a work visa some time back. Worked IT for an insurance company in Lexington, then met my skydiving friend Galen at the dropzone. His dream was to open a bourbon distillery and he wanted a business partner."

"And now you divide your time between here and the U.S.?"

"Yes. About six months each time."

"That sounds like an exciting life. I'm a little jealous." I folded my arms on the table. "Do you like the U.S.?"

"I love it. I can do all the things I can't do here, like skydiving. I also don't have my parents breathing down my neck."

"Oh, are they a bit controlling? They have to let you live your life at some point. You're what... thirty?"

He sipped more water. "Thirty-one. And that's just how Indian parents are. They're too old and set in their ways to change now."

"Anyone can change if they really want to." And I smiled.

⚜   ⚜   ⚜

It was almost dark when we returned to Aryan's house. He immediately poured glasses of brandy in the kitchen before joining me out on the couch.

"Thank you for coming with me today." He sipped his drink while kicking his feet up. "I like having you around."

"This has been eye-opening so far. I really can't thank you enough for all you're doing for me."

"Why wouldn't I? I get to spend time with a beautiful, adventurous woman."

There was no denying how uniquely desirable he was. I sought to memorialize this time spent with him, briefly forgetting all cares and concerns back home while wishing I could just stay in his presence.

"You have another day before I take you to Chennai. Do you want see Kerala tomorrow?

"As long as I'm not keeping you from getting your work done."

"Not at all. I'll be here for months."

"Do you think we'll see some tigers?"

"Possibly. I've only seen a couple during my life…"

His voice trailed off by something suddenly disturbing him. I was about to inquire when a knock at the door broke the silence, his friends stampeding inside with bags of liquor before Aryan could speak.

"*Machi!*" Kelvin clamored amongst the group.

I leaned over to Aryan. "Impromptu frat party tonight?"

He laughed. "Looks that way."

The guys raved it up for hours, just laughing, drinking, and goofing off. Though ignorant of the language, I appreciated seeing the interaction they had together.

"Hey, what do all the women do while you guys go out and party?" I addressed the question unanimously. "Are they stuck at home cooking and cleaning?"

"Yes," Kelvin answered impassively.

"That doesn't seem very fair. You guys are spoiled, huh?"

Sanjeev was staring at me wide-eyed like a ravenous beast, so I decided to say something. "Sanjeev, how did you meet your wife?"

Nishant translated as he didn't speak English as well as the others. "He says he found the diary of a girl who was contemplating suicide. She wrote about problems with her parents, so he found out who she was and ended up marrying her."

My mouth dropped. "That is the sweetest love story I've ever heard. He's like her hero. What about you, Nishant?"

"Mine was an arranged marriage actually. My parents are friends with Pretty's parents."

"Her name is Pretty? That's adorable. Did you know her for a long time?"

"No, we spoke for two months' time on the phone and I saw her picture."

"You didn't meet her in person until you married her?"

He bobbed his head, which I assumed meant no... at least in this case.

"Back in the States, people could live together for ten years and not be ready to get married."

"Yes, but here, divorce is not common."

"Yeah, you've got me there." I sipped more of my drink.

"Scaith, you play Truth or Dare?" Kelvin asked.

"Yes! You guys know that game?"

"Of course." Kelvin stood up and spun an empty beer bottle on the coffee table, the neck landing in Mango's direction. He picked dare.

"Dare you to eat a whole chili," Kelvin challenged him.

His head swayed nonchalantly. "Super. That is no problem." He headed to the kitchen, chewing confidently into a round red pepper from Aryan's fridge, but coughed and gasped a few seconds later.

"You grabbed a ghost pepper, dude," Aryan informed him matter-of-factly.

The guys erupted in laughter as Mango plunged his head under the faucet, sputtering under the rushing water.

Steny spun the bottle next and it landed on Sanjeev, who picked dare. Steny glanced over to me and smirked.

"I dare you to pick up Scaith and spin her around."

Sanjeev grinned, his mahogany eyes bulging, and lunged toward me like a raging lion.

"Oh god! No!" I protested and ran helplessly to the stairs, but was too late. Sanjeev snatched me around the thighs, bending me over his shoulder while twirling around. The guys all clapped and cheered him on.

"Just don't fart, Sanjeev!" I warned him. "My face is right by your ass." I clamped onto his shoulder as he lowered me, waiting for my head to stop spinning.

We sat down, continuing on with the chaotic, but entertaining game. My eyes circled the room, taking in each distinct personality. Nishant seemed like the mature one, and possibly the closest to Aryan. Sham was the shy, quiet one. Steny was the jokester, having earlier in the night danced while shaking his exposed jiggly belly. Mango was a bit goofy and awkward, though he was certainly polite. Sanjeev was the brute, sort of a 'shoot first and ask questions later' type of guy who would look right at home in the Marines, and Kelvin was the playful baby of the group. When it came to Aryan, he was the alpha male, without a doubt in my mind. The guys overtly looked to him as the leader, understandably with all his accomplishments and the way he carried himself.

Nishant's spin landed toward me next, causing the guys to flare up in whistling yowls and all drink glasses to clank.

"Okay, Scaith," Nishant started as they all settled down. "Truth or dare?"

"Truth." I sat up, mentally preparing myself.

He paused, eyes bouncing between me and Aryan with optimistic surmise. "Do you want Aryan to kiss you?"

I momentarily stopped breathing, my smile meekly retiring from the question I wasn't prepared to answer. What was worse, the room stood uncomfortably silent with all eyes upon me in thoughtful expectation.

"I, uh…" My gaze deliberately avoided Aryan's, the short pause feeling like an eternity. "I… think I ripped a stitch." I looked down to see blood slowly seeping through my jeans where the wound was located.

Aryan turned to his friends after seeing my affliction. "Hey, that's it for tonight, guys. We can do this another time." He helped me to my feet as his friends prepared to leave.

"Sorry, Scaith," Nishant empathized.

"I'll be fine, Nishant. No problem. It was fun. Thank you for the company."

Aryan assisted me upstairs while the guys paraded out the door, and he brought me straight to his room, helping me to bed with my leg outstretched. "Be right back."

He left briefly, returning with bandages, a wet rag, and small container. His hazel eyes deflected down to my pants and he stalled, not knowing how to handle the situation.

"It's fine, Aryan. Go ahead," I reassured him, dispelling any fear he might have about undressing me without permission. "You've already seen it. Remember?"

He grinned shyly, and I silently gasped when his fingers brushed over the bare skin of my hips. He removed my pants slowly, exposing my black panties... and bloody thigh. Luckily, he remained plutonic... and focused.

"It doesn't look like any stitches broke, but your skin did tear some." After cleaning the area, he sprinkled coffee powder to stop the bleeding before bandaging it.

"That's a neat little trick," I discerned.

"You'll want to keep this leg as still as possible, so just rest here." He pulled up the bed covers, tucking me in.

"What are *you* gonna do?"

"I can sleep on the couch tonight. You have everything you need?"

I appreciated his sincere concern, and responded honestly. "And then some, Aryan."

He nodded once and stepped over to the door, pausing against the doorframe while exhaling, running fingers through his hair as he stared down to the floor.

I rose to my elbows. "What's wrong?"

Another pause. "I'm not sorry I walked in on you."

It took me a second, but realized he was referring to the shower room where we had met only a day prior.

"You looked amazing." He lingered another second and left, shutting the door behind.

⚜   ⚜   ⚜

An hour later and I still couldn't doze off. The plush comfort of Aryan's bed should've mitigated me into a peaceful, impenetrable sleep, but I instead tossed and turned with instability. My thoughts kept drifting to Aryan... his kinds words and actions, delightfully flawless face, full yet masculine lips, the obvious bulge in his pants...

My cheeks flamed at the gratifying image. The sheets smelled of him, my body responding in a surprisingly unexpected way. Warmth rushed from deep in my chest down to my most sensitive flesh, breaths becoming more rapid the more I fantasized. I closed my eyes, imagining him in ways that Catholic priests would define as nothing short of sinfully immoral and wickedly obscene. My hand trailed slowly to my navel, fingers slipping down my panties...

My eyes sprang open, and I shook my head in self-humiliation while turning over. What the hell are you doing? I castigated silently. This is Aryan's bed.

A deep sleep followed soon after with minimal effort, though I can't say my dreams that night were pleasant.

8

"Scaith, what's wrong?!"

Aryan's face materialized in front of me, blurry at first, then clear enough for me to notice he looked concerned. My own nightmarish screams had awoken me in the middle of the night, breaths deep with anxiety as I scanned the room in a near-daze, almost forgetting where I was.

"Terrible dream," I revealed while shaking.

He sank to the bed, mindful of keeping his distance. "What happened?"

Feeling particularly vulnerable, I sat up. Childhood memories that never ceased to torment me sought to arise from concealment. I never talked about what happened to many people, but Aryan seemed a perfect exception to the rule. I bundled amid the blanket to stop quivering, and finally unshielded the pain that longed for release.

"It was a flashback." I wiped sweaty tears away, pausing before recounting the events. "My mother and little brother died in a car accident when I was twelve. Jimmy was only ten, but had already decided he wanted to be a movie star. Mom was driving him to an audition for a commercial when a semi struck their car on the freeway heading into Los Angeles, crushing them." I cried harder in overwhelming remembrance, hugging my knees. "I can't forget the look on my father's face when he came home to tell me. He was destroyed… just a wreck. It impacted him even more than it did me and he still struggles to deal with the trauma."

Aryan patiently waited to commiserate. "I'm sorry, Scaith. That's not an easy thing to go through at all." His apologetic eyes sheered deep into mine as he took my hand, his thumb stroking my knuckles lightly. "What can I do?"

I slapped hair from my perspired face and disclosed a bold request. "Will you stay with me tonight? Please?"

He studied my face in surprise. His obliging eyes told he me understood my plea and that it wasn't sex I was seeking, but the comfort of feeling close to someone I trusted, and in the mere days I knew Aryan, I already trusted him explicitly.

"Okay," his response hushed as he crawled into bed alongside me. Leading his arm around my waist, I closed any gaps between us, his body warm and scent earthy like sandalwood and spice. Though his hand sat just under my breast, not once did it move during the night.

⚜ ⚜ ⚜

I woke up to the smell of breakfast tantalizing my senses. Aryan wasn't in bed, so I followed the sounds of sizzling. He turned around as I entered the kitchen, giving me his full attention.

"Morning, Scaith. How are you feeling now?"

I leaned against the doorway and sniffed, running my fingers loosely through my hair. "Better. Thank you for being there last night. Sorry I was a mess."

He came and hugged me closely, a spatula still in his hand. "Don't ever apologize for that. It's sad to lose people, especially family." He took a step back while still holding my waist, his forehead pressing against mine. "You're strong, *Vellakari*. Time heals all wounds, right?" He returned to the counter. "Speaking of wounds, how's yours?"

"It's fine, thanks to you." I sat at the table as he set a plate and cup of chai in front of me.

"I made you a bread omelet." He sat across from me with a plate of his own. "You can rest today if you want, or if you don't feel up to going."

"No, I'm okay. I learned a long time ago not to let my negative thoughts keep me from living my life. I'd like to see Kerala today if it's still on the agenda."

Aryan nodded and started eating. "How is your father doing now?"

I sighed and sipped my chai. "Not sure. We haven't spoken for a while. Our last big conversation was an argument."

He kept staring, as if requesting to know more.

"Dad became really strict after Mom died. Very protective of me. When I was in high school, he caught me hanging out with a boy who was a Guatemalan immigrant, to which he disapproved of. He was so upset I thought he might disown me. So, at age seventeen, I moved out and in with my best friend's family until I graduated. We've barely spoken since then. He finally remarried, to a nice lady. I actually speak to her a lot more than I do him."

"That's a stupid thing to be upset about for years," he noted.

"It was," I agreed. "It is. But then I dropped more bombshells on him, namely joining the military. He thought I was ruining my life by not going to college. And yet, the military actually paid for my college, so it looks like it was the right choice."

"Seems like you've been making *all* the right choices."

I stared at my plate, still guilt-ridden over some of the choices I'd made. "I'm not so sure about that."

"We all just do the best we can. What else can you do?" He paused, deeply in thought, as if he had demons of his own to battle. "And then there's times we aren't left with any choice at all. That's when you discover just how strong you are."

⚜   ⚜   ⚜

After a forty-five minute drive, we pulled into a lush jungle area with several elephants freely walking abound.

"Whoa. What is this place?"

"An elephant rehabilitation center." He parked the car. "Come on. It's almost feeding time."

We crossed the field over to a couple workers. Aryan spoke, this time in Malayalam, and they motioned for us to join them. I probed Aryan as we walked.

"I meant to ask before. What are these rags called that men wear around their waist?"

"It's a *lungi*. If you see a fancier white one, it's called a *dhoti*."

"Do they wear something under that?"

He laughed. "Yes."

"Well, that's good to hear." I chuckled as well. "It's sort of like the Scottish kilt of India, then."

At the wooden fence, numerous elephants approached us from the other side, one holding out her trunk to me. I glanced over to Aryan, seeking authorization. "Is this safe?"

He assured me it was, stroking the trunk of another in illustration. "These are tame ones."

The men brought piles of tall grass, leaves, and bananas for feeding. I held a banana mid-air as the elephant snatched it with her trunk, bopping me on the head after.

"Oh! She just tapped me."

"She was thanking you."

I grinned. "I want to try something else." I grabbed handfuls of grass to continue feeding her.

"The guy says her name is Lakshmi."

I pet her trunk, admiring her small, glossy eyes and epic, flapping ears. "Such a pretty name. Look at you."

We were later led across the park and down a path toward a dramatic, surging creek surrounded by flat rocks. All the elephants followed.

"Now it's bath time," Aryan told me.

A couple elephants were immersed in the water already, men washing them down with soapy rags.

"A rehabilitation center? It's an elephant *spa!*" I pointed to the gathering. "Oh, look! A baby one."

The baby elephant dunked his head under and popped up, squirting water from his trunk in two long streams.

"You're probably so used to seeing elephants all the time that it's not a big deal anymore, huh?"

"It's still fascinating to watch. Historically, Indians used elephants to move logs. People also made rings with elephant hairs. It's supposed to protect from illness and bring good fortune."

"Sounds like Indians can be superstitious people."

"Especially in Kerala."

"Did you ride elephants when you were young?"

"All the time."

My grin curved in his direction, verging on provocative. "You really are a real-life Mowgli."

"Want to ride one?" he smirked.

I glanced up, Lakshmi towering over. "Only if you're coming up there with me."

"Of course." He spoke to one of the men and climbed Lakshmi's trunk as easily as if he were climbing a tree.

"Whoa!" I called out.

He hopped on her back, his arm reaching down to me. "Come on up."

"Are you kidding me?"

A worker backhanded the air, as if I didn't have any other option than to follow Aryan's method, so I cautiously crawled up as Lakshmi upheaved her trunk, bouncing me up onto her back. Aryan pulled me to a seated position in front of him.

I breathed deep. "This is really high. I'm not going to ask how we get down."

His arms circled my waist. "Hang on."

"Hang on to *what?*" I asked abrasively.

Lakshmi took a step forward and I gasped. "Oh, shit." Although her strides were slow, I still felt as though I might tip over.

"Relax, *Vellakari*," Aryan conveyed softly in my ear, his hand lightly stroking my hip. "I've got you."

Lakshmi followed the creek, sounds of a waterfall roaring off in the distance. Further out, wild boars and peacocks grazed in their natural habitat. Macaques were also playing about the area, picking bugs off each other and swinging from trees.

"Look at this place!" I stated in astonishment. "It's amazing. A zoo without the cages."

"That's the idea." A bird landed on Lakshmi's head, vibrant teal and burnt orange. "And that's a kingfisher."

"Hey, I tried a beer called Kingfisher once at an Indian restaurant."

"There's one called Taj Mahal, too," he laughed.

It was unfortunately time to head back when it started to rain.

"I kind of expected that," he told me despondently. "Kerala has far more rain than Tamil Nadu."

Within minutes, the sky darkened and began to downpour. We returned to the main center, Aryan sliding down Lakshmi's trunk as if a child at a playground.

"I'm opting for 'no' on that one," I refused over the patter of rain as they set out a ladder.

I thanked all workers exuberantly before skipping to the car, Aryan chortling a few feet behind me.

"Aryan, why would you ever live somewhere else when you have all this?" I raised my arms in the air, capturing raindrops while dancing in circles.

"Because I've always had it." He was still giggling at my antics. "It's exotic for you because it's different than what you're used to. It's fresh and exciting."

We got in the car and he drove off.

I brushed my hair back, giving a wet, sleek look. "Some people prefer what they've always been accustomed to, but I never understood it. If there's something I've never done, that's the first thing I want to do. Same with food. I don't want to be that person to say I've never tried something."

Aryan grinned. "I'm the same way."

My arm impulsively slid around his shoulders. "And look at you now, Aryan. This young boy from the jungles of India made it all the way to the U.S. and now owns a business there."

He smiled subtly, as though he'd never been praised before, but he certainly didn't seem to mind the accolade.

⚜   ⚜   ⚜

The rain stopped as we entered another parking lot, packed with crowds of people. The sun was just coming out, heating the humid forenoon period.

Aryan slid aviator sunglasses on while shutting his car door. "Up this mountain is the Edakkal Caves. I've never been here before, but my friends say it's a nice place." He took my hand as we shuffled through people. "It's the weekend, so lots of travelers. Stay close."

The shops and vendors were swarmed with unabated macaques, roaming the street and rooftops trying to steal food. Once again, all locals stared in my direction. A couple college guys even asked for a picture with me, at which, I glanced to Aryan, who grinned with approval.

After dodging many more photo op requests, we hurried up the mountain. A two-hour wait in line finally brought us up to a green-tinged cavern, the air inside slightly damp and cool. A dim light shone through bats flying with foot-long wingspans, circling above us.

I noticed some interesting inscriptions on the walls. "Hey, this writing looks Neolithic," I ascertained. "That reminds me, I read something a while back about a village in India that has hundreds of twins, even after generations. I think it's somewhere in Kerala."

"That's Kodinhi in Malappuram." He spoke faster than I could register.

"Uh, yeah sure. *That* place. Do people know why that is? Something in the water maybe?"

"No one really knows."

"I also read about some blood rain phenomenon that happened a few years ago. It rained red for days, staining everything pink." I climbed one of the rocks behind Aryan and sat down next to him.

"How do you know all this history stuff?"

"I study these kinds of things when I have time. Just for fun."

"Good hobby. Maybe you can teach me more about my own country's history."

"I'd love to. The best place to learn is being right where the history occurred."

     ᭡   ᭡   ᭡

Aryan had a special late lunch planned, and drove us out to the coast next. The salty ocean breeze caressed my face as I emerged from the car, the sound of waves crashing against the shore nearby. The pier was littered with palm trees and wooden boats. A man waved to us from the dock, trotting across the sand toward us.

"These are the Blue Lotus houseboats," Aryan informed me. "My friend Ganesh owns one and is going to take us out through the backwaters."

Ganesh smiled diligently as he approached, shaking my hand. "Nice to meet you, ma'am. Welcome to Kerala."

"Thanks, Ganesh. Happy to be here. Your state is gorgeous."

"Ah, super. Very nice to hear that, ma'am." He bobbed his head, still smiling. "Please, follow me."

We crossed the beach, stepping inside a luxurious houseboat with a bar and accommodating deck space. Ganesh moved to the front to drive as a waiter set out banana leaves on a table as plates.

"You arranged all this?" I asked Aryan as we sat down. "You guys really know how to take care of your guests."

The waiter brought out a couple dishes and served us.

"This is shrimp curry," Aryan pointed out. "It's made with coconut milk." He handed me the platter of flaky, doughy bread. "And this is paratha."

"This looks too good to be true." I salivated at the aroma.

"You want a drink? They have banana wine or toddy."

"What's toddy?"

"It's a coconut palm liquor. Very traditional drink of Kerala."

"Well, I'll go with that. When in Rome…" A decision I later came to regret as it tasted like a rancid lemon kombucha.

Our bellies were full to the brim when we walked the deck for an hour, taking in the huge Chinese fishing nets before heading back to shore. I thanked Ganesh and pranced across the beach, just as I had after seeing the elephants.

"Hey Aryan, how come you don't wear a *lungi*?" I called over to him while picking up a seashell.

"I don't like how it feels. It also doesn't stay on my hips."

"Is that the real reason? Or maybe you just don't want to show off those long, hot legs of yours."

We laughed. I was feeling a little frisky from the drinks. I watched Aryan walk with unabashed confidence, his whole persona different from most men. He saw the world in a realistic way, fraught with challenges to embrace and conquer.

He caught me staring and reached out his hand, bringing me closer as it encircled my waist, those scintillating, exotic eyes torturing mine.

"You having a good time?" his deep accent robust and hypnotizing.

I nodded, momentarily unable to speak.

His hand trailed up my back, under my swath of blonde hair. I thought he might kiss me until a bug whizzed between us, distracting our compromising position.

"What is that thing?" I swatted at it.

It landed on his arm, still buzzing. "It's a bee."

"Wait a sec." I lowered my face for a closer look. "It's blue."

"Correct," his answer lax.

"A blue bee? That is the coolest."

It flew off as Aryan shook his arm. "Come on. We have one last stop."

.◈.   .◈.   .◈.

The sandstone fortress before us was colossal, and a perfect place to go to end our day in Kerala. Aryan thought I might like it, being a historical military site.

"This is the Palakkad Fort. My uncle recommended it."

Eagerness stirred as I smiled, crossing over the medieval-looking drawbridge. In the moat below were hundreds of swimming turtles. Aryan gave me a bag of chips for feeding, the turtles scrambling and snapping at each other in claim of the crumbs. Before I knew what hit me, a large grey monkey jumped on my shoulders, ripping the bag from grasp before disappearing down the hill.

Aryan laughed hysterically. "Yes, that will happen."

I still had my mouth open in shock. "No wonder monkeys are portrayed as little thieves in movies. That's what they *are*."

"That one was a langur monkey."

I laughed, shaking my head. "What a little shit." Brushing myself off, I continued on with Aryan, who was still chuckling.

The complex accommodated several lookout posts, a small Hindu shrine, gardens, and a sub jail, which we took our time exploring.

Aryan took a few photos with his cell phone. "My uncle said the original fort on this spot dates back to ancient times. It's been used by the British and sultans of Mysore. There's a palace in Mysore you might like. We'll drive right past it on our way to Chennai tomorrow."

I darted to the top of a tower and stared down to the moat. He had just reminded me that I would be leaving in the morning. If it weren't for my government duties, I would've wanted stayed longer. I didn't feel ready to leave all this behind.

"What are you thinking about?" he asked.

The sunset glowed against the sandy-red lookout point. "Honestly, I wish I didn't have to leave yet. I love being here."

He nodded and leaned against the brick next to me. "I'd like you to stay, too, but the Army needs you. Hopefully you can come back to India sometime."

I smiled, envisioning another trip back here. "I'd like that." I leaned against the wall beside him, my face toward his. I shivered as the wind blew, though possibly caused from something else besides the weather.

"Are you feeling cold?" He came over, rubbing his hands against my arms. "Let's get you back."

.⚜.   .⚜.   .⚜.

An hour later, we were back at his house. Upon returning downstairs from using the bathroom, I overheard Aryan yelling into the phone, his

Tamil words blocking my assimilation. I crept back to my room as the argument continued on. A short time later, he knocked on my door.

"Is everything all right? Sounded like a nasty fight."

His head shook in annoyance with his arms crossed, leaning against the doorpost. "My aunt called my parents and told them you were staying with me, so I had to deal with them."

"Your aunt? Why would she do that?"

"Because she's a cunt," he shot out angrily.

"Whoa, you guys use that word here? How would she even know about me?"

"People talk. Everyone knows everything here."

"But I thought you didn't care what people think."

He gave no response, just glanced about the room, his demeanor distraught.

"You just don't want to deal with your parents, right? Or disappoint them?"

"This is why I went to the U.S. in the first place. There, I can do what I want."

"Man, I thought I had a strict parent. Here you are thirty-one years old and can't bring a girl home, plutonic or otherwise."

"That is how it is in India."

I sighed empathetically. "I'm sorry about all this, Aryan. I can't help feeling like I've caused nothing but trouble for you. You've been so nice and helpful, yet here you are dealing with family conflict because of it."

"It's not your fault at all, Scaith. Don't think that way."

"Wait…" I paused. "Where did your parents think I went when you took me away?"

"They thought we were on the way to Chennai already."

"Oh. Well, I'm leaving tomorrow anyway, so there's really no need for this."

"About tomorrow, Scaith, I need to deal with something at the rental property. Can we postpone leaving for just one more day?"

Two days ago, I would've objected amidst mild aggression, but now, I just wanted to stay with him a little longer… not that I needed an excuse. "I can live with that, Aryan. I do have concerns about the amount of time that's already passed, but I want you to be able to get done what you need to. I don't want to disrupt your life."

"Here." He pulled a scrap of paper from his pocket, handing it over. "This is the number to the Consulate. They'll be open tomorrow, so we'll call and let them know you're here."

"Okay, good." I slipped it into my bag.

Aryan was still staring off into space, mind obviously racing with thoughts of his last phone conversation as he tapped the wall ferociously.

"Goodnight, Scaith." He avoided my gaze as he exited the room.

⚜   ⚜   ⚜

I checked the clock, seeing that I had slept in later than usual, so I headed downstairs, curious if Aryan had left yet. He wasn't in the kitchen, so I returned upstairs to find him still lying in bed, an empty bottle of brandy on the floor.

I sighed, setting it on his bedside table. "Morning sunshine." He started to wake up as I sat at the foot of the bed. "Have a nice self-destructive night?"

He groaned, trying to sit up. I fetched his water bottle and he took several long gulps, carelessly spilling all over himself. If this had been a friend back home, we would've laughed it off as a fun morning-after, though with Aryan, I felt he was dealing with unresolved family issues that he didn't know how to handle on his own.

I took the water, setting it aside. "You okay?"

He gave a muffled "yeah" before turning over, trying to fall back asleep.

"Aryan, you said you had things to do today. Shouldn't you get up?" But he didn't respond. "Okay, then," I said under my breath, not wanting to force him. "Guess I'll check on you later."

I did some exercises in the living room before frying up a couple eggs for breakfast. Aryan faltered in as I sat down.

"You found something to eat?" He wasn't wearing a shirt and his hair matted to one side. Despite his rough edges, I had to admit, he still looked sexy.

He didn't say anything during the drive into the city. It didn't necessarily feel awkward, I just didn't understand what was going on. He stopped outside a large apartment complex, painted cobalt blue and surrounded by a chain-link fence.

"Wait here," he instructed. He walked into the building with a set of keys in hand.

Ten minutes of wild dog and chicken-watching later, a man came stumbling out the front door, dropping to the ground with Aryan tailing behind. He swung a rock up at Aryan's head, just narrowly missing him.

I bolted from the car, moving closer to see the commotion. Aryan grabbed the man's arm, shoving him down to the ground again as they both hollered at each other. The man scrambled to his feet, attempting to punch Aryan's face, but Aryan caught his fist and kicked him across the grass, hitting the chain link fence with a jangle. A curious crowd began to form as policemen arrived behind me. The man was apprehended and taken away while continuing to yell.

Aryan retrieved his key set from the ground and returned to me, a glower across his face. "I told you to wait in the car," his accent prominent as he scolded me.

"I could've helped had I known what was going on." I demurred his claim that I was undermining him as we got back in the car. "What did that guy do?"

He drove off without answering me, then called someone, speaking aggressively in Tamil for a while. He pulled up to a house next and parked, waiting. A police vehicle was situated not far down the street. We sat in silence as he stalked the house, a frown exhuming his face that looked both scary and dangerously magnetizing.

Two policemen burst out the front door while seizing a young man in a black t-shirt and red bandana. I wanted to ask Aryan what was happening, but just left it. He seemed interested in seeing this arrest transpire. The policeman placed the man in custody and drove off.

Aryan looked straight ahead, exhaling before he broke the silence. "Last week my fourteen-year-old cousin was assaulted by two men. Just yesterday, the police tracked down who they were. One turned out to be a renter of mine." His head shook in disgust. "I've been over to his place for dinner before."

"I'm sorry that happened to her, Aryan. Both of them are arrested now, so hopefully justice will take care of it from here."

"I wanted to come early and deal with him myself first."

"That's understandable. With how upset you were, I'm surprised you didn't kill him."

"I wanted to." His pause prolonged before he started up the engine, driving off. "I'm sorry if I was short with you."

I lightly rubbed his arm in an attempt to comfort him. "At least now I understand why." He took my hand in response, holding on for several seconds before letting go.

"I'll call the Consulate." He cleared his throat, pulling out his phone again. He dialed the number and handed it over to me.

"Hmm. It went to voicemail," I informed him.

"We'll try again later. The office might not be open this early." He put his phone away. "Today I have to go back to the coffee plantation. Just need a couple hours. Do you want to come along or stay at the house?"

"I'd like to come if you don't mind."

He smiled. I was relieved to see him slowly returning to the cheery Aryan I knew. "That's what I figured. I'll pick up Nishant on the way. He can keep you company."

⚜   ⚜   ⚜

Back at his coffee estate, Aryan worked inside while Nishant and I walked the gardens. The weather was near perfection.

"How is your leg feeling now? I'm sorry about that dare."

"I'm fine, Nishant. Don't even worry about that."

"We are all very sad to see you go."

I changed the subject, not wanting to admit how much I would miss them, too. I longed to stay in the moment. "What do you do for work?" I picked a wildflower and stuck it in my hair.

"I manage a resort in Jamaica. I'll be heading back next month."

"That's great. I managed a hotel back in California before I deployed. It's nice that all you guys can take off and come back to India for months at a time."

We continued deeper into the valley. I found Nishant to be very authentic and humble. He seemed to care for Aryan as a brother. He was a little shorter than him with a round baby face, pouty lips, and dimples.

"Want a banana?" he offered.

"Uh, sure," I answered while looking around. Not sure why I expected him to lead us to a shop somewhere. He simply climbed a tree, tossing down a couple bananas before dropping back to the ground.

"Are there other Indians in Jamaica, too?" I asked as we walked on, peeling my fresh banana.

"Yes, there are many. Lots of Americans, too."

"Maybe I'll come visit you guys sometime. I've got quite the travel bug now. I want to see everything I can."

"Yes, please do. Aryan is also like that. Even when he was a boy, he wanted to travel."

"How did his parents feel about that?"

"His mom was worried. His dad was just angry, like he always is."

"What do you mean by that?" I pushed him for a little more insight into Aryan's background.

"His father was not good person. He would drink very much and hit his family."

I stopped walking and turned to him with concern. "His father is abusive?"

"No, he is not now, but he was. He was police chief in Gudalur and would get very angry when he came home from work. Aryan would defend his mother and sister. Most of the town does not speak to his father, or his siblings. The Visu family owns half of Ooty and much of Gudalur. They are very powerful and corrupt. Aryan didn't want to be like that."

"Does Aryan get along with his father now?"

He bobbed his head. "It is okay. They do not talk much. His father just sits and watches TV. He expects his wife to take care of everything."

"Yeah, I guess I could see that. What does Sharvani think?"

"She does not talk to him much either. She married outside of caste, so their father was very angry about that."

"I can't believe how that caste system works here!" I scowled. "People should be able to marry whoever they want."

"Aryan never spoke of wanting to get married because he didn't want to deal with his father. He just wanted to move out of the country to get away from all that."

The more I learned about Aryan, the more I was intrigued. "Nishant, does Aryan date at all? There was this girl in Gudalur that threatened to kill herself over him."

"That was Prema. Her parents wanted her to marry Aryan, so she got the idea in her head for very long time, but he didn't want to marry her."

"Why not?" My hope stirred.

"Because she is traditional. Aryan likes adventure. I know he wants to meet someone more like him."

I smiled, wondering how Aryan felt about me.

Nishant stared, stepping a bit closer. "He doesn't want to see you go, Scaith."

I stared back, curiosity spurred further. "How do you know that?"

Before he could answer, Aryan returned.

⚜   ⚜   ⚜

Nishant was dropped off back at his friend's place in Ooty. I hugged him goodbye, promising to keep in touch. Aryan tried the Consulate one more time, but once again, went straight to voicemail.

"At least I'll see them in person tomorrow," I said, focusing on the positive side.

"You know it's a twelve-hour drive. Even if we leave early, we'll have to stay overnight in Chennai. My brother-in-law has a friend with an apartment we can use."

"You have a lot of good connections."

"There's one more spot here I'd like to take you before you leave tomorrow."

He drove us across town up to Doddabetta Mountain, placing a grey jacket over my shoulders to block the elevation-induced wind as we got out. We walked the brick path, stopping at one of the vendor tables of hand-crafted trinkets.

"Would you like something?" Aryan offered. "Maybe a souvenir to take back with you?"

The elderly woman smiled, showcasing the items for sale, but there was nothing I needed.

"That's okay, Aryan. You've done more than enough…"

He showed me a pair of gold earrings from the table. "How about these?"

"Oh, my god. Those look just like…" I held up my ring, comparing it to the peacock image on the earrings.

"Yeah, I noticed."

He stepped closer, tucking a strand of hair behind my ear as he inserted the earring. I glanced at the reflection in a small mirror. After wearing military fatigues in the desert for so long, they glistened more than they probably would have otherwise. I turned back to find Aryan had put the other into his own ear, and I burst out laughing.

"Your ear is pierced?"

"Yeah," he grinned, quickly removing it. "An impulse buy when I first got to the U.S."

"Aww. You should keep 'em. You look so beautiful." I stroked the side of his face while smirking. When his eyes moved down to my lips, I quickly retracted my hand.

Aryan bought me the earrings and we moved on, arriving at the summit after fifteen minutes of intense step-climbing. At the top was a sizable platform with hiking trails, park benches, and a lookout tower. Being a Monday, there were only a few other visitors.

"This is the highest point in the Nilgiris Mountains. You can even see my parents' home in Gudalur from here. Came here a lot as a child."

I pointed to the observation tower. "Can we go up there?"

He grabbed my hand, leading me inside where the walls suddenly blocked the wind as the door slammed closed behind us. I fixed my hair as we climbed to the top. A large gold telescope stood surrounded by a panoramic view of the valley enclosed in glass. We were the only people inside.

"What a view!" I gaped out at the mountainous jungle and cluster of pink rhododendrons below, flora native to California as well.

Aryan stared as I leaned against the railing, his saunter over self-assured and purposeful. My eyes found his as he reached up, stroking my hair. My heart fluttered, anxiously anticipating his next move when his hand moved to my face, his fist opening to reveal a small white butterfly.

"This was in your hair," he informed me with a smirk.

I chuckled, brushing back through my hair while feeling a little presumptuous. The butterfly flew off from his palm, returning outside through a crack in the glass. Though I had misunderstood Aryan's maneuver with the butterfly, he didn't disappoint, as the second I turned back to him, his lips were on mine.

9

"And then I told myself, if my cat doesn't even like him, then I'm not gonna go out with him again. *And* he was a total jerk. He was always like staring at other girls when we'd go out and then wonders why I'd get mad. I mean, come on."

I sipped my whiskey, wanting to drown out the sound of the girl's voice that resembled a rusted car door opening, but she babbled on, her hands gesturing wildly like a mindless psychotic.

"On top of that, he didn't even drive. He said he had like a bad eye or something, but I think he just didn't want to spend the money. Some guys pull shit like that so they don't have to pay for things. Like, are you kidding me?" Her break from loose vocals was only to sip her fruity cocktail before continuing on.

I sighed, sheer boredom and irritation washing over as I scanned the dimly-lit supper club, wishing I hadn't agreed to go on this date. I checked my watch, wondering how the distillery was doing. I could barely stand another minute with this girl and we hadn't even gotten our meals yet.

Her head brainlessly bounced about the room. "So like, where's our food? We ordered such a long time ago."

My forehead received an exasperated rub. "Was just wondering the same."

"So, that's really cool that you own that bar." She barely looked me in the eye. "You can like, drink as much as you want all the time, huh?"

"Yeah, if I want to see a reduction in my inventory."

"Oh my gosh, one time I got so wasted on tequila that I had a threesome with my best friend and her boyfriend."

Her chortle echoed as I near-choked on my whiskey. Our waitress set our orders down while grimacing over at my date.

"And it was totally weird to see them both after, but then we all laughed about it."

"Another one of these," I implored the unfortunate waitress.

She nodded in mutual understanding. "Anything else I can get for you both right away?"

"Um, this needs more cheese on it," Megan complained, sneering down at her plate.

The waitress remained impressively polite. "The spaghetti dish doesn't come with cheese, ma'am."

She appeared annoyed and inconvenienced. "Well can you add it?"

"Yes, ma'am." The waitress removed her plate, returning to the kitchen.

Megan rolled her eyes. "Who doesn't put cheese on pasta?" She twirled her hair in circles, as though her mind wasn't registering her surroundings.

I was tempted to leave, but decided to stay for the expensive prime rib I ordered. Megan's plate was brought back, now doused in shredded mozzarella. She said nothing, just hurriedly stuffed her face of spaghetti.

On her own, she wasn't a bad-looking girl. Her short, curly brown hair could've used some maintenance, dark brown eyes plain, and she was on the chubbier side. Her thick-rimmed glasses were cheap and black strapless dress covered in cat fur. If her personality wasn't such a flop, I maybe would've taken her out again, but as the situation stood, I couldn't get out of there fast enough.

I quickly finished dinner and signaled for the check.

"Hey," Megan objected. "I'm not even done yet."

"I have to leave early. There's an important event going on at the distillery."

"Huh? I don't even know what you're saying. You have like a really thick accent."

I paid the tab and got ready to leave.

"Hang on a sec," she grumbled as she put on her faux-leather jacket, which I didn't bother to assist her with.

We walked to my silver KIA Sportage in the lot. Immediately driving away was tempting, but I had to take Megan home. Her gripes and "misfortunes" of her life were something I didn't want to hear about on the way home, but luckily she didn't live far. I left my engine on when I stopped in front of her apartment building, hoping she'd get the hint that I was calling it a night.

"So, you coming in?" She leaned close, her alcohol-scented breath saturating my car. "I'll let you meet my pussy."

If she was trying to sound seductive, I couldn't think of anything that would've had more of an adverse effect on me. "No, Megan." I didn't bother to look at her. "I'm not interested."

She bounced back in her seat, scowling at being spurned. "Are you kidding me?" She acted like she had never been turned down before, making me question some of the standards of other men out there.

"I told you I needed to go to my distillery tonight." I spoke calmly, though I would've preferred to yell at her while kicking her out of my car.

Her eyes reeled like an entitled, spoiled child. "Whatever." She stumbled out. "I can't even understand you. And you're fucking boring anyway!"

She slammed the door and stormed off. I shook my head in disbelief at a woman so insecure and fragile that even common civility offended her.

∴   ∴   ∴

It was just getting dark when I arrived at my bourbon distillery. I drove past the white picket fence, up the hill to the tasting room parking lot in back. I unlocked the door and stepped inside the modern rustic lounge area to see my partner Galen behind the bar talking with Alex, both sipping beers.

"Hey, dude." Galen looked perplexed. "What are you doing back here? Thought you might pull an all-nighter with that girl."

I joined them at the bar, shaking my head with dismay. "She was a nightmare. Dating is a waste of time and money."

Galen handed me a much-needed Belgian lager from the cooler. "She seemed cute and sweet when she was here with her friends."

"Yeah, we probably shouldn't take out customers anymore. I knew that was a bad idea."

Alex spoke up. "Actually, I met Marcy while I was working at Walgreens. She'd come in all the time to see me until I finally asked her out."

"You've been married twenty years, Alex," Galen pointed out. "Things have changed now. Women these days want a rich CEO that looks like Johnny Depp. They won't settle for less."

Alex sipped his pilsner. "Aryan's a stud, though. The girls line up for him."

"These girls are either superficial, stupid, or snobby," I told him. "I don't want."

Alex was about ten years older than Galen and I. Sometimes he played dad to us whenever we were acting too crazy. His usual look was a flannel to go with his dark goatee and beer gut. He managed the tasting room and knew most of our regular customers. Galen was my age, but stood taller with pale skin, a thick mahogany beard, and bald head. He never had any trouble with the ladies due to his undaunted, entertaining personality.

"How'd the Wiedmann event go tonight?" I asked them, sipping my beer.

"Same shit, different day, dude," was Galen's response. "Bunch of rich corporate pricks that don't tip, but we did book some ayahuasca group meeting for next weekend. They're looking for a regular monthly venue."

"That's good," I commended. "What's ayahuasca?"

Galen smirked, as if he had some good stories to tell. "It's a natural psychedelic drug made from this plant in South America. A bunch of us took a trip down to Peru last summer and tried it. They had this whole tribal ceremony."

Alex frowned. "What happened? What did it do?"

His smile widened. "Dude, it was like nothing I've ever tried. I was somewhere else in this complete out-of-body experience. I saw my whole family and these like Native Americans showed up and told me I didn't belong there. It was crazy."

Galen was well-versed in the world of illegal drugs. He used cocaine on a regular basis; even bought a small school bus and transformed it into a party on wheels with TVs, stereo systems, and flashy lights.

"You excited about going back to India?" Galen asked, not leaving any room for me to answer. "I've always wanted to go to Goa, chill out on the beaches and just get fucked up."

"Too bad you can't join me next month. We'd be leaving Alex to run the distillery all by himself."

Our gazes shot over to Alex. I think both of us were being partially serious.

"Absolutely not," Alex objected.

Galen turned back to me. "How are the girls over there, dude? Some of them are insanely hot."

"They all just want to get married and have kids." The statement couldn't have been more true in my experience.

"You don't want kids, man?" Alex asked.

"No way."

"Do your parents know that?"

"No. I don't talk about it with them."

"Dude, you're like an Indian rebel," Galen remarked. "You don't want kids, you drink, you eat beef, and you date American girls."

I shrugged. "I was meant to be an American, I guess."

"You know, we've got that bachelorette party tomorrow afternoon. There should be some hot girls there."

"Aren't you still with Stacy?" I verified.

"I'm talking about for you, bro. Brush this shit date off and go out with a better one."

I changed the subject, not wanting Megan's voice to invade my mind again. "Did you close out already?"

"Yeah, man," Galen confirmed. "It was a good Friday night. Had a lot of walk-ins."

Alex turned to me. "You should grow back your beard, Aryan. Now you look like an altar boy."

I laughed, stroking my bare chin. "If I do, then I look like a terrorist."

"Oh, chicks dig dangerous-looking dudes," Galen assured me.

"How about scary bald ones?"

"Hey, this bald head does it for me. Remember San Diego? That skydiver Becca couldn't stop rubbing my head all day."

Alex's opinion chimed in. "That's some weird fetish, man."

"Nah, that's not weird," Galen opposed. "I once brought home a chick that wanted me to take a brush to her pubes."

"Did you do it?" I asked, not really wanting to know the answer.

Galen chuckled with pride. "Hell yeah. She loved it."

I had to admire their dedication in ensuring I learned American culture to the fullest.

⚜   ⚜   ⚜

My condo in the Southeastern Hills of Lexington was a fifteen minute drive from the distillery. Many of my neighbors were regular customers, horse racing and polo often their topic of choice. My place was small, but completely functional for a person that resides only half the year. I knocked out some push-ups while watching a George Carlin skit before heading off to bed.

I was the first to arrive at the distillery the next day, as usual. Morning was spent at the nature sanctuary for a jog and shopping at the Indian grocery store, catching up with Gujarati owner Vivek for a while. I now sat in my office, completing reports in a crisp, aubergine shirt over black slacks.

By early afternoon, the place was hopping with customers. Multiple walk-in groups showed up and the scheduled bachelorette party was already underway. Galen and I assisted our bartenders sporadically as more people arrived and I finished up several tastings before the crowds started to die down.

The place became relatively quiet until the bachelorette party started playing some drinking game in the lounge area by the fireplace, their animated laughter echoing throughout the building. I walked over to check on them. There were fifteen girls, all wearing micro-scale, tight dresses and skirts with plastic princess crowns. One was an Indian.

"How are we doing over here, ladies? Have everything you need?"

Some continued to laugh and chat while some just stared back.

A girl with florescent pink hair spoke up, and a slight southern accent unfolded. "Well, how did we miss *you*, honey? Are you a manager here?"

I smiled professionally. "I'm one of the owners, ma'am."

A pair of girls gasped, whispering amidst giggles. One stood, pulling me towards them by my arm.

"Will you take a picture with us? We want a hot guy to be in it."

I laughed modestly. "Sure."

The sloshed, overly-exhilarated group crowded around me. At one point, my ass was also pinched. As one girl prepped to snap the picture, Galen interjected, snatching the camera away.

"I've got this. You can get in there, honey." He shot me a smirk while snapping some photos with the digital camera, the following gratitude from the girls slamming us in the form of group hugs and canoodling.

When Galen returned to the bar, I tried to follow, but one girl's inquiry stopped me.

"Hey, where are you from?"

"India."

Several mouths dropped in intrigue.

"Sutton here is from India, too." She pointed behind her.

I extended my hand to the visibly Punjabi woman, greeting her in Hindi. She was reasonably good-looking with shiny onyx hair and a short stature. Her sheer, forest green dress was classier than the outfits of her friends, possibly signifying elevated affluence, and she was adorned in silver jewels. We continued a brief exchange in Hindi, and I learned that she moved to the U.S from India at a young age.

"Whoa, that was so cool," Miss Pink Hair stated. "I've never heard Indian spoken before."

Sutton corrected her. "There's actually no language called Indian, Brooke. That was Hindi we were speaking. Aryan is from a different part of India, but he speaks my language."

"Well, enjoy the rest of your evening, ladies. Let us know if you need anything else." I strode back my office, first checking the bar to ensure employees were handling business okay. "You guys good up here?" I called out.

"Yeah, man," Alex responded from behind the bar. "Got a couple tours soon, but Galen's got the front covered."

I worked in the office for about an hour when Galen entered. He held up a business card and read the name aloud, "Sutton Singh," and tossed it to my desk. "She wants you to call her sometime."

I retrieved it. "She's a real estate agent."

Galen gave a smile of satisfaction and approval. "That's an improvement, right? Wasn't that chick from last night unemployed?"

I sighed, focus still at my computer. "Sutton seems nice, but I don't want to go out with an Indian."

"Are you serious, dude? She's cute. Why wouldn't you?"

I shrugged. "Indians are too much work and they're bossy. Especially the ones that live here in U.S."

Galen crossed his arms. "You're the most critical, particular guy I know. At least take her out once, man. If you don't, I'll call her myself."

"Fine, Galen." I saluted him from my desk, as if I were a soldier obeying orders.

⚜   ⚜   ⚜

That evening, I prepared a pot of goat curry at home while flipping through TV channels. I contemplated calling Sutton when I was unable to find anything decent to watch. Galen's officious words played in the back of my mind as I pulled out her business card, so I dialed her number.

"Hello?"

I responded in Hindi. "*Namaste*, Sutton. *Kya haal hai?*"

"I'm fine. It was nice to meet you tonight." She didn't sound like an Indian as her accent was full American.

"Would you want to go out sometime next week? The distillery is closed on Mondays and Tuesdays. Would that work for you?"

"Yes. Tuesday would be fine."

"I was thinking we could go for a walk at the arboretum, then have lunch at Carson's."

She was silent for a moment. "Actually, I don't really want to go walking. How about we just go to dinner at Ruby's?"

"Sure, we can do that. I haven't been there yet."

"Okay, then you can pick me up at my place on Tuesday at seven."

She gave her address and we said our casual goodbyes. The interaction replayed in my mind as I ate dinner because it sounded more like a business meeting than a date.

⬥   ⬥   ⬥

The next day was business as usual. Having caught up on a lot of my office work, I spent the afternoon behind the bar. Sundays typically consisted of older crowds, so I was answering a lot of questions about the distilling process to customers over fifty.

"Oh, this is very smooth," a silver-haired women said aloud, sipping her bourbon sample. "Which one is this again?"

I held up the bottle at a slant. "This is our fifteen-year rye whiskey. It has notes of black pepper, cedar, and pear. You might taste some clove, mint, malt, and a little honey on the finish."

The woman's husband inspected his snifter, swirling the golden contents before taking a sip, grinning with contented endorsement. "Ah, yes, this is very nice."

I brought out the next bottle for sampling and poured into each glass while explaining the product. "This next one is our double oaked bourbon. On the nose you may get notes of plum, caramel, chocolate and honey. For the taste, a mix of full-bodied vanilla, hazelnut, and cinnamon."

"How long have you guys been open?" the woman asked.

"Three years, ma'am."

"It looks like you guys are doing very well. How did you come up with the name?"

"So, a burble is like a dead pocket of air above you when you freefall during skydiving. My friend Galen and I own the business together and we're both skydivers, so we just thought to name it Burble Distillery."

"Oh, that's very clever and unique. Ron and I are visiting family here. We're actually from Boston. Tomorrow, we'll visit the Woodford Distillery."

"They have very good bourbon there as well. Ask for Scott and tell him I sent you. He should offer you a discount."

"Wonderful. And what was your name again?"

"Aryan." I shook her hand.

"Well, Aryan, this is a wonderful place. I'm Janice. Very nice to meet you."

I shook Ron's hand as well. "Likewise. Thank you both for stopping in."

⚜ ⚜ ⚜

Tuesday night came around and I was busy preparing for my date with Sutton. I put on a sapphire shirt and steel-grey slacks, picking up half a dozen white roses before arriving at her house.

House was hardly the appropriate term for it. I pulled up to an epic-sized mansion, a towering bronze gate surrounding with an intercom and security cameras.

"Yes, who is it?" a male voice spoke through as I pressed the button at the gate entrance.

"Uh, hi. This is Aryan Visu. I'm here to pick up Sutton."

The gate steadily opened and I drove onto a cobblestone driveway past an elegantly-lit fountain, a marble Aphrodite statue looming up from the center. I approached the door of the luxurious stone mansion with white trim, a man in a black suit answering when I knocked. He was around my age, fit, and considerably handsome, his jet-black hair pulled into a long ponytail with a diamond stud in his ear.

"Good evening, sir. Please come in. Sutton will be with you shortly." Whatever accent he was trying to mimic, he was doing a terrible job.

I stepped inside, flower bouquet still in hand. The crystal chandelier above me shimmered like diamonds, an Oriental rug lolled over a checkered floor of navy-blue and maroon tones. Sutton appeared at the top of the white spiral staircase. Her red lace dress clung just above her knees as she descended the steps in matching red heels. Glistening jewelry covered her from head to toe, including her loose bun. She smiled and walked over to me with her jewelry clanging, and kissed my cheek.

"Hi, Aryan. Thank you for coming."

I felt underdressed, but smiled back, handing her the roses. "You look nice. This is your house?"

"Yeah, I live here alone," she replied, then glanced at her doorman. "Well, me and my butler Ares."

I looked back at her butler, who was still standing by the door like a fourteenth century guard, his hands interlocked in front of him.

I turned back to her. "Is that his real name?"

She laughed out loud, as though I said something ill-founded. "No."

⚜   ⚜   ⚜

I was busy searching for a parking spot on the street when Sutton intervened. "Why don't you just valet?"

My head bobbed in compliance. "I could do that, I guess."

After being handed a fifteen dollar valet ticket, we entered the restaurant, and I immediately noted the premier and elite vibes it gave off. The interior was sleek with substantially long wine racks and impressionist paintings decorating the walls.

Sutton opened the wine menu right after we were seated at a round corner booth.

"This is a very fancy place," I distinguished, though it was something she unarguably knew prior.

"Yeah, I come here every weekend."

"You do?" It was a tad intimidating, seeing how wealthy this woman was. She was clearly used to this upper class lifestyle.

Our waiter arrived, young and handsome with black hair and indigo eyes, possibly a college student. I found Sutton's smirk in his direction a tad dubious.

"Hi Chase. How's it going tonight?"

"Livin' the dream, Sutton. What'll it be for you tonight, honey?"

"A bottle of the Chateau de Dufort Bordeaux," she relayed articulately.

"Wonderful choice, sweetie."

I checked the wine list, noting it was an astonishing eighty-nine dollar bottle.

The waiter turned to me, though was still gawking at Sutton. "And for you, sir?"

"Uh, I'll have an Old Fashioned."

"Any appetizers to start off with this evening?"

Sutton ordered before I could blink. "The steak tartare with quail egg, please."

Chase nodded, jotting in his notepad before walking off. She laid down her menu and smiled, her fingers interlaced on the table.

"So, Aryan, tell me about yourself." She spoke English to me this time.

I cleared my throat. "I'm from the Ooty area back in Tamil Nadu, but grew up in Gudalur. I came here on the H-1B visa, working IT for Cambridge Insurance before opening a distillery with my buddy."

"It's a nice distillery and looks like business is good." We perused the menus while chatting. "What do you do for fun?"

"I like to skydive. In summer, I try to go every week. My friend Beau owns the dropzone near Versailles. Then in winter, we take trips up to Paoli Peaks to go snowboarding."

"Do you play tennis or golf at all?"

"No, I'm more into extreme sports, ones with adrenaline."

"Hmm." Her chocolate eyes trailed over my shirt, though I doubt she was finding my buttons interesting. Thorough analyzation was sprawled all over her face, or possibly deep-rooted judgement.

"Do you own a house?" she went on with her interview-interrogation.

"I have a condo."

"Just a condo? Why don't you have a house?"

Her question came off as irrationally strange. "I don't need a big house, Sutton. Why would I when it's just me? I'm rarely home anyway. Most of my time is spent at my business."

Our waiter returned with drinks. "Okay, are we ready to order our meals?"

"Yes," Sutton chimed in, unsurprisingly. "I'll do the grilled portobello."

"And I'll do the stuffed chicken breast with fries."

"Excellent." He removed our menus. "Your tartare should be up momentarily."

Sutton sipped her rich, heady wine. "Tell me about your childhood back in India. I was too young to remember much before my family came here. You have any fun stories to share?"

I grinned, sipping my boozy, orange-infused cocktail. "Actually, yes. One time when I was nineteen, my friends and I were playing cricket down in the valley by my grandfather's house. This gigantic tusker elephant came out from the bushes and chased us. I was scared, because this one had been attacking people for a while and causing all the destruction in our neighborhood."

"How did you get away? You finally outrun him?"

"My neighbor Leela set off firecrackers. Eventually, he got scared and ran away."

"That sounds crazy living amongst all those wild animals."

"It is, but I like living in both places."

"I like it here in the U.S. My parents moved to Kentucky and I never left, but they're in Fort Lauderdale now."

"You're a real estate agent, right?"

"Yeah, I sell luxury homes."

I studied her as she shared more about her profession. She obviously came from a wealthy family, and although she seemed nice enough, there was no apparent chemistry, at least from my end. I found her questionable displays of fondness for good-looking men a bit problematic as well.

After our appetizer arrived, a strapping man in a business suit approached our table. "Evening, Sutton."

Sutton looked up, gasping subtly. "Nick. How are you?"

She stood and embraced him, kissing his cheek a little too close to the mouth. His eyes were sky blue and tan hair nearly full grey, making him a good example of the American silver fox.

She rubbed his muscular arm, then turned towards me. "Nick, this is my date Aryan Visu. He's also from India."

I arose to shake his hand proper. "Nice to meet you, sir."

Sutton went on, "This is Nick Collins, my ex-husband."

I sat down, stunned to hear she had already been married... and divorced.

Her gaze snapped back to him. "What are you doing at Ruby's tonight? Did you have another client meeting?"

"Yes, but it ended. I was just heading out and saw you over here." He checked out her dress. "You look gorgeous as always, dear."

"Aww, thank you, Nick. I'll walk you out."

She escorted him outside, leaving me hanging for a good fifteen minutes. She returned slightly out of breath.

"Well, that was nice running into him." She avoided my glance, serving herself some tartare.

"You were gone a while. Everything okay?"

She waved her hand, brushing off the inquiry. "Oh, it's fine. He has a lot of cases right now and is really under pressure. He needed someone to listen."

"He's a lawyer?"

"Yeah. He's a partner at Collins & Brix. He specializes in copyrights and trademark."

"Why did you two split up? You seem to get along well."

"Oh, we're just too different."

I assumed there was a lot more to the story, but I didn't ask, nor did I much care.

⚜ ⚜ ⚜

I was intending to walk her back to her door that night, but she remained in my car when I parked.

"Hey, why do you drive a KIA? You own a distillery. Why not get a luxury car like a Lexus or Mercedes Benz?"

"I like the KIA. It drives just fine. I would rather save my money for things I want more, like travel and skydiving."

She tilted her head, stroking her fingers through my hair in a sudden change of mood setting. "You're *very* sexy, Aryan. You know that?" Her seat belt unlatched and she bent over, her lips meeting mine. They were soft and tasted like berries. I didn't necessarily want this to go any further, but I continued in the moment while her hand slid brazenly down my pants.

"Wait," I whispered, glancing over to her front door.

"It's fine. He's not there." Her palm squeezed my cock, exposing it.

"My god. You're so big," she gasped softly. "And uncircumcised. That's hot."

Her mouth went down upon me. I took a deep breath, while silently deciding to never call her again.

10

NILIGRIS, SOUTH INDIA
MAY, 2009

Aryan caught me off guard, but his determined move came as a welcome one, his kiss intense, passionate, and fervent with claiming hunger. My arms circled his shoulders, his mouth pressing harder against mine. His brisk beard brushed against my delicate skin, tingling my pleasure sensors, his earthy scent now steeped with permeated pine and spring water.

I was unsure how much time had passed, but it started to rain, temperatures now falling drastically. Aryan stepped back, his jacket swinging over my shoulders. He then embraced me, and I snuggled into his rock-hard chest, the warmth from his body flaring my nerve endings. Rain pattered onto the tin roof as my mind drifted to an almost meditative state. For the first time, I felt unconditionally accepted and secure, like reaching nirvana.

His lips brushed my hair, then fell hotly to my neck. "Do you want to head back?"

My eyes closed. "Not just yet."

Being in his arms, I felt like I was seeing the world from a new and refreshing point of view. Traumatizing memories, feelings of guilt and shame, the unachievable strives to be perfect… it all faded amidst his enfold. Never had I felt more connected with someone I was so enticingly drawn to.

An unforeseen wave of sorrow hit as my slow strides drifted across his living room later. I would be leaving tomorrow, and the probability of never seeing Aryan again was heartbreaking. In the few days prior, I had grown to care for him, as well as his circle of family and friends.

I was deeply reflecting on our earlier encounter, and assumed he was doing the same. His keys dropped to the table, and a charming smile in my direction lifted my spirits as he strolled up the stairs, clearly intending for me to follow.

The evidence suggested our thoughts kindred as we blatantly stalled by our separate rooms, blistering tension overfilling the hallway. My back shifted to the wall as he approached, his hopeful gaze locking onto mine… and my responding, exceedingly-subtle smile was the green light he needed.

His mouth came down upon my mine, the kiss respectfully rough and purposeful with his tongue slipping through softly. The mass of his body rubbed against mine, his hardened member jabbing my side teasingly as I craved his overpowering strength. My palm brushed over his sizable bulge as I suggestively tugged at his shirt, but he abruptly stepped back.

"Are you sure this is what you want?" he whispered, with both eagerness and consideration.

My eyes darted to his perfect, full lips. "I'm sure."

"You don't owe me anything, Scaith. I was happy to help you."

"I know that. I can assure you… it's *you* I want." After I said it, I realized I might have meant for more than just one night.

He sighed, his gaze dropping. "I just want to make sure you won't have any regrets. You'll be going back to the other side of the world soon."

I tilted his head up toward mine… and whispered back. "I don't have regrets."

Although unsure of what would happen between us after I left India, it didn't matter. In this moment, there was nothing I wanted more. No guilt, shame, or remorse invaded my thoughts this time as it had in the past. I hung close to the freedom of my choice instead... and I was choosing him.

His lips curved to a longing smile, and I was whisked up, my legs wrapping around his waist. His thickened groin pushed against my sweetest spot, intense heat rushing down to my toes in reaction. I tingled, wanting desperately to feel him inside me.

I was carried off to his dark bedroom with only a hint of light flooding in. Those gentle yet fierce lips continued to play atop mine as their owner sprawled me atop the bed. He crawled over at a gradual pace, his hands igniting desire in every inch of skin they explored, and I relished the solid weight of him on top of me. His mouth drifted down my neck as I groped his firm ass mounds.

I was pulled to a seated position and blouse unbuttoned, my ruby red bra exposed. A warm hand stroked my cheek and moved down, caressing over my strained cleavage. One-handed, he unhooked my bra, slipping off shirt and bra together, tossing them across the room. His gaze settled over my naked chest in cherished acclamation, and he reached down to cup my plump breast, pinching my throbbing nipples to tips.

I slid his fitted slate t-shirt off, my fingertips traversing over his firm pecs and ripped abs. His smooth, caramel skin had a light dusting of hair that spread across his chest, trailing down to his groin where I could tell it thickened. My own skin appeared distinctly pale against his in a beautiful display of our bodies entangled.

My pronounced exploration of his physique excited him and he wet his lips, lowering them over my breast while his scorching-hot tongue wagged tauntingly at my nipple. My fingernails dug into his broad back as the button of my pants unsnapped. Aryan slipped them off before moving onto my underwear, his muscular arms brushing along my lengthy, toned legs as they came off. He then straddled one leg, hastily shoving them apart.

I inhaled sharply, whimpering in carnal need as I watched his head dive. I sucked in a thrilling gasp when his tongue darted inside, my fists clenching his hair and tugging hard from gratification. Two fingers slipped within my velvety pool, his thumb feeling my wetness while circling my clit. His mouth advanced up my leg… and I jolted when he reached my unsightly stitched wound.

"Sorry," my apology faint.

Part of me was self-conscious. Aryan's body was coveted perfection and here mine was tainted with a distasteful injury, reminding me of just how broken and flawed I was. He reacted to my despondency, adjusting his body to lie next to mine, and stroked my cheek.

"Don't disparage yourself, Scaith. Every part of you is incredible… even your scars."

Without time to react, his mouth returned to my sex, teeth nibbling at me. His fingers delved back inside, now caressing rapidly with full force. My head bounced back, almost pounding the headboard as he ravished me, my breaths expeditiously increasing the longer and rougher he went on. I soon squirmed under him, screaming out as I came while slamming the headboard. The removal of his fingers was slow, his warm palm resting over my sex as I savored the intense seconds following my orgasm, my entire body still quivering. He glanced up and smirked, immense satisfaction consuming his mystifying hazel eyes.

With my body now having calmed down, I shot up and kissed him with vigor. Shoving him onto his back, I unzipped his pants, tearing them off with his boxers as if in a fitted rage. The coarse black hair above his huge brunet dick made me rampant with ceaseless insistency. I was hungry for more of this incredibly sexual, foreign beast.

"Stand up," I whispered in subtle, but impatient demand.

He complied, his bronzed naked body facing me with his cock fully erect. I laid back, my feet turned away and face forward, upside down of him. My head bent back, taking in the ridiculously sultry body towering above, ready to service any desire at my request. Although his stance was dominant, we both knew I now held all the power.

"Come here," I continued.

He stepped closer and I reached up, grasping both his hips. I tongued the tip of his engorged cock, sliding his foreskin back with my lips, then plunged him downward, his stiff phallic flesh sinking down the length of my throat. Pleasurable groans echoed while he lurched forward, continuously impaling my mouth, and I savored all his untamed, masculine sensuality.

Unable to contain his urge, he rapidly pulled out, slapping my leg as he swung me around. I was hurled over on all fours and head pushed down, my ass now in the air for his unrelenting use... and with no time wasted, he slid into me, simultaneous moans to follow. He rammed against my backside like a brutish caveman, a fucking maharaja that was now spreading my thighs further apart, and repeatedly reentering me.

His speed intensified and I tightened my vulva, my fingers reaching back to the glazed, swollen cock within.

"Oh, fuck!" his deep voice cried out, a result most likely heard within a mile radius.

I flipped over as he slid out, him squeezing my arm as he ejaculated over my chest. A breezy gasp of staggering gratification shot out from my lips in the seconds ensuing, my lady parts still feeling the effects of his generous girth.

"Holy shit," he stammered, dropping to the bed beside me.

Recuperation was definitely in order from both parties, and the room stood still as we both breathed deep, the magnitude of our coupling now abating.

"Wow, Aryan." I broke the silence minutes later. "I've never had anything quite like that."

We chuckled together softly, then he grinned deviously, pulling my face close so he could kiss my lips. "I'll take that as a compliment, *Vellakari.*"

"Oh, it was." I cleaned myself off with a tissue, turning back as he lay flat on his chest.

His finger bopped my nose. "That had to be the best time I've had, Scaith." He then kissed the palm of my hand. "You're the most beautiful thing I've ever seen."

I would normally shy away from flattery, but with Aryan, there was nothing he did or said that made me uncomfortable in any way. His erotic, accented words and actions were complete intoxication. In one night, he managed to shame every man that came before him. My memories of them dissipated in his shadow.

"What are you thinking about with that adorable smile of yours?" he grinned.

I giggled sheepishly. "Actually, last night when I slept in your bed, I nearly touched myself while thinking of you."

"You what?" He sat up on his elbows, his interest highly piqued. "What stopped you?"

I let out a humorous scoff. "Respect and common decency. Here you were helping me out and I go and…"

"Are you kidding me?" he interrupted. "Having a gorgeous woman masturbate in my bed is unbelievably hot. I'm so happy you told me."

I smirked shyly, thrilled to see I had elevated his ego. No one was more deserving.

He brushed hair from my face. "I can't believe a woman like you exists. How lucky am I?"

We both just laid in bed, admiring the akin nature we found in each other. I never wanted the night to end. I rested my hand under my head. "So, what do we do now, Aryan? Just fuck off into the sunset?"

"We'll figure it out," he assured me, stroking my cheek. "I know I don't want to lose you. You have to return to Iraq. I understand that. We need to go our separate ways for a while." He leaned over, kissing my forehead as he pulled the covers over us. "Just trust me, okay?"

I did, and I couldn't say the same for too many others in my life. I kissed his cheek back. "Thanks for a great night."

He enclosed me in his arms and smiled. "Oh, *anytime, Vellakari.*"

⚜   ⚜   ⚜

I was still wrapped within Aryan's arms when the morning sunlight shone through. I turned over, his striking face meeting mine.

"Good morning, beautiful." He stretched and yawned, a little smile still showing. "What time is it?"

I read his bedside clock. "Almost six-thirty."

"Okay, we should get up. Get on the road early like we planned."

I stood up from bed, still naked, and retrieved my clothing.

He leaned on one elbow, plainly admiring the woman he successfully seduced, though I had to admit, he didn't have to try very hard. Between his looks and personality, it was a no-brainer.

"Can't believe I had this amazing woman in my bed last night."

I leaned over, pecking this mouth. "See you downstairs soon." And I was met with a slap to ass as I left.

I packed up my few belongings and got ready, meeting Aryan at the base of the stairs.

He tossed his overnight bag over his shoulder. "You ready?"

I wasn't, but I knew I had to be. I glanced over his house, my eyes scanning the kitchen, living room, and staircase, each area holding a different happy memory. I wanted to remember this place in case I never found myself back here.

Aryan dropped his bag and hugged me. "You'll come back, Scaith. I promise."

I sighed. "Let's get this over with."

And we left the house, driving back down the road with Spydo and Chestnut barking behind.

꧁ꞏ   ꧁ꞏ   ꧁ꞏ

An hour later, we swung by his parents' place for breakfast, and to say goodbye. I waved out to Mani, who was collecting sticks in front of the tea factory. Aryan's mother emerged in a pink floral sari to open the gate for us.

I stepped out, greeting her with my palms together. "*Vanakkam*, Auntie."

She smiled, bobbing her head as usual, then Aryan hugged her, saying something in Tamil. We removed our sandals and entered the house, burning incense perfuming the space. His father ignored us as we sat down, his attention still affixed to his damn TV, and he and Aryan made no attempt to speak to one another. His mother provided us with dosa and onion chutney, and they spent time conversing before our exit.

I wondered if she was still upset with him for lying to her, but she didn't appear to be as they were laughing together in a friendly manner.

As we headed back to the car, Mani showed up at the gate, a yellow wildflower clutched in his hand that he held up to me. He smirked bashfully, his fist half covering his face.

"Oh, Mani." I pressed it to my heart, blown away by how thoughtful he was. I moved to hug him, and this time, he let me. "Thank you for saving my life," I whispered. I knew he didn't understand me, but I thanked him, nonetheless.

He scampered back to the factory and I began to cry, watching my protector as he disappeared up the hill.

Aryan walked up behind me, taking hold of my hand. "You okay?"

I paused, still watching the factory. "Guess I didn't realize how impactful a few days in a new place could be."

He nodded. "Every day counts, Scaith. Sometimes we meet people that drastically change our lives for the better, and a chance encounter is all it takes."

I turned to him, my palm resting atop his chest. "You're his boss. Promise me you'll take good care of him."

He reached up, wiping tears from my cheek. "I will. I promise."

．０．　　．０．　　．０．

The Indian countryside whisked by from my window. Certain things that I saw, I deemed physically impossible, but as was the case in India, people utilized every resource at their disposal. I first witnessed a family of five, including an infant, riding a motorcycle while gripping a goat across their laps. If that wasn't shocking enough, a guy was even carrying a small cow on his, and we hadn't even been driving an hour yet. The vehicles swerved around each other in a fast-paced, but impressively safe manner. With the staggering number of people in this country, they made things work for them.

My attention drew back inside the car and noticed I was still gripping the yellow flower.

"Aryan, can I ask you something personal?"

"Anything, Scaith." His arm rested on the door.

"What's your relationship status with your dad? It's pretty obvious that there's some unspoken tension there. You just got back from the U.S. after months of being away and he's barely spoken to you."

He sighed heavily, looking out the window as he drove.

"If it's none of my business, you can say so. I'll get it."

"No, it's not that. I usually just tell people he's a great guy. I don't speak badly of my father to others. And he does have some good qualities. When he was police chief, he was very hard-working and tough."

"But I mean his personal relationship with you. Do you guys do anything together? Have real conversations?"

"We talk when we have to. We used to get into big disputes about the family properties. His brothers and sister also got involved with some of them trying to steal deeds, signing them over to themselves."

"Is it all settled now?"

"Most of it has. He sold some land shares to an entrepreneur from Sri Lanka. The rest he'll pass onto me, anything my grandfather didn't already hand down, and their house will go to Sharvani."

"Oh, speaking of which, can we call her?"

"Sure. I'll call her now." He dialed and handed the phone to me.

"Hey, Sharvani?"

"Scaith, how are you? How was your stay?"

"It was amazing. I'm forever grateful."

"Good. You go back to Iraq and finish your job, then come back to India. You can visit my family here in Coimbatore. I am pregnant now."

"Really? Congratulations." I glanced over to Aryan. "Your brother will be an uncle. Awww."

"I have to go, but you take care and have a safe flight back. And come visit us."

"I will, Sharvani. Thank you again." We both hung up and I gave back the phone. "Your sister's pregnant now. How do you feel about that?"

He shrugged. "That is fine. She can have. That will make our parents happy, because I'm not going to."

My face lit up. "You don't want kids?"

"No way," his answer quick and confident.

I smiled admirably in his direction.

"What's that?"

"Nothing. I'm just thinking you're the epitome of the perfect man in my eyes."

He lifted my hand, kissing the back as his thumb grazed over. "That makes me happy to hear."

⚜   ⚜   ⚜

A couple hours more and we were driving through Mysore, the City of Palaces, and it accommodated more people than Ooty and Gudalur combined.

"We're in the state of Karnataka now, so locals will be speaking Kannada."

"And you can speak Kannada, right?"

"Yes. That is actually my mother tongue."

My head shook. "You're incredible. I can barely speak Spanish and I'm from California."

We passed colorful street markets, restaurants, horse-drawn carriages, and tourists roaming around on camels.

"You have camels here, too?"

"In the cities, yes, but they are mostly in North India where there's more desert."

"I actually saw a white one once... in Iraq."

"They bring good luck," he enlightened me.

"Ahh, so it is true." I tsked. "Wish I still had my camera."

He handed me his phone. "Here, you can use the camera on this. I'll make sure you get them."

"Thanks. Which phone is this?"

"That's Apple's iPhone 3G."

"Hmm. I'm not good with tech items. Never used an Apple product before. How does it work?"

He tapped on an app, displaying the camera function, then pointed outside. "This is the Mysore Palace I was telling you about."

"Perfect." I snapped shots of the enormous, elegant red and beige palace surrounded by a large courtyard, manicured royal gardens, and lion statues inside a fenced area. Once out of the city, I checked the road signs, getting a sense of where we were.

"So, you said we're in the state of Karnataka now. This is where Hampi is located, right?"

His eyebrows raised. "You know Hampi?"

Now I was glad I had done some research on the history of India in years past. "Yeah, I read about it once. It's an ancient village and UNESCO World Heritage Site. I created a list of historical places around the world that I found fascinating, hoping to check them off like a bucket list."

"I'd like to see your list sometime. There's quite a few spots I'd like to go as well."

"Sure, I'll email it to you. What's our next stop?"

"Bangalore. I lived there during college. We'll reach in another four hours maybe. It's a big city and the capital of Karnataka. We can stop for a late lunch. I know a good place."

"Sounds like a plan, Aryan. You've got this under control, as always." I drank from the copper water bottle and yawned.

"If you're tired, now's a good time to nap."

I nodded in agreement. "I think I will." I leaned my seat back and turned toward him, stroking his arm. "Do you get enough sleep, Aryan? You're always so busy."

I noticed him grin. "I like to stay busy."

I nodded, more to myself. "I get that."

Despite the consistent horns honking, I managed to drift off.

.₫.   .₫.   .₫.

"Scaith, we're here." I felt Aryan's hand on my shoulder as I leisurely awoke. I yawned and stretched. "Okay, coming."

I smoothed my hair and got out of the car, the overpowering noise of the big city packing my eardrums. Modern skyscrapers abutted the chaotic traffic and wandering cows and dogs of the streets. These metropolitan surroundings looked completely different from the jungle-abound India I had seen so far.

Aryan clutched my hand tightly, navigating me down the busy sidewalk while dodging through countless pedestrians.

"Be careful here. It's very busy with lots of pickpocketing."

"You lived here? Looks like a pain in the ass to get anywhere with all this commotion. What are all these little yellow cars called? Tuk-tuks?"

"We call them auto rickshaws here."

We continued along and he pointed up to a white building with elegant black archways, hanging plants, and fountains on the front patio.

"We're heading here, the Lotus Pavilion."

Before walking up the steps, I noticed a man in his mid-forties on the sidewalk, talking with locals. He had on a nice black suit jacket over a navy-blue dress shirt, his skin light tan and sported a dark grey donegal tweed hat.

"Hey Aryan, one second." I let go of his hand, approaching the man with curiosity. A black sign displayed behind him reading 'Hughes Foundation' in white and red lettering.

The man turned to me and smiled politely. "Hi there, welcome to India." His accent was American.

"Hi, are you from the States?"

He nodded. "I live here now, but I'm from Minneapolis."

Aryan stepped up behind, listening in.

"I'm happy to see someone from my country. What are you out promoting today?"

"I run an AIDS foundation." He handed me a pamphlet. "I contacted HIV twenty years ago, so now I raise awareness and promote safety measures to avoid the spread of AIDS in India. I have an office in Nagpur called the House of Hope."

"I assume you're Mister Hughes?"

"I am." His smile charming as he shook my hand. "Jerry. And you are?"

"Scaith. I'm just visiting here as a tourist, so to speak."

"Pleasure to meet you, Scaith."

"Likewise. And good luck with your foundation. This is a great thing you're doing. Keep it up."

"I appreciate your support. Enjoy your stay."

⚜   ⚜   ⚜

We sat under the grass-roofed outdoor pavilion of the restaurant, glancing over our menus.

"There's some American options here as well," Aryan told me. "What are you in the mood for?"

"Would you really like to know in this public place?" I winked suggestively. "And for the record, I prefer Indian... and not just the cuisine."

He chuckled. "As much as I like where your head's at, I'm not on the menu right now. We can take care of that later."

"Looking forward to that." I blushed behind my menu.

"Would you like to try *thali*?"

It didn't take long for the assorted platter of traditional South Indian dishes to arrive. Aryan introduced me to the sampling feast of medu vada, papadam, vegetable poriyal, sambar, rasam, curd, and payasam.

I dug in, excited to indulge in some never-tried items. "So, does Bangalore hold a lot of memories for you, being your college town?"

Aryan sipped his water. "My friends and I got into a lot of trouble. Very much drinking, stealing bikes, and bar fights."

I frowned in concern. "You guys got into fist fights?"

He chuckled at himself. "One time in school, my friends and I made a plan to attack teachers that we didn't like. We were going to burn their bikes. They were all so scared when they came to know about it that they slept at the school overnight."

I gasped. "You were a bully."

He agreed. "I had no patience. My friend Sunil and I got kicked out of school. He eventually drank so much he got a stroke and now his parents have to take care of him."

"Your mother must've been furious. Being the son of a police chief back in your hometown, I'm sure you thought you could get away with anything."

He laughed, as though he's now come to terms with it. "Yes. I was a spoiled brat."

I studied his face and demeanor. "You're from a higher caste, aren't you?"

He nodded, confirming my suspicions, but had nothing to add.

"It's hard to imagine you doing these things, but sometimes past anger can arise once we're out in the world on our own." I crossed my arms on the table. "Aryan, did your father used to hit you when you were young?"

"Yeah, he did," he replied casually. "My mother hit me much more though. I was a bad child."

The confirmation was concerning. "Regardless of what a child does, causing intentional physical harm isn't the answer. It's a form of control and fear. If children are beaten for not obeying, how will they react when they are in an adult relationship and are beaten for same reason? Will they simply tolerate it?"

"Oh, the teachers beat the students here, too."

My mouth dropped in horror. "They shouldn't be allowed to do that!"

"They don't do it much anymore, but it happened a lot when I was in school."

I rubbed the sides of my temple in distress. "Glad to hear it's at least being phased out. But honestly, Aryan, abuse can have long-term negative effects. You come off as strong and unbothered by it, but sometimes that's a person's cover to hide how resentful they actually are."

I was met with the infamous Indian head bob, so I dropped the topic, not wishing to damper our last day together before my exit.

-♦-   -♦-   -♦-

The last leg of our road trip was the longest haul, another six and a half hours to Chennai. By the time we reached his contact's place, we were both exhausted.

We brought our bags down a narrow alleyway, and up the stairs of an apartment complex. Aryan obtained a key from the neighbor and let us into a tiny apartment with orange and white walls and one bedroom. Hindu pictures and statues graced the walls, tables, and window sill. The air was humid and stale with saturations of aromatic curry wafting past from the street carts outside.

"I'll be right back," Aryan informed me. "Gonna head down to the street market quick and pick up a few things to eat in the morning."

"Oh, a couple bananas, please."

"Sure." His lips pecked my cheek before he walked back out the door.

I changed my clothes and washed up for bed. Aryan returned only a few minutes later, a solemn look on his face.

"What is it?" I asked, worried.

He leaned against the doorway, crossing his arms. "I wasn't sure if I should even tell you. Sharvani just called me." He stalled.

"Yes? And?" I grew nervous and anxious.

"She was watching the news and a picture of your face showed up. They held a military funeral for you in the U.S. yesterday."

"What!?" I covered my mouth in shock.

"It's my fault. I didn't get you here on time."

I walked over to him. "No, it absolutely wasn't. You got me here when you could. I might not have made it here at all if not for you and the circle of people you're associated with."

He didn't look convinced. He remained leaning against the doorway with his arms crossed and face down.

I buried my face in my hands, trying to process. "My god. Everyone would come to know this news by now... my family, friends. They all think I didn't survive."

Aryan reached out and held me tightly, rubbing my back. "I'm sorry, Scaith. Let's get some sleep. The Consulate isn't far from here. We can show up early and see someone right away." He stepped back and lifted my head in his hands. "Everything will be fine. We'll get you where you need to be and make sure this is sorted out."

I nodded, trusting his words. I was used to being the strong one in my life and here I had found a man that was strong in all the areas where I was weak. If that plane crash wasn't some weird twist of fate, I don't know what was.

⚜   ⚜   ⚜

We arrived at the General Consulate of Chennai just before it opened. Aryan stopped at the security shack and spoke to the guard, showing his aadhar card before continuing through the opened gate. I noticed the orange, white, and green flag of India waving in the wind next to the American flag. We entered the building and went through the security scanner, our bags and clothing inspected.

We walked up to the receptionist at the front desk, a young Indian woman in a black business suit.

"Morning. I'm reporting in as a missing American citizen."

She looked up from her computer. "Can I have your passport, please?"

"I don't have any ID. I was a passenger on the flight that crashed in the Nilgiris Mountains a few days ago."

She typed something on her computer. "Emirates Airlines Flight 204?"

I nodded.

"We were informed by inspectors there were no survivors of the crash."

"That information was reported wrong. A villager pulled me from the debris before the craft exploded. I don't think anyone else made it out."

Her eyes turned to Aryan in suspicion. "And you are?"

I continued, "He's the one who helped me get here."

"One moment." She picked up her phone and turned away while talking to someone. I looked to Aryan, who was signaling that everything was going to turn out all right.

After a few minutes, the woman hung up and stood up from her desk. "Okay, ma'am, you can follow me." She pointed to Aryan. "He can wait here."

Aryan pursed his lips. "It's fine. I'll be right here."

He went to the waiting area as I was led to an office down the hallway. A man in a black suit stood up and shook my hand.

"Good morning. Please have a seat. I'm Guy Carlton, the Management Officer here."

"Scaith Donegal. Thank you for seeing me."

"I hear you're the sole survivor of that plane crash from New Zealand. Is that correct?"

"As crazy as it sounds, that's correct."

"Well, without proper identification, we do have a number of processes you'll have to go through so we can verify your identity. Did you sustain any injuries?"

"It's been taken care of."

"We'll still put you through a physical before we can send you back to the U.S."

"Sir, I'm actually an Army Sergeant stationed in Iraq. Is there a way I can contact my unit and let them know I'm okay?"

"Not until we verify who you are first." He took a notepad out of his desk. "Who would be the best contact that's stateside?"

"Try Melissa Ryder. She's the Brigadier General of the 134th Combat Aviation Brigade in San Jose. I don't know the number off the top of my head."

He wrote down the information. "That's fine. We can look it up."

I looked at his desk phone longingly. It was frustrating knowing he had the capability of calling someone right now, but couldn't.

He typed on his computer. "Would you like some coffee?"

"No, thank you. I just want to get this done as soon as I can."

᪻   ᪻   ᪻

For the next four hours, I filled out paperwork, signed documents, and was issued a temporary U.S. passport. I returned to Guy's office after completing my physical and fingerprints.

"All right, Miss Donegal, looks like we're almost done here. This process normally would have taken a lot longer, but since you're a deployed soldier, we'll get you out of here as soon as possible. We've booked a flight for you leaving tomorrow morning at nine a.m. with a layover in New Delhi. Your hotel arrangements for tonight are printed inside and a car will pick you up by six a.m. to bring you to the airport. I reached General Ryder in California and she notified your Commander in Balad, so they know you're coming."

"My unit's been informed?"

"Yes, I spoke with them not long ago. They're looking forward to having you back."

I sighed with relief. "Good. That was concerning me the most."

"Looks like our government jumped the gun and gave you a proper funerary procession already based on the misinformation they received from India."

"I heard. Guess I can understand how it was reported that way."

"My card is in this folder in case you need to reach me. Is there anyone else back home you'd like to call before flying out?"

I thought for a moment, and though I hadn't spoken to this person for almost a year, there was no one else more deserving of a courtesy call.

"Graham Donegal in San Jose," I finally answered.

Guy typed on his computer again, retrieving the number. "Thank you for your service, by the way. I'm an Army veteran myself. Served during the Gulf War."

He brought me down the hallway to a separate room for more privacy.

"Just dial +91 before the number. You can take your time, and bear in mind it's the middle of the night there." He held out his hand and shook mine. "Good luck to you, Sergeant."

I sat down as he left, feeling winded as I dialed the number. I was nervous. He would've been officially informed of my supposed passing from the Army by now. I cleared my throat as it rang, not knowing exactly what I would say.

"Hello?" he mumbled, as though just woken up.

The lump in my throat swelled at the sound of his voice. "Dad?" I said softly. "It's Scaith. I'm sorry to call in the middle of the night, but…"

"Scaith?" There was a moment of silence followed by labored breathing.

"Dad, it's me. I'm calling to let you know…"

"What is this?" his tone flared in distress. "My daughter died in a plane crash last week. What kind of sick…"

"They made a mistake, Dad," I almost shouted. "I survived the crash. I'm here at the Embassy in India."

There was another moment of silence. "No! No!" his voice crackled, unable to accept the revelation. "These two men in uniform came to my house and said…"

"I know. They received wrong information, Dad. I'm sorry to have put you through that." I could hear him crying, causing me to tear up as well. I sniffled, wiping my eyes before proceeding. "Dad, I can't talk long. I just needed you to know I was safe."

He sniffled as well. "I'm so glad you did, lassie. I'm sorry. I'm so sorry about it all. I just want you to come back."

"I will. I'll be back in a month. I need to return to Iraq and finish my tour, and then I'll be home. Is Linda around?"

He blew his nose. "She's sleeping. I'll tell her the news."

"Thanks, Dad." I paused, wishing I could hold him. "I love you."

I could hear him crying harder. "I love you, too, lassie."

⚜   ⚜   ⚜

Aryan drove us toward the hotel after waiting so patiently. "We're going to make a quick stop. There's someplace I want to bring you."

"Oh, okay." I was confused. I thought he wanted to get to the hotel as quickly as I did.

Fifteen minutes later and he was parking alongside a silver warehouse. Through the side door was an area that looked like multiple movie sets.

"What is this place?"

"It's a studio. They film movies here."

"Like Bollywood?"

"Yes, but here in Tamil Nadu, we call it Kollywood. I contacted the director earlier and he agreed to film you in a commercial. I thought it would be a way to honor Jimmy's last day alive."

I gasped and covered my mouth. "Are you serious?"

An Indian man in a tan suit approached me. "Miss Donegal?"

"Yes?" I replied, still reeling in shock.

He shook my hand. "You can come on back. I'll get you into makeup before filming."

I followed the man while glancing back at Aryan, my face exuberating sheer enthusiasm.

"Have fun, *Vellakari*."

⚜   ⚜   ⚜

Morning approached too soon. It had been a night of bliss with Aryan, ordering room service, mind-blowing sex, and staying up late chatting.

He stood with me in front of the hotel as I waited for my ride to the airport. I was never skilled with goodbyes, and I was awkwardly running through things in my head to say before deciding I would say them all wrong.

His arm slid around me. "Well, this is it, *Vellakari*. I've kept you long enough."

"It's been an adventure, Aryan."

"Thanks for deciding to land in my country."

I chuckled, trying not to cry. "Yeah. Next time it'll be on purpose."

He smiled, his eyes searching mine. "I'm glad there'll be a next time." He tucked hair behind my ear, revealing the earring he had bought me.

"Thank you, Aryan. I love your country. Love your people. Love your family and friends. And I love y…" My voice trailed off, and I turned away flabbergasted. The words almost just flew out of my mouth.

To my consolation, a black towncar pulled up to get me. We had exchanged contact information prior to morning, so I was free to leave with a clean slate. I took a deep breath and faced Aryan, getting one more hug.

"I'll miss you, *Vellakari*. Go continue being a hero. We'll talk soon."

I held back tears and quickly got in the car, lowering the tinted window so I could take in every remaining moment as the car started to drive off.

"Scaith…" he called out, stepping onto the road. "I love you."

11

ARYAN

*W*ind rushed through my hair at an incredible speed, intense adrenaline pumping through my body. My arms and legs spread out wide above the clouds and sapphire blue skies, the Pacific Ocean extending forever in the distance. Freefalling was my happy place. I felt on top of the world without cares or concerns. It was just me and the sky, and it was incredible.

I checked my altimeter. At three-thousand feet, I deployed the parachute and floated down to the dropzone, taking in the mesmerizing view while descending. Galen's neon-green jumpsuit and matching canopy landed several meters away. I pulled the straps of my harness and my feet touched the ground, running for several feet as the canopy floated to the field behind me in a large puffed ball. I rounded up my navy-blue parachute, returning to the hangar with a wide smile on my face.

Galen met me halfway across the field. "Hey, dude." His fist bopped mine. "How was your jump?"

"It was awesome! Amazing view. Glad I got my C-license before this trip. Eighteen-thousand feet is much better."

"Yeah, San Diego's great. Sometimes they do helicopter jumps, too. When we hit up the Phoenix dropzone on the way back they'll have hot air balloon jumps and shit."

"I'm excited for that. I'll have two-hundred jumps by the time this road trip is over."

"You're on your way, man. Your form is getting a lot better. We'll do some more formations this afternoon."

We entered the hangar, setting our canopies on the mat area while rock music from the sixties blasted from an old stereo in the corner. Huge flags hung down above us representing the U.S., state of California, and a black POW flag.

Our friend Tad approached us in full gear, ready to fly through the sky. "Hey guys, could one of you do a gear check? I'm on the manifest for next flight out."

I stood up, inspecting Tad's gear as Galen packed his canopy. "What's Logan doing?"

"He's at the Sky Bar. Where else?"

Galen spoke up from the ground, tightly rolling his canopy. "I'm so ready for a drink, but we've got hours of sunlight left. I want to get at least four or five more jumps in today."

I was the skydiving newbie of our group. Hairy Bob was a world-record holder in the sport with almost two-thousand jumps. We learned tricks and safety tips from him on a regular basis and he earned his nickname after years of record-breaking naked skydives. He seemed particularly proud to show off his hairy, grey, eighty-year-old body. A few years back, he base jumped with the prince of Dubai from the top of Burj Khalifa in wing suits. I've considered him my mentor and personal hero, aside from having to see him naked often. The five of us had arrived in San Diego the night prior after a long road trip from Lexington in Galen's school-turned-party bus. Logan wasn't a skydiver, but came along for the adventure.

I pat Tad's shoulder. "Okay, looks good. You're all set."

Tad walked off to the runway as a female skydiver approached the mat area in a dusty pink jumpsuit. Since meeting her at the dropzone in the morning, she hasn't been able to leave Galen's side.

"Hey, Galen." She flung her auburn ponytail off to the side, blatantly flirting. "Mind giving me a gear check?"

"Sure, Becca. One sec." He finished wrapping his canopy with thick rubber bands before standing up, and I crouched down to begin packing mine.

Galen finished Becca's gear check and said, "You're good to go. Have a good jump."

She smirked at him adoringly. "Thanks, Galen." She stroked the top of his head and walked off to the plane.

He glanced back at me and grinned, the wrinkles from his smile raised high up on his cheeks. "That chick loves my bald head, dude."

"Go for it, Galen. We're on vacation. After we open the distillery next month, we won't have as much time to go out. We'll be too busy working."

"Yeah, but owning a distillery is gonna open up a whole new window of chicks."

"We should be careful taking out customers, though. That could backfire."

"Hey, there's a seafood place here that's said to have a good distillery. Figure we could go there for dinner and check out the operations before heading back to the hotel."

"Sure. You planning to bring Becca along?"

"Yeah, I'll ask her. Maybe she can bring a friend or two," he smirked, suggestively.

"I'll pass on that. I just want to skydive this weekend."

.&.   .&.   .&.

By late afternoon, I was geared up alongside Galen, Tad, and Hairy Bob for one final jump of the day, our freefall circle formation planned prior to boarding. Galen and Bob opted for a naked skydive, so I of course chose to sit several feet away. There was no chance I'd ever do a naked skydive, and would probably never change my mind.

Fifteen minutes in the air and the yellow light turned on, winds of about a hundred miles per hour blasting into the cargo hold as the door slid open. Bob got up first, his wrinkled, furry ass on display, and crouched by the opened door, waiting to jump as his goods hung between the harness. Those of us remaining hunkered down in a line behind him, a couple other fun jumpers ready to go after us.

As the light turned green, Bob dived off the platform, his dick immediately flopping in the wind. Galen and Tad followed with me jumping last. After picking up terminal velocity, we all soared towards each other and clasped hands, forming a perfect circle mid-air. We held the formation and performed different maneuvers, gaining several points with each stunt. I flew towards Galen and locked palms, spinning in several full circles while the camera atop Tad's helmet captured the moment. Once reaching agreed altitude, we broke off and deployed canopies, floating to the ground simultaneously.

After changing and packing our gear, we left the dropzone and hopped into Galen's party bus. I could hear Logan grunt as he stumbled at the steps, having drank most of the day away.

"What's wrong, Logan?" Tad teased him from the fuzzy pink sofa inside. "Did you hit your chode, sweetheart?"

He grabbed his crotch, squinting in pain. "Fuck you. That really hurt, bro."

Galen skipped up behind him and slapped his ass. "Get up, dude. Let's go."

He got behind the wheel and blasted Rob Zombie through the stereo system as he drove off. I sat on a tan loveseat across from Tad while Hairy Bob laid down on a pew in back, smoking a cigarette.

Galen had done quite a few alterations since first buying the broken down elementary school bus. His artist friend painted one side of the exterior when she was sober and the other while high on cocaine, quite an ostentatious sight for people on the road. Aside from the random furniture pieces bolted inside, there was also a twin bed. Beads hung from the ceiling in the form of rosaries, hare Krishna, Mardi Gras, and anal beads. Several dicks, boobs, and turds were spray painted along the inside walls and a blowup goat with a retractable butthole sat atop the cargo compartment like a mascot. Out of all the people I've met from around the world, skydivers were by far the craziest and most eccentric.

"Hey, Aryan," Bob's raspy voice called up. "Wanna grab me a beer?"

I stood up, handing him back a Blue Moon from the cooler.

"Thanks, man." He blew a puff of smoke. "You're looking good up there. Just remember to keep your body loose during freefall. You're still a little stiff and that'll stop you from turning more fluidly."

I sighed, my denial giving in to agreement. "Yeah, I know. I'm trying really hard to work on that." I returned to my seat, noting Logan passed out on the floor.

Tad called to Galen. "Hey man, you invite that Becca chick tonight?"

"Yeah, dude. She's gonna meet us there."

Tad then turned to me. "Aryan, you wanna toss me a beer, too?"

He took it and cracked the cap off with his teeth, a monstrous burp released following a long swig.

"Galen, why didn't Alex come with us on this trip?" I shouted over the music.

"Cause Marcy's got his balls chained up. Last time we went out, he got home late and she threw a fit. Now he can't go anywhere."

I shook my head, feeling sorry for him. "I never want a woman like that."

"Good luck finding one, man." Tad took another swig. "Madison always has to approve of my friends before I can hang out."

Hairy Bob spoke up from in back. "Is that why we've never met her?"

Tad turned around and grinned. "Yup."

⚓   ⚓   ⚓

Twenty minutes later and Galen pulled into the upscale Mariner's Cove, a red and white striped lighthouse just behind it. Logan was still passed out in the bus, left to his slumber while the rest of us went in. Nautical antiques decorated the interior with fish taxidermy and a wooden mermaid mounted above the bar.

We were seated with an overlook of Ocean Beach Pier, the chairs and tablecloths pine green with candle centerpieces burning low.

"Nice place," I told Galen. "Good view of the waves from here."

Hairy Bob picked up a menu. "I'm in the mood for some crab."

Galen smirked. "You've gotten crabs twice already, Bob. You want it again?"

I watched the surfers below. The lavish orange sunset extended in the reflection of the ocean, creating a glowing mass. We ordered pitchers of beer along with shots of their signature craft whiskey. The menu read more like a book with the first couple pages dedicated to the history of the restaurant's owner, Laurent VonRutenburg. Several pictures of his family were littered throughout.

"What the hell is this?" Tad asked aloud, also browsing the menu. "A menu or family photo album?"

"They own a few seafood places in San Diego," Galen said. "They're supposed to be good."

Tad laughed. "There's a picture of some old fat dude at the beach in a speedo next to the appetizers."

When our waiter returned, we ordered some crab cakes, clam chowder, grilled scallops, and stuffed salmon, all to share.

Hairy Bob sipped his beer and glanced over. "So, you guys ready for this new venture coming up?"

I nodded zealously. "We're just about done. There's a couple more permits we're waiting on. Otherwise, the bourbons are good to go."

"I'm excited, man," Galen expressed to me. "Always wanted a distillery. Glad you've partnered up with me."

"Me, too. Glad you can accommodate my India trips."

"That's no problem. Alex can help cover."

Becca strolled in with a lanky brunette, both wearing skin-tight, low-cut shirts that perversely perked their boobs up.

"Hi guys," Becca said excitedly, her entrance adjuring a need for validation. "This is my friend Chelsea."

She sat next to Galen as he grabbed an empty chair for her friend.

"How are you lovely ladies this evening?" Hairy Bob was trying to sound charming. In his younger years, I'm sure he had gotten a lot of girlfriends. Even now at age eighty, he thought he still could, and I found that rather amusing.

"Can we get you some drinks?" Galen asked them.

"Yeah. Prosecco, please." And Chelsea nodded in agreement.

"Are you ladies fun jumpers then?" Hairy Bob probed.

"*I* am," Becca responded. "I've been jumping since I turned eighteen."

I silently laughed, wondering if that was just last year.

"I don't skydive," Chelsea spoke up. "I'm terrified of heights. I prefer to go waterskiing."

"Are you both from San Diego?" Tad asked, fixing his golden blonde hair.

"Yeah. We're both servers at the yacht club."

Our food was arriving just as Logan wobbled in, pulling a chair up next to mine.

"How was your beauty sleep, princess?" Galen taunted teasingly.

Logan was already resting his arms on the table, his eyes bloodshot and drooping. "I need a beer," he groaned.

We passed the food around, serving ourselves as I poured Logan a beer that he obviously didn't need.

Becca held her plate up to Galen. "Scallops, please."

Chelsea sat timidly in her seat, smiling at me from across the table.

"How long are you guys in San Diego for?" Becca asked our group.

"We're leaving tomorrow at sundown," Galen told her. "Gonna get one more good day of skydiving in."

"Oh, well in that case, I'll get to see you guys again tomorrow."

Logan chugged his beer and let out a vomit-inducing belch. "I wanna go to SeaWorld."

Chelsea's face kindled. "I'd love to go to SeaWorld." She looked to me. "Are *you* gonna go?"

"No, I'm skydiving all day tomorrow." Way to go, I mocked myself. Always letting down the ladies.

"Mmm. This is good crab." Hairy Bob was having a moment of self-indulgence.

"You guys are from Kentucky, right?" Chelsea directed the question to me, but Tad answered.

"Yeah, Lexington. We all skydive there together." He gestured to Logan. "Except for this stubby little shit stain. He works the dropzone, cleaning toilets and mowing the lawn."

He laughed sarcastically, raising the glass to his mouth again. "Go eat a dick, man."

Our waiter approached with a bottle of Prosecco and two flutes. "How is everything so far this evening, folks?"

"Really good," Galen commended. "And I have a question. Could we possibly get a tour of the distillery tonight?"

"I can ask my manager, but I'm sure it won't be a problem."

"Thanks." Galen poured the flutes for the girls as the waiter left.

"So, you guys are driving all the way back to Kentucky?" Becca asked.

"Yeah, in Galen's party bus." Tad opened the topic for conversation.

Chelsea took a bite of salmon. "You guys have a party bus? I'd like to see it."

"Trust me, you don't," I warned her, shaking my head in aversion.

A few minutes later, a man in his early twenties came to our table in a business suit, his hands eloquently folded behind his back.

"Good evening, folks. I understand you'd like to take a tour of our distillery. Go ahead and finish your dinner, then ask your waiter to come get me. My name is Neil."

"Are you one of the owners here?" I asked.

"I am of the family, yes. My grandfather was Laurent VonRutenburg." He grinned passively and left.

Galen was paused in thought for a moment, then asked, "Anyone else notice that he looks like Jared Kushner?"

"*That's* who I was thinking of!" Tad exclaimed, slamming his hands on the table in recognition. "I kept trying to figure out the name of the guy that he looked like."

"Who the hell is that?" Logan asked, practically falling asleep at the table.

I took a shot of whiskey and smiled. "That's good whiskey they have. Smooth."

Chelsea was still glancing over at me. "Hey, are you from India?"

I nodded, swigging my water. "Yes."

"Land of the Kama Sutra." Galen winked at me.

"That's really cool. What's the Taj Mahal like? I want to go there."

"I've never been."

"You've never been to the Taj Mahal? But you're from India."

"I'm from *South* India. The Taj is up north. India is a big country with separate states, just like here. It would be like visiting New York and being asked how you liked the Golden Gate Bridge."

"Oh, okay. Yeah, I guess." My response seemed to ruin her perception of me. Once again, I'd managed to let down the ladies.

"Who farted?" Galen's nose darted up, sniffing the air.

Logan's arm rose straight up, his head still resting on the table.

Hairy Bob scowled. "Geez, man. You had to go and bust that in front of these lovely young ladies?"

"Actually, I think we're done here now," Galen announced to the group. "We can go get Neil to give us the tour."

For the next hour, we toured the distillery while taking mental notes of the processes and operations. Galen ended up going home with the two girls, and I drove the party bus back to the hotel for the night.

⚜   ⚜   ⚜

After knocking out another fun-filled day of skydiving, we packed up, crossing the border into Arizona by sundown. We stopped at a hotel in Yuma for the night, getting an early start the next day.

Along the way, we checked out an old abandoned silver mine and military consignment shop with a small museum, buying some bags of jerky to snack on. I sat watching the desert pass by as I gnawed on a strip of wild boar, admiring the tall cactus plants that towered towards the sky from the dry, barren sand.

"Hey man, how much further to Phoenix?" Tad called up to Galen.

"About two more hours. We'll stop soon for lunch. I want to find some good Tex-Mex."

"I'll look it up." I pulled out my phone, searching nearby restaurants, and came across some other fun activities. "Hey, there's sand dunes nearby. You guys want to do some off-roading?"

"Oh, hell yeah," Galen responded. "I'd be down for that. You guys in?"

"I'm all in, man." Tad said, sitting up in his seat.

Hairy Bob was chilling in back, smoking another cigarette. "Sure. Let's go."

"I wanna drive the ATV," Logan spoke up.

We stopped for lunch and headed to the nearest ATV rental spot.

⚜   ⚜   ⚜

"Woohoo!" Galen bellowed out as his dirt bike went flying over the rippled dune, leaving a dusty trail of sand behind.

He and I had rented dirt bikes while the rest of our crew rode in the ATV, Logan the driver. The sand was hot from the blaze of the midday sun. It had been a while since I had this much fun on a trip. Having grown up riding motorcycles, maneuvering along the sand was no issue. I popped my bike up into a wheelie as I soared over the dune behind Galen, my engine roaring and tires spewing sand. The ATV followed with Tad and Bob poking through the open top, calling out with adrenaline.

"Arizona, bitches!" Logan cheered. "Wooooooo!"

The ATV passed us and circled along the sand. I noticed a steep dune ahead, so I accelerated and raced my bike up and over, just narrowly missing the ATV. Tad and Hairy Bob ducked out of the way as I landed on the sand a few feet ahead of them.

I rode up next to Galen. His face shot over and helmet opened.

"Holy shit, dude! That was fucking awesome!"

⚜   ⚜   ⚜

We made it Skydive Arizona by late afternoon, dropping off our gear before visiting a nearby ostrich ranch. The cages were extensive, packed with ostriches, goats, deer, and a bird habitat swarming with colorful parrots. Ducks, geese, and turkeys also roamed free amongst the farm.

"Do you think we can ride ostriches here?" I asked, stepping off the bus.

Galen grinned. "Let's ask. That would be sweet."

He went to the ticket counter, the rest of us going to see the ostriches. Logan stepped up close, trying to pet one.

"Careful, man," Hairy Bob apprised him. "They're known to bite."

One darted forward, snapping at his beaded bracelet and shattering it apart, sending beads flying in all directions.

"Oh, you little fucker!" he hollered. "My girlfriend gave me that."

The rest of us laughed. "That's what you get, Logan," I sassed him.

"Since when do you have a girlfriend?" Tad remarked teasingly.

"Okay, whatever. Ex-girlfriend."

Hairy Bob managed to pet one on the head without being bitten. "See, Logan? They like charm, which you obviously lack." His hand brushed down its long neck. "They're quite ugly up close, aren't they? This one looks like my third ex-wife."

Galen returned, his smile triumphant. "Hey, guys. They don't normally give ostrich rides, but the owner's a skydiver, so he made an exception for us. He'll be out here to meet us in twenty minutes."

"Awesome," I exclaimed. "I'm excited to try it."

"Let's go see the goats next," Tad suggested.

A hundred goats crowded towards us as we approached the cage, scrambling on their hind legs and tongues waving out. I took a handful of food pellets from the nearby bucket.

"Hey, what would they do if I farted?" Logan bent over with his ass against the cage, forcing out a loud, squeaky fart. A goat bleated while another suddenly snatched the top of his jeans, pulling roughly. "Shit. He's got me." As he scrambled to get away, we all laughed hysterically. He was eventually dropped to the ground, his jeans halfway down his ass, a dimpled crack exposed. He reached back, pulling his pants up one-handed. "Oh, man. He ripped my jeans."

Galen walked over, offered his hand while still roaring in laughter. The owner met up with us and set up our ostrich rides. Galen and I were the first to try it, and each of us required two guys to heave us atop. I held on tight to its feathers as the gate raised, sending both ostriches out running with incredible speed.

"Whoa!" I called out, barely holding on. My body slid off and I toppled to the ground almost immediately, rolling along as Galen's ostrich kept charging past to the other side, leaving a trail of dust behind. A couple minutes later, he strolled back smiling as I stood up, brushing off the sand that covered me.

"That was the best! I was hauling ass, dude!" He gave me a high five.

By morning, I was the first one to arise in our tent, and I was eager to skydive more.

"Hey, are you part of Galen's group?" A flannel-wearing hipster with glasses greeted me from behind the front desk.

"Yeah, we got in last night." I shook his hand.

"Welcome to the dropzone, buddy. I'm Randy Hass. If you're ready to rock, I can get you set up in our system. You guys want to try the hot air balloon jumps this morning?"

"Definitely!" my answer intensely deliberate.

At close to start time, our group stood geared up for safety briefing, huddling in a circle as the burner filled the hot air balloon, the vibrant colors glowing in the sunrise. We went up after briefing, each leaping off at five-thousand feet. I spun in circles during freefall, the bright colors of the balloon occasionally popping into view. I deployed my canopy and settled down towards the ground, overlooking the hazy desert. I always admired seeing different parts of the world from the sky: oceans, deserts, forests, snow-capped mountains… all from a bird's-eye view.

We continued skydiving past sunset before retiring to the hangar for the night, joining several other fun jumpers for drinks and games.

Randy joined us on the couches. "Hey guys, how were your jumps today?"

"The gravity was good, man." Galen held up his beer. "This is a great dropzone. We'd stay another day if we could."

"Hope to see you all back sometime. I'll introduce you to some of our regular local crew." He pointed to a few people within the hangar. "The big dude in the corner is Shawn. Guy's an ex-Marine with eight kids. The Homer Simpson lookalike over there is Carl and the redhead next to him is his wife Hailey. The two playing corn hole are Dewey and my wife. You can call her Giggles."

I walked over to the corn hole match as Randy continued chatting, hoping to play the next round. Dewey threw his hands in the air after scoring, tearing his shirt off.

"Ha!" he shouted with victorious gloat, tossing it at Giggles. "That's how it's done, Giggles. You should know not to mess with the man!" He danced in circles, his beer belly shaking.

"You know what, Dewey?" she snidely retorted, lifting her shirt to expose a boob. "This."

I glanced back at my crew to see Galen coming over. "Hey, I'll play the next round with you, man."

Giggles turned to us. "You guys want to play?" She tossed a sandbag to me. "Go ahead. I'm done with this idiot."

We played a few matches while Carl came over to watch, sipping his Pabst. "You guys are from Kentucky? My uncle owns a horse farm in Louisville." He pulled a blunt from his pocket and lit up.

Galen tossed his bag, missing the hole completely. "Fuck, Aryan, you kicked my ass on that one. Not a single point."

"You lost the game with zero points?" Carl verified. "We have a rule at this dropzone: anyone that loses corn hole with no points gained has to run around the airfield naked."

I dreaded the ardent grin that arose with Galen's ratifying rapport. Everyone in the hangar condensed, cheering and whistling as he stripped off his clothes. I silently cheered to myself for winning, happy it wasn't me having to strip down. His exceptionally tall, skinny white body took off running, several people filming his stunt with their phones while in hysterics.

We all sat around the campfire that night, roasting marshmallows and hotdogs, most of them stoned or drunk... or both. I don't remember much of the remaining night, but I was pretty sure my memory would serve me the next day. If not, I had a twenty-seven hour drive ahead of me to figure it out.

12

The Kuwait Towers came back into view as the plane descended onto the runway, their sharp dignified points piercing the sky. It felt strange being back, as though much time had passed, yet, as if I had just left. Removing my bag from the overhead bin, I exited the plane. The flight from New Delhi had been around three and a half hours and I managed to sleep through most of it, now feeling ready to face whatever craziness came with my return.

I headed toward the gates, expecting to see a C-130 on the tarmac bound for Iraq, but something else caught my eye. Commander Ryder stood amongst a group of reporters and a three-star General. He noticed me and smiled with satisfaction, raising his hand in my direction.

"And here she is arriving now."

"Oh, fuck." My bag dropped to the floor with a thud as several reporters raced over and engulfed me, flashing their cameras and bombarding me with invasive questions.

"Miss Donegal, how did you survive the plane crash?" one woman shouted. "Were you injured at all?"

A man chimed in from behind. "What happened while you were in India? How did you get back so quickly?"

I squinted as another shoved a microphone in my face. "How does it feel knowing you were declared dead, only to turn up alive? Do you believe this was a terrorist attack?"

My hands raised in expectant dismissal. "If you all don't mind, I'd really like to get back to my unit."

I retrieved my bag, shoving through the inconsiderate crowd with the cameras still flashing. A smug Ryder was now being interviewed, smiling proudly for the cameras. General Larsen stood beside him at parade rest like a crusty old fancy set piece.

"Oh, you know she's one of our best soldiers," Ryder stated into the microphone. "She trained in an outstanding unit. We knew she would pull through and we're all very happy to have her returned to us."

I glared daggers, though he was too preoccupied to witness it. This was his opportunity to shine and boost his career. It was no wonder he had come to Kuwait himself. He loved the spotlight and would never miss taking advantage of some publicity.

After a while, the hordes of reporters and crowds of onlookers dissipated, and I stood waiting with my arms crossed. Without any conversation in my direction, Ryder walked alongside General Larsen, laughing and patting his back while I trailed behind. The flight back to Iraq was no different. His tongue was so far up the General's asshole, I wanted to puke in my lap. He shook the General's hand once off the flight line back in Balad, then finally turned to me.

"Sergeant, go over to Medical to get looked at, then come to my office."

Before I could acknowledge, he darted off in the General's direction. I rolled my eyes and walked off with my flip flops briskly sifting through the sand.

-✤-   -✤-   -✤-

After a quick shower, I underwent a physical from the medics, and got the stitches removed from my thigh. I passed a few soldiers on the way back, smoking on a picnic bench below the hanging tarps. A couple whispered, both glancing in my direction suspiciously.

"Hey, Sergeant Donegal." One stood up in recognition.

I smiled at the friendly face before me. "Hey, Private Williams. How was your trip to the Philippines?"

He puffed his cigarette. "It was awesome, Sergeant. Can't wait to tell you about it."

"Please do. I've got someplace to be right now, but I'll catch up with you later."

"Um, just real quick… did you really survive a plane crash?"

I paused and nodded, though I really didn't want to discuss it, and he could sense that.

"Glad you made it back, Sergeant."

◦⚬◦   ◦⚬◦   ◦⚬◦

I entered Ryder's office without knocking. After the stunt he pulled earlier, I wasn't in any mood to play by the rules, not that I ever did. His head popped up from his desk and he laughed almost sardonically, shaking his head.

The door slammed behind me. "Something amusing, sir?"

He sighed. "Ahh, my Scaith. Didn't I tell you not to do that to me again? Within a month, you managed to get yourself almost killed twice. I really need to keep a closer eye on you."

I stood at parade rest, my face void of any unsuited hilarity. "Some things are out of our control, sir."

He nodded. "Well, the unit is glad you're okay. You gave everyone quite a scare." He tapped his pen, studying my demeanor. "How's your wound? Better?"

"Fine, sir. The Indian locals took care of everything."

"We heard." He typed on his laptop. "I'll need you to fill out an incident report explaining what happened after you left New Zealand. Make sure you include as many details as you can remember, such as who you met, where you stayed, and so on."

"Roger, sir. I'll get it to you tomorrow."

"Was your duffel bag the only military equipment you brought with you?"

I pressed onto more important matters. "Sir, I'd like to discuss the crash with you."

He swigged his canteen. "What about it?"

"I don't believe it was an accident, sir. I've been thinking about it and there's far too many things that don't add up."

His look suggested I may have lost my sanity along the way. "Such as?"

"For example, how often does an aircraft explode due to faulty maintenance *after* it crashes?"

"It's happened before."

"Not often, sir. I think explosives were rigged inside the cabin and set to go off after someone tampered with the craft, causing the plane to go down. The explosion destroyed all evidence."

He exhaled, as if I were wasting his time. "Scaith, both the NTSB and UAE's aviation safety boards inspected the debris. If foul play was involved, they would've discovered something to the effect."

"Yes and I believe certain parties involved were tipped off. That plane carried mostly Western tourists. Someone might have also known an American soldier was on board if an insider had access to that information. You said yourself that Abdel Karim has yet to be captured and his brother sits wounded in Iraqi custody. Did you really think there wouldn't be retaliation against those responsible for his arrest? Hezbollah attacks have been on the rise and they have followers worldwide, gaining new recruits all the time. They also have a headquarters in Dubai where the plane was headed."

An absurd smirk played about his lips. "You're gone for three weeks and now you're a conspiracy theory expert?"

"It's not a conspi..." I wanted to shout, but restrained myself. "Sir, you specialize in counter-terrorism. Please just look into it. That's all I'm asking."

He stared at me while contemplating, that damn pen of his tapping the desk again. "I'll make some calls if that'll make you feel better. In the meantime, you should get some rest. You look exhausted."

My head bobbed. "Yeah, a lot has happened in the last few weeks."

"You're acting different, too. What's going on?"

I didn't respond.

He sat up, his palms rubbing together as he looked me over. "You've been missing something, perhaps?"

I noticed the blue Post-Its on his desk and was suddenly enraged, my previous conversation with Perez looming in the back of my mind.

My eyes blinked up to his. "That won't be happening again, sir. On a personal level, you and I are done. It shouldn't have occurred at all, but at least I can admit it was wrong and move on."

He frowned. "What are you talking about?"

I stood my ground, refusing to let him intimidate me. "I said this affair is over, sir. That's all it was. No more private late nights in your office, or my hotel. No more personal calls."

He scoffed. "What fresh hell is this? You find God over there or something?"

"No sir, I found *myself.* And I'm choosing to no longer be involved with you. From now on, address me as Sergeant, one of your NCOs. That's as far as it's going to go. You didn't expect me to be your piece of patch forever, did you?"

His expression hardened when he realized I was serious and sprang from his chair, his face suddenly two inches from mine. "You wanted it as much as I did. Don't act as though you're an innocent bystander here."

"Irrelevant, sir. And I'm not excusing my actions. I know what I did and you should acknowledge your part in it. I was only twenty-four years old. You knew the effect you had on me and took advantage of it, but as my Commander, you never should have touched me."

He still seemed unconvinced of the validity in my words, and an infuriating grin ensued. "You always say this, Scaith. And you always come back to me. I know how you are."

"I'm not bluffing, sir. You come near me again, it's your career in the shitter."

He cornered me against the wall, his rage starting to simmer. "And you'll bury *yourself.*"

"That's fine with me, sir. Perez is aware of what's been going on. I'm willing to accept whatever punishment may come my way."

He wet his lips and leaned closer, still misconstruing the situation. "And what punishment would that be? My huge dick destroying y..."

I instinctively punched him across the jaw. He grunted, stunned for a moment before huffing back to his desk.

"You can leave now, Sergeant." He avoided any further eye contact. "And remove those earrings. They're not up to military standard."

I scorned at how the news had gone over, and bolted to the door absent a salute.

"And you can kiss that E6 goodbye!"

I stopped to glare back at him. "You can shove that E6 up your ass, sir. I'll consider that as my punishment for being so stupid and weak when it came to you. Give it to someone who's willing to suck your dick for it, cause it won't be me."

I faced the door and stalled, wanting to say one more thing.

"You know what? I remember the first time I met you. Your wife was screaming like a lunatic and stormed out of your office after you had disappointed her again... Now I'm finally starting to understand why."

"Didn't I tell you to get the hell out?" he shouted without glancing over.

I swung the door open with a bang, turning back to him over my shoulder. "Go fuck yourself, sir!" I yelled, not caring who might have overheard.

I stumbled outside and breathed deep, slapping my forehead as I dropped to a nearby bench. Despite the uncomfortable exchange, I did feel somewhat relieved and empowered, knowing it was the right decision.

⚜   ⚜   ⚜

I stepped back in the S4 office after cooling down. Some of the supplies and equipment were already packed up, sitting in preparation for our upcoming return home.

"Crash and burn, Sergeant Donegal!" Belinsky's arms flew up in his usual fashion. "Way to survive a plane crash and come out *unscathed.*" He pointed with both hands, his mouth hanging wide open. "Eh? Get my joke? Huh?"

My lips curled to one side. "Missed you too, KGB."

VonRutenburg astonishingly stood up. "Sergeant Donegal." His hand shook mine. "It's good to have you back, soldier."

I appreciated his small, rarely seen gesture of compassion. "Thank you, sir."

I felt a welcoming presence behind me, and turned into Perez's compressing hug.

"Thank God," he whispered. "You have no idea how much it hurt to hear that you didn't make it, Don." He released his grip on me. "Why did you decide to come back, *amiga?* They reported you legally dead. You could've started a new life if you wanted to."

"I couldn't skip out on you yet, Master Sergeant. You're not very good at handling the CONEX reports. I felt guilty leaving you tasked with it so close to our return home."

He laughed, nearly in tears. "Hopefully that's not the only reason."

It was a heartwarming moment being reunited with my team. When the LTs became re-occupied on their computers, I discreetly spoke to Perez.

"By the way, that little situation we discussed..." He clearly knew what I was referring to. "It's over. Just ended it."

"Good for you, Sergeant. I'm proud of you."

"Hope I never let you down again."

His thumb bopped my chin. "Just keep doing what you're doing. I don't have any doubts you're on the right track."

"Becker in the supply room again?"

"*Si, soldado.* You can head over there. She's anxious to see you." He pat my shoulder as I stepped toward the door. "Glad to have you back, Don."

⚜   ⚜   ⚜

I quietly entered the supply office and found Becker seated on the floor, sifting through piles of equipment and taking notes.

"Corporal, I'm here to report that one Army duffel bag has been killed in action."

She gasped. "Oh, my god!"

I was eager to embrace her. She leapt up and raced over, tugging me into her arms.

"Babe, what happened?" She let go and pulled up a chair. "Tell me everything."

We both sat as she handed me a Gatorade from the cooler.

"Well, what exactly were you told?"

She sighed, still somewhat frantic. "So, you were supposed to return a few days ago. Ryder tasked Perez with finding out what happened. He called the airline and they either didn't answer or said they didn't know yet. Then the Indian government contacted the State Department because your name was on the manifest, reporting that the flight crashed in the mountains. Ryder held a formation and told us you were on that plane and..." her voice crackled, and she paused to compose herself.

I leaned over to grip her arm. "It's okay, hon. I'm right here. I'm fine."

She sniffled. "I almost fainted in the middle of formation, babe."

"I'm so sorry you had to go through that." I wiped a tear from her eye.

She cleared her throat. "But then yesterday, Ryder came in and told us you had been found alive."

I nodded, staring off in remembrance. "It feels like a long time ago. After the crash, I somehow landed far from the impact site. It was just a whirlwind of events from there." I stood up, wanting to continue the conversation back in our room. "We can get going, by the way."

"Good." She sniffed again. "Let's get out of here. I've been counting this shit all day." She rose and returned my rifle to me.

"Hello, Xena." I swung her over my shoulder as Becker logged off her computer. "You hungry?"

"Yeah, just gimme a second."

"Afterward, I think I'll swing by and say hi to Dee. He messaged me after I left and I never responded."

Becker paused, suddenly looking perturbed.

"Uh-oh," my observation overpowered with worry. "What's wrong *now?*"

She seemed remorseful. "Babe, Dee was in a bad attack a couple days ago in Basra. He went on a convoy mission as the acting mechanic and an IED went off at the checkpoint, striking his Humvee."

I covered my mouth, verging on panic. "Is he okay? Please tell me he's okay."

She shook her head. "Not really. He survived, but suffered horrible injuries. He had severe head trauma, lost an arm…"

"Oh, no!" My mouth fell in shock.

"They already sent him to Walter Reed."

"Noooo…" I slowly sank down to the chair, my face drained of color. "Poor Dee. I didn't even get to speak to him and here I completely brushed him off when I left. I feel so bad for him." I sat in silence, processing the unfortunate news. "Maybe we could contact his family, tell them how sorry we are and what a great person he is."

"Yeah, babe. Think they'll appreciate that. Vernon and I talked about doing something similar. His unit is really upset about it."

I sighed. "I don't think I'm hungry anymore."

"Come on. We can take something To Go. You'll feel better if you eat."

She pulled my arm, and practically dragged me to the mess hall as my stance resembled that of a zombie.

-♦-   -♦-   -♦-

We brought containers of chicken strips and fries back to the room. I set down my rifle, changing into PTs.

"Whoa!" Becker cringed at my uncovered thigh. "Your scar is gnarly, babe. Does it hurt?"

"Not anymore, but it does itch and smell like butthole." I popped a fry in my mouth.

"More care packages came this morning from the VFW." She shuffled through a box on her bed. "Here. Your favorite." She tossed over a bag of homemade roasted sunflower seeds. "There were chocolate chip cookies, too, but I ate those earlier."

"Figures." I set it aside for later. "Thanks."

"How was your time in New Zealand?"

I had almost forgotten about the trip preceding the accident. "Met some great people, saw animals, drank wine, skinny-dipped under a waterfall... I got pictures."

Becker giggled. "Naughty, babe. I love it. Did you meet any hot guys... or girls?" She winked in wishful thinking.

I stared off and smirked, picturing Aryan's face. I wondered what he was doing right now. I was still in shock about Dee and wished I could hug him for comfort.

"So you *did.*" She smiled, readjusting herself on the bed while awaiting my response. "Who was he? One of the Kiwis or a traveler?"

"A local from India, actually. He took me into his home."

Her face lit up. "Details, babe. Did you guys fuck?"

My eyes rolled racily as I laughed, feigning coyness.

"You did?! Oh, my god. What's sex like with an Indian guy?"

I blushed. "I can always count on you to make me laugh, hon, no matter what state I'm in."

She studied my face, her playful demeanor transposing as she reached a realization. "Babe, it wasn't just sex, was it? You fell for the guy."

I paused, biting my lip. "Yeah, guess I did. I keep thinking about him, but not sure if I'll even get to see him again. Might just forget about me after a while."

"Did you guys make plans to keep in touch?"

"We exchanged info. He has a home and business in Kentucky."

"Well, that's promising that he can come to the U.S. when he wants. What's gonna happen with Ryder now? You planning to end things?"

"Already did." I bit into a chicken strip.

"Really? What did you say to him?"

"To put it mildly, I told him to fuck himself."

Becker laughed as though I were kidding, but then saw my reaction. "Wait... you're serious?"

"Yeah," I responded casually. "Punched the bastard's face, too."

Her mouth dropped. "You've got serious ovaries, babe. How'd he react?"

"Oh, he's fine. It's a temporary dent in his ego. He'll get over it."

"Suppose it's for the best, like I said. You're getting out of the Army soon and won't have to see him anymore."

"Being with Aryan, I just…" my voice trailed off for a moment. "It's different."

"What's he like? He's hot?"

"Definitely, but he's also adventurous, smart, and… sweet. He's confident, but sort of shy, too. He's like this ambitious entrepreneur and thrill-seeker. He skydives and travels… oh, and he doesn't want kids. I mean, how often does a guy like that come along?"

Becker stared, pleasantly stunned. "Normally I'd be puking right now, but I'm actually really happy to hear this, babe. He sounds perfect for you."

I looked at the clock. "He wouldn't even be back home yet."

"Shit. You know what, babe? I told Vernon I'd come over after work." She stood up and grabbed her rifle. "I'll tell her you're back safe. You gonna be okay here by yourself?"

"Yeah, I'll browse the net a while. You go ahead."

"Be back later." She hugged me and left the room.

I turned on my laptop, perusing through Facebook while lying back. Gin and Clark were now in Thailand, pictures posted of them swimming at the beaches in Phuket. I smiled, clicking through their photos, seeing adventure after adventure, and even saw a few with me in New Zealand. I checked Aryan's page next, seeing only a few pictures, all of them skydiving. There was a video of him flying through the sky when he was in San Diego, and he was smiling in every picture.

I liked seeing him happy. Out of curiosity, I pulled up the Burble Distilleries website, reading through his bio, history of his business, and details about the products he and his friend produced. I admired him for everything he was.

Upon checking my email, I noticed a message sent:

Hey Vellakari,

I stopped at a coffee shop on the way back. Hope your flight went well this time. I'm sure the other soldiers in your unit are happy to see you. I want to thank you again for staying with me. My home is going to feel empty without you. My friends are already calling and asking when you'll be back. As I said before, I'll be here for another few months and will return to the U.S. We can plan to meet. In the meantime, I'll be thinking of you. Please message me anytime. I meant what I said as you left. Can't wait to see you again.

- Aryan Visu

I opened the attachment, containing a few pictures I had taken with his phone. I closed my laptop, setting it aside before falling asleep, Aryan weighing heavily on my mind.

⚜ ⚜ ⚜

It was the day of our scheduled return home and our entire brigade was busy packing up, finishing last minute details. The majority of our equipment had already shipped home with our advance party and our remaining bags sat in a pile outside as we cleaned up the office.

"Hey KGB, what's the first thing you're gonna do when you get home?" I asked while sweeping.

He stood up from folding a table. "First, I'm going to the bar to get me a hot girl. Then, a hot Super Star burger from Carl's Jr."

"Sounds about right." I turned to VonRutenburg. "What about you, sir?"

"I'll be attending one more drill with you all before heading back to San Diego, then I'll continue managing my family's restaurants. How about you, Sergeant?"

I leaned against the broom, surprised that I hadn't really thought about it. "Uh, probably just start working at the Hilton again, after I pay a visit to the bar, of course."

Perez and Becker walked through the door. "Okay, supply room is all set to go. We almost done in here?"

"Just finishing up, Master Sergeant," I told him.

"The first C-130 is leaving in an hour. You all can grab your bags and wait on the flight line. I'll stay back and catch the next one to ensure everything is loaded properly."

"Then I guess we'll see you in Kuwait." I set my broom aside and turned to leave as Perez gently grabbed my wrist.

"Don, wait..." His dark eyes were troubled, yet wholeheartedly sanguine. "Please, just... be very careful. I couldn't bear losing you again." He gave me a snug hug and whispered, "Your father has been a fool. Anyone would be fortunate to have a daughter like you."

My tears of joy flowed, and this time, I didn't care who saw me.

⚓   ⚓   ⚓

Our unit stayed overnight in Camp Buehring's transient housing before shipping back to Kuwait City's airport. The soldiers remained seated, now settled on our commercial aircraft, waiting to fly out once the Commander arrived. I sat between Becker and Perez, glancing out at the Kuwait Towers for what would probably be the last time.

"Did you say goodbye to Vernon?"

"Yeah," Becker's reply bittersweet. "She was a lot of fun. I'll miss her."

"Maybe you guys can keep in touch."

"Nah, I don't do long distance." She changed the subject. "You nervous about the long flight, babe?"

I bobbed my head. "I'll be all right. Pam and the family coming to the welcome ceremony?"

"Yeah, they'll be there."

I glanced around the eerily silent cabin, only a few soldiers chatting quietly over the hum of the plane's engine. Many were already asleep. It had now been a full year that we were away from home, and were all exhausted. I'm sure mixed emotions were being experienced across the brigade.

Ryder hopped up through the front door, the welt on his chin now mostly healed. "Good morning, 134th. Let's do a quick headcount before we leave. Sound off."

Each soldier counted off until we got through the entire cabin, accounting for everyone.

"All right, we have three layovers with stops in Hungary, Germany, and Iceland before we have boots on ground back home. You *will* have the opportunity to get out and stretch your legs, grab something to eat, and use the restroom. Let's have a good flight."

He sat down as the plane pulled out toward the runway. I watched out the window as it took off, eventually leaving the desert behind.

·Φ·   ·Φ·   ·Φ·

"Hey, babe. Wake up." I felt my arm shake as I opened my eyes to Becker. "We're landing back home!"

I yawned, glancing out the window to see the San Jose National Guard Armory expand as we neared the runway. Excitement brewed throughout the cabin as soldiers were already gathering their bags and watching for friends and family on the ground. It had been several long flights with an overnight, but we were home now, and I couldn't wait to hug Dad… and take a long shower. Crowds had gathered outside the armory, waving American flags and banners welcoming the soldiers home. We landed to the cheers and screams of people as the door swung open. Ryder exited first and stood by as the rest of us filed out, each soldier racing over to their loved ones.

I emerged amidst the crowd, taking in the California summer sun that no longer felt as hot as it once did. Becker stepped off behind me. I located Dad and Linda right away and ran up, embracing them both in a bear hug.

"Scaith!" my dad cried out, kissing my cheek. "So good to have you back, lassie. It's been too long."

I hugged him so tightly, I nearly picked him up off the ground.

"Welcome home, sweetheart," Linda said politely, a bouquet of wildflowers in her hand. "We were so worried about you."

"I missed you guys. Feels amazing to be back." I sighed from the overwhelming excitement and looked up at the armory, mass memories flooding in. Becker was busy greeting her family next to us, and they all came over to join our circle. Becker and I hugged for the hell of it, both feeling ecstatic. I couldn't have made it without losing my mind had Becker not been by my side.

"Welcome home, Scaith." Pam embraced me next. Her brother and parents were also present.

"It's great to be back." I looked at their brother. "Now it's your turn to go play in the sandbox, Mike."

"I hope so." He hugged me as well. "Welcome back, Sergeant."

Dan, Cody, and Ellie had also shown up. They moved slowly through the crowds to greet us while waiting for us to finish being reunited with our families. Several news reporters and journalists had showed up to interview soldiers along with military organizations and locals from the community who wanted to show their support.

"Why don't you all join us for dinner tonight?" Becker's mother offered.

Dad wrapped his arm around my shoulder. "Thanks for the offer Beth, but I think we'll stay together as a family tonight. Lot of catching up to do."

"Of course. Another time perhaps."

I glanced back at Perez with his wife and son, tears running down as he hugged them both. Lieutenant Belinsky was busy head butting a friend of his and Lieutenant VonRutenburg was already leaving with his family.

I smiled, appreciating all the love surrounding the homecoming. I noticed Commander Ryder off on the sidelines, shaking hands with the visiting civilians, his wife nowhere in sight.

"Uh, just give me a moment guys."

I walked over to him. Though he was greeting everyone with a smile, a sadness exhumed from his face and I couldn't help but feel pity, so my hand extended up to him.

"Welcome home, sir."

He smiled in pleasant surprise, and shook my hand. "Welcome home, Sergeant."

I nodded and smiled back, indicating a cease fire between us before returning to my family. We enjoyed each other's company for a while and caught up on funny stories before heading to the car.

"Scaith, we'd like to take you out to eat tonight," Dad told me as we walked to his car. "Your pick."

"I'd like that." I grinned as I thought of a place to go. "How about Indian?"

13

GUDALUR, NILGIRIS, SOUTH INDIA
JUNE, 1998

ARYAN

My face stung on impact as my mother's palm slapped across it.
"Why do you do like this? I taught you how you should behave.
Is this how you will act at college? Stealing bikes and plotting with
your friends?"

I waved my arms in defense. "It wasn't me, *Amma*. It was Sunil and
his brother."

"You need to hang out with better friends. Those tribal boys never
behave good. What would *Appa* do if he would come to know this?"

My mother's scoldings always cut deeper than my father's did. Most
of the time, I would devise excuses as to why I misbehaved, usually
blaming others to get out of beatings.

Not wanting to wait around for my father's belt, I darted out the door
and raced up the hill, my mother still screaming from inside the house.
Past the abandoned tea factory, I entered the dense jungle and ran until I
reached my favorite spot. The sun shone down through the large guava
tree as I climbed to the top, my legs hanging down over the thick branch
as I sat.

I closed my eyes, breathing in the crisp, oxygen-rich air. Here, it was
peaceful, away from the noise and chaos. It was just me in the wild with
birds singing, bugs whizzing by, and monkeys leaping from tree to tree.
Two white gravestones loomed up through the tall grass below, ohm
symbols gracing the front face of both.

No more than ten days ago, I buried my grandfather here, next to my grandmother who had passed before I was born. I missed spending time with him. No matter what I was dealing with, *Thatha* always knew how to make me feel better with his long talks of wisdom, perfected over the years. I had yet to meet someone that I connected with as much as I did him. Now gone, I felt lost, as if part of me died along with him. Being at his house in Ooty, I felt more at home than I ever did in this place, but I made the most of it. Soon, I would be off to college to make new memories.

I bent my leg up to scrape a leech from my toe. Monsoon season was just beginning and the leeches were coming out in droves. After some time, I swung from the branch, dropping to the ground with a thud before heading further up the trail. It was still early afternoon and I wanted to see my friends again.

Thirty minutes of running later, I arrived in the mountainous village of Kurumbar. My parents disapproved of my friend choices as they were tribal people of the lowest caste possible and didn't want our family to be associated with them, but I didn't care what they thought. These friends were adventurous and spontaneous like I was.

"Machi!"

Sunil stuck his machete in the log he was chopping and walked toward me, wiping sweat off his brow. His skin was much darker than mine, heavily scarred, and his facial features resembled that of a Neanderthal. He had just turned nineteen, the same age as me, but was far less educated. By some miracle, he managed to get accepted into college and was bound for the Tech Institute in Bangalore, the same place I was headed.

"Hey Sunil, where did you hide the bike?" I asked him eagerly.

"Come. I'll show you." He grinned, leading me into one of the huts. He removed the tarp to reveal a brand new Yamaha RX-100, which he had stolen earlier whilst in town. Though I was with him, I now got to take a closer look, my fingers trailing over the smooth, shiny black and magenta detailing.

He had escaped punishment for his actions, but I was not so lucky. Everyone in town knew my face and who my father was. No sooner than a minute after the act had someone called my mother to inform her of my involvement, though I doubted she would tell my father of it. Despite her constant bickering and seemingly controlling habits, I knew she loved me and would protect my reputation, even if that meant keeping secrets from my father.

The people of Sunil's village, however, didn't seem to care what he and his little brother did. Being dirt-poor, they stole on a regular basis just to survive, often taking fruit and wood from nearby privately-owned or government lands. When their mother was killed last year, having been trampled by a wild elephant, their father became a drunk. Even now, he stumbled around the village, clutching a bottle of brandy.

Sunil's little brother entered the hut, gripping a machete.

"Hey, Mani," I greeted him. "It's a nice bike you guys got."

Though the brothers were the ones who stole it, I fully intended to make use of it as well.

Mani smirked, as if he knew a secret that we didn't. "I just left flowers for Neharika," he giggled. "She took them and smiled at me."

Mani was always shy around girls, so this bold step came as a surprise to me. He was a couple years younger than us, stronger and much better-looking than Sunil, giving him far more chances of getting married someday. Tribal people only married within their own tribe as no outsiders would ever consider them as options.

We all peeked outside to see Neharika sitting under a tree, sniffing her yellow flowers as a smile graced her lips.

"That looks promising, Mani," I told him. "She seems happy."

Sunil brushed past us hurriedly, pointing towards something else. "Guys, check it out! They just caught a cobra!"

"I want to see!" I shouted with excitement.

We raced over to one of the villagers as he maneuvered sticks, trying to take hold of a king cobra going wild. A crowd started forming around him as the cobra barred his fangs, snapping at anyone who came too close. We moved in, trying to catch a glimpse as the villager dodged its bite, dancing around and eventually catching it by the head.

Mani stepped up with confidence. "I can remove it, Uncle. I will take it to the river."

He was one of the bravest kids I knew. If adventure and danger struck, he was always there to swoop in and handle it. He also knew the jungles of the Nilgiris better than anyone.

I stayed in the village for the better part of the afternoon and returned close to dark. I rinsed my sandals and feet in the washroom by the old tea factory before heading back to the house. I walked in to find my mother on the couch, sipping chai with her friend. My father hadn't come home yet, which only meant one thing: he was out drinking.

My mother frowned with concern. "Why are you coming home this late? What are you doing all this time now?"

I stormed across the room, slamming my bedroom door behind.

.⚜.   .⚜.   .⚜.

The sound of news playing loudly awoke me Saturday morning. My dad had weekends off and would waste all of it watching TV. My mother had dosa and coconut chutney waiting for me in the kitchen.

"Aryan, *Appa* is taking you to Ooty today to do some work at *Thatha's* house." She handed me a plate, her voice much calmer than yesterday.

I started eating, my father strolling past me while dragging his slippers and hacking his throat. He leaned over and spat out the window, dropping his dirty plates on the table before returning to the TV room, leaving a trail of farts behind.

I wasn't looking forward to spending the day with my dad, but I longed to be in my grandfather's house again. *Amma* was on the phone with Sharvani now, talking about how college was going in Coimbatore. I was surprisingly missing my sister a lot. She always managed to get me out of trouble with our parents and now she was no longer around to defend me.

I took a quick bucket bath and dressed into a blue t-shirt and dark grey cargo shorts, brushing my thick, curly hair on the couch as Dad talked about the news.

"Look at this," he mumbled, his eyes never meeting mine. "American troops were attacked in Saudi Arabia. Muslim terrorists again."

I slipped into sandals while sitting. His complaints against Muslims often bothered me, but then, I was the type to judge people on their character, not their beliefs. An entire group of people shouldn't be held responsible for the actions of a few.

"Not just Muslims are terrorists, *Appa*," I reminded him. "Hindus and Christians can be, too."

"No, Christians cause no problems," his voice agitated, most likely because my logical comments challenged him. "It is these dirty Muslims that cause so much brutality. In January, they killed Kashmiri Hindus in Wandhama… women and children. Slaughtered them like goats. It was the Lashkar-e-Taiba again. They are the start of all these things happening."

"And remember that bombing in the U.S. a few years ago in Oklahoma City? They weren't Muslims, *Appa*. They were citizens."

He didn't respond, which was probably for the best. I didn't like our constant bickering. He had his own opinion about things and there was no changing his mind, especially at his age. The news often made him grumpy, but unfortunately, that was all he usually watched.

"*Appa*, when are we going to Ooty?" I was anxious to leave.

"In some time," he replied.

I knew what that meant. It could be anywhere from two to five hours, so I headed to Nishant's house to wait there.

‑◆‑   ‑◆‑   ‑◆‑

Nishant's parents didn't live far, and I often hung out there when I wasn't in Ooty. Walking up to their yard, I immediately regretted my decision when I noticed Prema on the porch.

"Hi, Aryan!" She waved and set down her tea, running up to me. "Come on. I'll make you some chai." She was pulling me towards the house by my shirt.

"Is Nishant here?" I groaned, looking for an escape route.

"He's in back."

"Then that's where I'm heading. See ya."

I scurried to the back of the house, leaving Prema hanging. Nishant was chopping up a jackfruit on a tree stump.

"Morning, Aryan." He continued chopping.

"Why is Prema here?" I complained, skipping the formalities.

"She came with her mom. Probably to talk about her marriage to you," he laughed.

I shook my head, feigning indifference. "No way is that happening. I told my mom this. She doesn't listen."

"You might be out of luck, *Machi*. Sounds like this is already arranged."

"And it's *my* life. I should decide what goes. I really wanna move to another country so I can do what I want."

He handed me a jackfruit pod. "Hey, what happened with the bike yesterday? Sanjeev said you and Sunil stole one."

"How does Sanjeev know about that?"

"All of Gudalur knows that, Aryan. You know nothing can be kept secret in this town."

I sighed. "I can't wait to go to college. Too much drama here." I bit into the jackfruit pod, popping the pit out. "What are you doing today? I'm going to Ooty with Dad, whenever he decides to get ready. You want to go with?"

"Yeah, sure." He brushed off his dark green, long-sleeved shirt. "I need to pick up some snacks for my mom."

Nishant was the child every parent in India wanted to have, the epitome of the American golden son. My parents loved him because he came from a good background, education, and was a high caste, like me. We got along great, but sometimes he played by the rules more than I would've liked, which is why I often steered towards the Kurumbar tribal villagers.

‑⚜‑   ‑⚜‑   ‑⚜‑

I stared up at the white and teal house in Ooty a couple hours later. I hadn't been back since he died. His warm and inviting home now stood empty, but my memories with him remained. Leela Auntie would often pick me up on rainy days so I could join *Thatha* for chai and onion pakora on the porch out back.

Gangatharan Uncle waited for us by the door. "Ravi, sir," he called to Dad as we stepped out of the car. "We have a problem. Your sister is here making a fuss."

No sooner than a couple seconds later, Meena Auntie stormed out. Her name suited her well as she was the meanest person I knew. Growing up, she couldn't help but insult me and my sister. If it wasn't my mother fighting my dad, it was my aunt who was stirring up trouble.

"What is this now, *Thambi*?" she grumbled, flapping her arms like a crazy person. "You give our father's house to your son? I am the eldest child. How dare you! You stole this house from me and my children." Her dyed red hair was messy, the bags under her eyes more prominent than usual.

"This house was never yours!" he scolded back. "*Appa* wanted Aryan to have it. This was his final wish."

Despite the heated argument, I suddenly felt exhilarated. This was the first I had heard that my grandfather wanted me to inherit his home. I turned to Nishant with a grin and took him by the arm, gesturing towards the house. We raced through the front door, leaving the adults to sort out the dispute amongst themselves.

"Did you just hear her? *Thatha's* house is going to be mine!"

"Super, *Machi*," his dimples deepened. "We can all come and hang out here."

"Too bad I'm leaving for college so soon. Now I want to stay and work on this house." I looked around, envisioning what changes I would make. "I want to paint it dark blue, put in modern furniture, fix the balcony out back…"

"Wait, *Machi*. You always get ahead of yourself. The house isn't yours yet. You have to deal with your aunt first, and she won't let it go so easy."

I brushed it off. "My dad will fight her. And if he doesn't, I will. I'm taking this house no matter what."

All three adults charged through the door. Gangatharan was unsuccessfully trying to keep the peace between the siblings.

"You think Aryan can manage a house?" Meena's griping continued, her high-pitched, threatening voice bouncing off the walls of the foyer. "He can't even stay out of trouble. He brings shame and embarrassment to our family. He doesn't want to marry Prema and here she is too good for him like anything."

She turned to me with fire in her eyes. "How did you even get into college with your grades, Aryan? You are spoiled degenerate! You took advantage of your grandfather to get this house!"

I had heard enough of her accusations and lunged at her in full force, shoving her back several feet. "You're a bitch! No wonder your husband killed himself. You torture everyone. Do you have any sense at all, Auntie?!"

My uncle pulled me back, dragging me out to the balcony while I protested. I wanted nothing more than to put my aunt in her place where she belonged. Everyone in my father's family was the same, lacking manners and common sense. My grandfather's accumulated wealth had caused nothing but problems over the years with each member trying to snatch the biggest share, and I was always stuck in the middle as his supposed favorite.

"Violence is not the way to resolve this, Aryan." He was ever the peacemaker. "It's true your aunt is jealous. You will have a future and life that she never had."

"*I'm* violent?" I seethed at the accusation, retorting with snark. "Wonder where I leaned it from."

Nishant joined us outside. "She just left, *Machi*. Your father struck her."

"Good," I snapped. "She deserved it."

"Nephew, sometimes you have to behave as the bigger person," my uncle's tone still relatively calm. "Anger and revenge do not solve problems. You must think like this when you go to college for there will be many more examples like that."

I paused and looked up at him, slowly calming down. "Did *Thatha* really give me this house, Uncle?"

"Yes. I will be your Power of Attorney while you are gone. I'll help manage the place and estates."

I raised an eyebrow. "Estates?"

"Your grandfather has also gifted you the titles of his land and estates."

I gasped in surprise. "All of them?"

"Aryan, now is not a time to celebrate or gloat," he warned. "There is much work to be done and you must be ready for the battles that will come."

"I'm not worried about her, Uncle. She's hated me her whole life, but she's never broken me."

"It's not just your aunt you should be worried about. Your father's brothers are also not happy about this, especially Bala. He has already raised alarm within the family and will likely try to cheat you out of the deeds."

My father joined us on the balcony as rainclouds covered overhead, the Muslim call to prayer sounding off from the city.

"Come, let's head down to the valley. An elephant damaged the fence again."

⚜ ⚜ ⚜

"You have everything prepared for college, *Thambi?*" my sister inquired over the phone. "Bangalore is a big city, not like home."

"*Ahmahm, Akka.* I just want to get away from Gudalur. I'm sick of the family."

"I understand, *Thambi.*"

It was dark and dingy inside the empty tea factory, if a tad creepy, but it was one of the few places in Gudalur I could enjoy some privacy. The cobweb-ridden machines were old and outdated, and I found myself imagining what it could become now that I was inheriting the place. I had never seen it in operation before, only as a familiar childhood hangout. It had been weeks since discovering my inheritance and I was already making plans for once I returned from school.

"Sharvani, would you talk to *Amma?* She still wants me to marry Prema, but I don't want."

"Aryan, I will support you with anything you choose. I've told *Amma* this. Just keep doing things as you want. It is your life. I will deal with our parents."

I nodded, despite her not being able to see me. *"Nandhri, Akka."*

"You take care, *Thambi*, and I will see you next week to take you and Sunil to Bangalore."

"Sarri, sarri."

I hung up and sat in silence to ponder, the chirps of lizards echoing throughout the eerie factory.

⚜ ⚜ ⚜

After some time, I decided to head back to Kurumbar. Fifteen minutes of trekking and I froze on the path, almost certain something was tailing me. Trees and shrubs often concealed any wild elephants lurking nearby, and after being chased by the one near my grandfather's place recently, I wasn't in any hurry to have the situation revisited. I often encountered elephants while trudging through the jungle, but they weren't usually a bother unless provoked, often staying further up the mountain. Just the other day, a neighbor complained of a tiger eating his goats, so I certainly hoped it wasn't that.

I continued on, but suddenly found myself on the grass, my head smashing against the ground. Something had knocked me over, and was now pinning me down with incredible force. A strong hand came down and encircled my throat, my mouth prying open to call for help, but only gasped. I was helpless in the moment. Someone wanted me dead badly enough that they followed me into a dangerous jungle, a place where bodies go to disappear.

My legs thrashed in panic, my upper body barely moving under the intense grip. I tugged at the arms around me as a tingly sensation shot through my head, a haze of white flashing from nothing external.

Grip released before the sharp, rusty blade of a machete came into my line of sight. My eyes adjusted to the person wielding it, and I screamed.

"Stop, Uncle!" my hysterical cry echoed.

Bala's eyes were filled with rage and determination. Despite my pleas, he looked hell bent on overseeing this task to completion. The machete came down, slicing the ground as I rolled to the side, avoiding its destructive intent. I managed to stand up, desperately gasping for air. He lunged again, his brawny, hefty build narrowly missing me as I darted behind a tree.

"You will never get what belongs to my family, Aryan!" he barked, chasing me deeper into the jungle.

I outran him until a root disrupted my footing, sending me several feet down a steep, rocky cliff. I toppled over the dirt and sand, landing near the raging river, my uncle not far behind. I stumbled to my feet as he came at me again, his machete high in the air. I caught his arm as it lowered above my head, using every muscle to keep the blade at a distance. After inevitable defeat seemed to close in, a wasp flew onto his face, distracting him long enough for me to swipe the machete, flesh tearing as I tore it from grasp before losing my footing.

I fell back and screamed, blood spurting profusely from the resulting gaping hole in his neck, and I nearly threw up at the horror before me. I had slit his throat. He dropped to his knees, blood continuing to flow. Had it not been for the rushing sounds of the river flowing behind me, my whimpering would have been the only noise. The machete dropped from my hand as Bala fell face-forward, his body mildly convulsing.

Another rustling noise rang out from the bushes nearby. I quickly retrieved the machete and planted my feet in preparation of self-defense, but it slipped from my fingers again, this time in relief.

It was Mani. I sighed as he approached me, surveying the scene. He didn't have to comment as he already knew what had happened.

"You okay, Aryan?"

My head swayed, mind panic-stricken. "No." My body shook in fear. "My father will beat me senseless for this."

Mani stepped closer, analyzing the situation before placing a palm on my shoulder. "Then you shouldn't get caught."

He set down his own machete and tightened his bandana before taking hold of Bala's now-lifeless body.

"What are you planning to do?" I asked, though I had a feeling I already knew the answer.

"Grab his legs," his instruction dauntless.

I complied and he led us further down the river, a long trail of blood flecking the grass behind. We set my uncle's body down inside the local manganese cave, just enough so no one would see, though not many people came to an area this remote.

Mani then grabbed my arm. "Come and sit." He brought me to a large rock on the opposite side of the river and we both sat, waiting.

"What's going to happen now?" I asked, my heart still racing.

"Shh…" His finger raised to his lips. "Just wait."

Minutes later, he started sharpening his machete with a small rock, each stroke causing a faint screeching sound. We waited for another half hour before something approached from up the river.

Mani stood up on the rock, looking like a true jungle wanderer. "Look, Aryan."

I stood up next to him to see a tiger prowling towards the cave, and I squeezed my fists, unsure of how to feel. The tiger sniffed the body and soon dragged it inward, disappearing from our view.

I turned to Mani. "Will this work?"

"Yes," he stated confidently. "No one will ever see him again."

14

"What do you feel is one of the most important qualities a manager should have?"

"Oh, there are many, but I believe trust is very important. Your guests and employees need to trust you. In turn, they will trust you back. It must be earned through hard work, dedication, and loyalty, and the manager must set the example."

My interviewee was a lovely, classy woman with mocha skin and a shaved head, huge gold earrings dangling. Her burgundy lipstick matched well with her black and red floral dress. She exhumed pure, untarnished confidence, her mind was sharp, and presented an impressive background having managed hotels both in the U.S. and Africa.

I leaned over my desk, hands folding together. "Fatima, I must say I can think of no one more qualified to fill the Night Manager position. You have all the credentials, fill the requirements necessary, and have the right personality for the role. I'd like to formally offer it to you if you are still interested."

"Oh!" Her bright white teeth emerged through her beaming smile. "I am *very* much interested." She stood up while shaking my hand, her accent thick Kenyan. "Thank you *very* much, Miss Donegal."

I returned the smile, reveling in her joyous attainment. "I have no doubt that you'll be a great asset here. You'll receive an offer letter from me via email within the next two days. I look forward to meeting with you again to go over your employee paperwork."

She continued smiling. "Oh, thank you, madam. Thank you."

I walked her back to the lobby, shaking her hand once more before approaching Hazel at the front desk. "Hey, you just get in?"

"Yes, dear. How did the interview go?"

My elbow fell to the counter. "It went well. I offered her the job. I think she'll do great."

"That's wonderful news. We need a good steady manager back up here, though no one can replace you. Patricia's okay, but she really wants to get back to Sales and Marketing."

"Things should return to normal soon. Just hang tight a little while longer."

"It's been so nice having you back, Scaith. How has Human Resources been treating you so far?"

"I really enjoy it, having my own department and space to work. It's been nice getting to know the employees better."

I tapped on the counter, as if to say, "See you later," and swung by Bill's office before returning to mine. He had lost quite a bit of weight in the last year.

"Hey Bill, I just made an offer for my old position. Once she starts, I can help her get trained in. Shouldn't take more than a couple weeks."

"Glad you found someone. Patricia was about to pull her hair out with you gone for so long."

I snickered. "Yeah, it's no easy role. Takes a toll on you."

"How's HR going? You liking it?"

"I do. Thanks again for the opportunity. Do you need anything? Otherwise, I'm gonna take off."

I checked my email once more back at my office. Aryan had sent a message about the improvements he was making at the estates and that he was getting along great with his father lately. We had been connecting every day since I left.

My desk phone rang as I was shutting off my computer. I leaned over and answered.

"Scaith Donegal, HR department."

"Hello lassie, are you still working?"

"Hey Dad, I'm just leaving actually. What's up?"

"I'd like to invite you over for dinner tonight. Linda's making an Indian curry for you."

"What's the occasion?"

"Well, we just feel like we haven't seen you for a while and wanted to catch up."

I chuckled. "I was over last week, Dad, but that's totally fine. I'd love to come over again. What time?"

⚜   ⚜   ⚜

I met Becker at Cinebar for a quick drink as we had already made plans.

"Sorry hon, tonight is gonna have to be a one drink max. Got dinner at my dad's place."

I removed my teal peacoat and studied her demeanor after ordering my usual Grenache.

"You seem a little down tonight. What gives?"

She sighed. "I just found out Lucille died."

"Oh, I'm so sorry. She was such a nice lady."

"Yeah, guess it was just her time."

"I'm sure she missed you while you were gone. Glad she got to spend more time with you after we got back. She clearly loved you like a granddaughter."

"I was thinking about getting a different job now. I only have a year of the Army left, so I might try for a corporate job as grounds maintenance."

"You'd be good at that. I can help you look for an opening if you want. I'll go over your resume, too. Get it updated."

"Appreciate that, babe." She sipped her Guinness. "How does it feel to be Director of HR now? Been enjoying civilian life?"

"I like working a regular schedule again, having my weekends open. I've been brushing up on my Spanish now, too, with so many Spanish-speaking employees. There's freedom in running my own department, though I may need an assistant soon. It's a lot of work."

"A lot of work? You're good at that, babe. They picked the right girl for the job."

"Yeah, but I like traveling, too. That's the downside. I can't leave when I want to."

"Speaking of travel, how's Aryan? Isn't he coming back to the U.S. next month?"

I smiled at the sound of his name. "He's doing great. We haven't made any definite plans, but we'll figure it out." I sipped my wine, noticing Becker's sudden smirk. "Hmm. What's that face? What have you gone and done now?"

"I meant to tell you sooner, but I have a girlfriend now."

"You what?" I set my wine down. "Like, an actual girlfriend? When did this start?"

"A couple weeks ago. I thought she was gonna be another fling, that's why I didn't bring it up. Her name's Sarah, and you'd like her. She spent a year in Colombia with the Peace Corps and manages a catering company. She's really into wine, studying to become a sommelier."

I was intrigued. "I like her already. Colombia, huh? If she knows Spanish, maybe I can practice with her sometime. When do I get to meet her?"

"She'll be at the Halloween party, but I'll probably bring her over before then."

Becker had purchased a house not long after our return from Iraq. Having missed living together, I was renting a room from her for the time being.

"I'm happy for you, hon. Glad you found someone that you might want to stay with. I know the feeling."

"Hey, I forgot to tell you. Commander Ryder got a divorce."

"When was this?" I was pleased to discover that I really didn't care that much.

"Perez told me at drill last weekend. Guess he filed just after we got back."

I shrugged. "Good for him, I guess. I actually messaged Dee last week and he's back home now. The Warrior Transition Unit has been taking care of him and he's doing a lot better."

I finished my wine, checking my watch. "I've gotta head over to Dad's place. Sorry I had to cut this so short."

"No problem, babe. I'm gonna stay a little longer. I've got this one."

"Thanks. See you back home."

-❧-   -❧-   -❧-

Linda answered the door wearing a light pink sweater dress and denim jacket, her smile adorable as ever.

"Hello, sweetheart." I hugged her as I stepped inside.

"Hi, Linda. New dress?"

"It is. I actually got this one from the mall. On sale, of course."

Linda had made a lot of positive changes to my father's house over the last few years. It had a pleasant, feminine touch, fading away the emptiness the walls once held within. I passed the stone mantel above the fireplace, reminiscing over the framed picture of my family from years past; my parents, myself, and little Jimmy together. I no longer dwelled on the painful memories of loss, enjoying instead the memories of great times we shared together.

Dinner was being served in the dining room. "That smells great, Linda. Chicken curry?"

"It is. I researched a recipe and picked up a few things from the Indian grocery store."

"That's so sweet of you. Thank you for this." I walked around the table, kissing my dad on the forehead. "Hey, Dad."

He set aside the newspaper he was reading. "Evening, lassie."

I sat down. "How's work, Dad? Those product launches going well?"

"Aye. We're coming up with new lines of the iPod, Apple TV, MacBook Air, and early next year, we'll announce the iPad 2."

"Glad you're enjoying it, Dad. I know Aryan really wants to talk to you about your work. He likes using Apple products."

"How is Aryan, sweetheart?" Linda asked. "Is his business going well?"

"Which one?" I laughed.

Dad interjected. "You know, Scaith, Blair's son has been asking about you again."

I scoffed in response. "Dad, we've been over this so many times. Tristan's a nice guy, but he's not for me. I'm dating Aryan, remember?"

"I know, I just thought you might like to date someone that's more available to you. Someone who actually lives here."

"I don't necessarily want to live in just one place, Dad. I want to travel. And the thought of dating an Irish Catholic hermit who wants half a dozen kids doesn't appeal to me."

I started eating, hoping to move on from the subject. "Mmm. This is fantastic, Linda. Very authentic."

"Thank you, sweetheart." She sipped her glass of milk. "So, your father and I were discussing a possible trip soon. A nice little beach getaway for the two of us."

"Really? That would be great for you guys. Where you going?"

"I'd like to see the Caribbean. I've never been there. We also never really had a honeymoon, but now with your father's job going so well, we can take a nice vacation."

"Anywhere you want to go is fine with me, love," Dad told her.

I thought for a moment, reflecting on my last conversation with Nishant. "What about Jamaica? I know someone that manages a resort in Montego Bay. He could help with arrangements."

"Well, that would be just wonderful!" She turned to Dad. "Wouldn't it, Graham?"

"Yes. That sounds very nice, love. We can go there."

I was elated at seeing my father happy again. He had spent so many lonely years in denial and now had a fulfilling career, caring wife, and his health was improving overall.

After a few minutes of eating in silence, Linda spoke up. "How about a toast? I know we don't drink, but maybe we could still toast." She held up her glass of milk as I chuckled. I adored Linda. She was a nerd at heart and one of the kindest people I knew.

"Sure." I held up my glass of water while Dad did the same.

"To family, to making new memories, and to Constance and Jimmy. May they always remain in our hearts."

I glanced over to Dad, witnessing his reaction. He wasn't always able to handle hearing their names mentioned, but this time, he smiled.

⚜   ⚜   ⚜

A few weeks had gone by and I was sitting in my office with my arms crossed, an exasperated look crossing my stern face. The two housekeepers in front of me were giving me a headache.

"… and you take all my toilet papers and shampoos! Then you don't fold *toallas*." Yudisley screamed at her coworker. "What is wrong with you, *Puta*?"

"Hey! Hey!" I put my hand up, interjecting. "I won't tolerate any name-calling here."

"You are one that keeps taking my toiletries!" Binh snapped back at her.

Yudisley rolled her eyes. "Why don't you go find work at nail salon!?"

I slammed both hands on my desk. "Okay, that's enough of the cultural insults. You two need to start getting along. This brawl has been going on for far too long and it's disruptive to the entire staff. I don't ever want to have to bring you two back in my office over this pettiness. This happens again and I'm writing you both up, handing out possible suspensions."

I continued my lecture as they started to calm down. I despised dealing with internal fights at the hotel. Many were a waste of time with nothing ever solved, causing me to seriously reevaluate this role.

I also had more on my mind to torment me. It had been two weeks since I heard much from Aryan, and I was starting to worry. It wasn't like him not to call or email every day.

I finished up with the housekeepers as Fatima walked in. "Miss Donegal, would you assist me at the front desk? I need your help for a moment." She was always dressed so elegantly.

"Sure. What's the problem?"

"You may have already told me, but I forgot how to enter that promo code for our guests from Epic."

"I can show you."

I stood up, locking my office door behind. One of the new guest service agents was walking in our direction as we headed down the hallway.

"Oh, Miss Donegal," he started. "You have a visitor."

"Okay, I'm coming," I told him and turned to Fatima. "I'll meet you in your office in a sec."

I approached the front desk and found myself face to face with the one person I wanted to see right now more than ever, his features and clothes looking better than I remembered.

"Hey, *Vellakari.*"

15

"It's indescribable." I sat on the bench, awestruck by the historically significant wonder before us.

Aryan took hold of my hand. "I heard a legend once that Shah Jahan planned a black Taj Mahal to be built across the river."

My eyebrows raised. "Interesting. I haven't heard that story."

Aryan checked his watch to see it was nearing noon. We had walked the grounds of the complex since early morning.

"You hungry, sweetie?"

"Yeah," my response bittersweet. "I could honestly stay here all day, but guess it's time to go."

His hand brushed under my hair, stroking my back. "We can always return sometime. Maybe your family will even join."

I chuckled. "I don't see that happening."

We leisurely headed for the exit, passing the reflection pool along the way. I turned back for one last glance of the mausoleum before recognizing a couple faces no more than a meter away.

"Oh, my god!" I shouted out, racing across the ivory-white marble path.

"Scaith?" Gin's eyes widened when she saw me and outstretched her arms for lovable impact, catching my embrace.

"What are you guys doing here?" I reached over to hug Clark as well. "You've been out traveling this whole time?

"Yes, love," her smile bright. "We reached India a few days ago. Looks like our few months of traveling turned into a gap year. We've been all over Asia and it's just been an absolute adventure. So much to catch up on."

"Yeah, I've been following your travels on Facebook, but I didn't realize you were stopping in India. This is so great running into you guys."

Aryan stepped up alongside me. Gin shot a smirk and suggestive eyebrow raise in my direction.

"And who might this handsome man be?"

I curved my arm around his waist, smiling back at her. "Guys, this is my husband, Aryan." I turned to my spouse. "Hon, this is Gin and Clark, the British travelers I met in New Zealand."

His smile gleamed as he shook their hands. "Nice to meet you both. Scaith talks about you a lot."

"Lovely to meet you, Aryan," Gin told him jubilantly. "I'm so happy Scaith has found herself a wonderful mate. Now if only this one here would propose." She twisted her lips, gesturing toward Clark.

He chuckled markedly, enfolding his arm around her shoulders. "There's no rush, darling. I have plans in place. Don't you worry about that."

"Where are you off to next?" I inquired. "Are you leaving the Taj now?"

"Yes, love," Gin answered. "Looking to have a little nibble."

"Us, too. Would you like to join us for lunch?" I glanced over to Aryan to ensure he concurred with my offer.

"That'd be lovely," Clark responded. "There's a fantastic spot near our hostel."

"Great. Let's sod off," I teased.

⚓ ⚓ ⚓

The four of us enjoyed our drinks on the patio near the courtyard gardens of the restaurant, catching up on the events of the last year.

"...then we left New Zealand a few days after you did and headed straight to Thailand," Gin explained while I nodded, absorbing her stories. "... at least two weeks, then traveled through Cambodia to see

Angkor Wat, then Vietnam and Indonesia. Now, we'll be in India for a couple more weeks before heading back to London."

I sipped my mango lassi. "What else do you plan to see while you're here?"

"We go to Rajasthan tomorrow," Clark answered.

"Jaipur is a nice city," Aryan informed them. "They have good food and textiles. Great palaces, too."

"We've heard the same," Gin said. "Hoping to make it as far as Gujarat before heading back to Delhi."

"When did you two get married?" Clark asked us.

"Last week," I responded with a smile. "In California. We took a weekend trip to Napa Valley. It was nothing fancy, which is how we wanted it. Aryan's mother wants a big, traditional Hindu wedding here in India soon."

"Oh, Indian weddings are incredible," Gin enthused, staring off as if tranced. "The colors and rituals, jewelry, music… We're hoping to attend one while we're here."

"You'll be more than welcome anywhere you go," Aryan assured her. "Just find a wedding and show up. Anyone can attend. Weddings are big news here."

Our waiter dropped off entrées as Aryan's phone rang.

"That's a California number, hon," I told him while glancing at his screen. "I'll take it. Be right back, guys." I stood up, slowly pacing the courtyard as I answered. "Scaith, here."

"Hey, Don. Enjoying your honeymoon?"

The voice was indistinguishable and welcoming. "Great to hear from you, Perez. How's your family? How's life?"

"Everything's good here. I can't talk long, but I had some information you might be interested in hearing."

"Sure. Fire away."

"It turns out you were right. Everything you told Commander Ryder checked out about the plane crash. The Hezbollah admitted responsibility after one of our soldiers informed them you were on that plane."

"One of *our* soldiers? Who was it?"

"Zack Williams."

My mouth dropped at the bombshell, and I stood stunned in place. "Wait... Private Williams?!"

I wasn't sure if I had heard him correctly. I couldn't believe that the friendly, cheerful young man who seemed so eager to stay in a beach hut would be involved with a tyrannizing foreign militant group.

Perez continued explaining. "He was cleared to go to the Philippines for his R&R, but he never went. Instead, he traveled by car to Baghdad and met with Abdel Karim where he helped coordinate the attack. He was recruited into their organization a couple years back by an Islamic extremist in the States."

My mouth was still open from shock. "I just... I can't believe it. He was such a nice kid."

"And impressionable. He was feeding all kinds of intel to the Hezbollah while we were deployed."

"Where is Abdel now?"

"In a holding cell in Tehran. Soon he'll be transported back to the States to await trial for his role in the Khobar Towers attacks. Commander Ryder tracked down his location to the Iranian town of Kashan."

"*Ryder* found him?"

"Yeah, he's been working with the Bureau of Counterterrorism to track down his movements as part of a special investigation."

I scoffed slightly. "I'm surprised he got involved. Didn't think he took my speculation seriously."

"From what I understand, he started looking into it the day you got back to Iraq. He's been working tirelessly on it since. I was hoping this news would bring you some comfort and closure. I know you had questions that remained unanswered."

"No, of course, I... I'm glad you told me. Something just didn't seem right." I sighed and shut my eyes, horrified at knowing the crash was intentional, and that someone we should've been able to trust had betrayed us. All those lives lost, and for what? Senseless retaliation that would likely result in revenge, contributing to the endless cycle of prejudice and war in our world.

"Ryder wanted me to thank you," he went on. "Had you not voiced your concerns, he never would've looked into it."

"I'm just happy to see these guys aren't running around freely anymore." I paused for a moment to reflect. "Perez?"

"Yeah, Don?"

I glanced over to Aryan, his smile and wave immediate.

"Um…" As I thought about my prior relationship with Ryder, I concluded that there was no reason for us to ever speak again. I had everything I could want in the man smiling back at me. "Just tell him thank you."

"I will, Don."

"Give your family hugs tonight. Let them know how much you love them."

"Always. You enjoy yourself over there in India. Let me know when you're back in town. We'll catch up."

I hung up and remained in place, watching my husband and friends laughing together in conversation, the smile on my face matching theirs.

EPILOGUE

*W*e arrived home in Ooty after days of touring North India. It was dark out, and Spydo and Chestnut sat waiting patiently by the door to greet us.

While still in the car, Aryan leaned over and kissed me. "Welcome home, sweetie."

We stepped out, and I glanced up at the navy-blue house as if I'd never left. We brought our suitcases and got settled in. The place looked just as I remembered a year ago, every room bursting with happy memories.

"We can unpack tomorrow," Aryan told me. "It's been a long day. I'll make a little something to eat."

We sat on the porch outside with chai and onion pakora, watching the sunset cast shadows of scarlet and marigold across the valley below.

"The last year just flew by." I sat awestruck, sipping my chai. "Can't believe I'm back here."

"I'm so happy you are." Aryan smiled, kissing my hand. "Thank you for being my wife."

I smirked back. "Like I'd ever let *you* get away."

"Galen called earlier. He's looking forward to meeting you."

"Likewise. I'm sure I'll like Kentucky. Get to see my baby in action at his successful distillery."

"It's your distillery now, too."

I looked out into the valley as a figure crossed my vision. I stood up and walked to the edge of balcony, mesmerized by the beautiful creature below.

"There's a tiger," I whispered as Aryan joined me. "And it's free, roaming in the wild."

"I'm glad you're able to see one. I haven't since I was about nineteen."

We watched it prowl further up the mountain before disappearing amongst the trees.

"I have something for you." He left and returned with a gift bag of items from the house.

"What's all this for?"

He smiled. "Just for being you. A collection of things I thought you'd like."

We sat back down as I pulled out the first item: a dried yellow flower, pressed between glass. "Is this... the flower Mani gave me?"

"Yes. I saw it in the car after you left for the airport. Thought you might like to keep it."

"That's so thoughtful. I love it." I reached inside for the next item, a framed photo of my family, the same one as on the mantel back at my father's home. "Aryan, how did you..?"

"I contacted your dad for a copy. Now you can keep your family here with you in India."

I reached over and kissed him. "Thank you. You always think of everything."

"There's more," he urged me. "Keep going."

I next pulled out an envelope containing two tickets to Cairo for next month. "What?" I gasped. "You're taking me to Egypt?"

"Yep. You still want to see the pyramids, right? It was on your travel list."

This time I leapt into his arms from excitement, kissing him all over his face.

"Hey, wait. There's still one more thing."

The last item caused me to burst out in laughter. "Chat Pack?"

He grinned. "I know it's just something silly."

"Not at all. These are fun. I know we're both tired, but can I ask just one of these questions?"

"Sure. You can do that."

I popped open the plastic container and held up a card, but frowned at my unfortunate first pick.

"Oh, boy," I mumbled. "The question's a little heavy for this time of night."

"What does it say?"

I sighed and handed it to him, which he read aloud: "What's the worst thing you've ever done?"

Although there were many things that could fit the bill, one significantly stood out from the rest. I clutched Aryan's hand as I answered the question first.

"Aryan, before I met you, I may have done some things you would hate hearing." I glanced back at the valley. "A few years back, I started an affair with my married military Commander. It shouldn't have happened, but it did. All that matters now is that it's over. I ended it the moment I returned to Iraq."

I looked over to gauge his reaction, but he was staring off, his reaction blank.

"Please don't think less of me," I kept on. "It's in the past now and..."

"I killed my uncle," Aryan blurted out, his expression unchanging.

My eyes darted up to his. "What?"

He didn't respond.

"Aryan, are you serious?"

His confirming nod was tenuous. "The details don't matter. What's done is done. As I told you a year ago, time heals all wounds. Mine are healed and I'm not the same man I was." He turned to stroked my hair. "You don't have to fear me, Scaith. I'll never raise a hand to you. I was tired of the violence in my earlier life. It has no place in my life now."

I stood up and hugged him compassionately. "Thank you for telling me. I trust you, Aryan. You're not trapped alone in your anger and resentment anymore."

We both stood up and he kissed my cheek, holding the sides of my face.

"We come from different worlds, but our struggles are the same. I love you, my *Vellakari.*"

I closed my eyes, the evening breeze running through my hair... and had not a single regret in sight.

*A*nna Siduri was born and raised in Silicon Valley, CA. She wrote her first novel, *Vellakari*, while quarantined in India for a year during the Covid pandemic. It recounts many real-life inspired experiences while deployed to Iraq, adventures in New Zealand, and her connection with the people inhabiting the deep jungles of South India. After serving ten years in the U.S. Army, she owned an Indian restaurant, managed at several hotel chains, and holds an MBA in Human Resource Management. Though she has a home in the Midwest, and one in South India, she often travels the world alongside her India-born husband in search of more adventures.